**Praise for Carolyn Haines and
the Sarah Booth Delaney mysteries**

The Devil's Bones

"Lively. . . . Cozy fans will have fun."
—*Publishers Weekly*

"Wickedly entertaining, intelligent, and consistently com-
pelling . . . . ach of a cozy."
. . . . *iterary Review*

"Distinctive characters and an atmospheric setting el-
evate this paranormal cozy. Series fans and newcomers
alike will be satisfied." —*Publishers Weekly*

"A dark mystery, effectively framed by its well-drawn
Mississippi Delta setting." —*Booklist*

A Gift of Bones

"Haines's longtime admirers will be thrilled to spend the
holidays with their favorite characters. New readers
looking for an engaging story can start here."
—*Library Journal*

"Infused with Southern charm . . . A stocking stuffed with
something for everyone." —*Kirkus Reviews*

Sticks and Bones

"Many well-drawn characters . . . help bring this Southern tale to colorful life."   —*Publishers Weekly*

Bone to Be Wild

"Haines shows Sarah at her madcap best . . . in this clever adventure. This is a crazy cozy with a little something for everyone: paranormal doings, plenty of Evanovich zaniness, and a cast of eccentrics."   —*Booklist*

"Engaging."   —*Publishers Weekly*

Booty Bones

"Delightful . . . [a] satisfying beignet of a mystery."
          —*Publishers Weekly*

"[Haines] delivers a riveting love story alongside the mystery, leaving her readers in hot anticipation of her next novel."   —*Mississippi* magazine

Smarty Bones

"Raucously entertaining. This entire series is filled with mystery, humor, and more than a touch of the romantic South . . . not to be missed."   —*Criminal Element*

"If you enjoy mysteries with rich Southern settings, fascinating history, and quirky characters, you'll devour this one quicker than a plate full of buttermilk biscuits."
—*Mystery Scene* magazine

"The South's answer to a feminine Sherlock Holmes, the marvelous and smart Sarah Booth Delaney is on the trail of another fun and fascinating mystery."
—*Fresh Fiction*

"A satisfying mystery framed by a well-drawn small-town Southern setting."
—*Booklist*

Bonefire of the Vanities

"Delightfully fun."
—*New York Post*

"Wildly entertaining."
—*Criminal Element*

"We have to admit being hooked by the title, but even urbane Tom Wolfe would get a kick out of this delightfully fun twelfth installment of Haines's Southern mystery series."
—*New York Post*

Bones of a Feather

"A lesson in lying, Mississippi style . . . Haines diverts the reader . . . with great dollops of charm."
—*Kirkus Reviews*

"Sarah Booth Delaney has a funny way of ending up in extremely strange situations . . . a perfectly written mystery with a cast that is humorous, charming and deadly. Haines certainly is one of the best mystery writers working today."
—*RT Book Reviews*

Bone Appetit

"Distinctive characters and a clever cooking background make Haines's tenth Sarah Booth Delaney mystery the best yet in this Southern cozy series."
—*Publishers Weekly* (starred review)

"A whole lot of Southern sass . . . Haines's novel is definitely a page-turner."
—*Jackson Free Press*

Greedy Bones

"The cast is in fine form (including the helpful ghost, Jitty), and it's good to be back in Mississippi . . . One of the more entertaining episodes in the series."
—*Booklist*

"Jitty, Dahlia House's wonderfully wise 'haint,' [is] one of the best features of this light paranormal mystery series infused with Southern charm."
—*Publishers Weekly*

"Funny, ingenious . . . and delightful."

—*Dallas Morning News*

"*Wishbones* is reminiscent in many ways of Janet Evanovich's Stephanie Plum novels, only fresher with a bit more of an edge . . . Light, breezy, and just plain fun. Call Haines the queen of cozies."

—*Providence Journal-Bulletin*

"Stephanie Plum meets the Ya-Ya Sisterhood! Non-Southerners will find the madcap adventure an informative peek into an alien culture."

—*Kirkus Reviews*

ALSO BY CAROLYN HAINES

SARAH BOOTH DELANEY MYSTERIES

The Devil's Bones

Game of Bones

A Gift of Bones

Sticks and Bones

Rock-a-Bye Bones

Bone to Be Wild

Booty Bones

Smarty Bones

Bonefire of the Vanities

Bones of a Feather

Bone Appetit

Greedy Bones

Wishbones

Ham Bones

Bones to Pick

Hallowed Bones

Crossed Bones

Splintered Bones

Buried Bones

Them Bones

Charmed Bones

NOVELS

A Visitation of Angels

The Specter of Seduction

The House of Memory

The Book of Beloved

Familiar Trouble

Revenant

Fever Moon

Penumbra

Judas Burning

Touched

Summer of the Redeemers

Summer of Fear

The Darkling

The Seeker

NONFICTION

My Mother's Witness: The Peggy Morgan Story

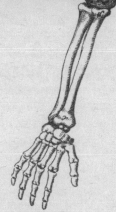

A Garland
of Bones

CAROLYN HAINES

St. Martin's Paperbacks

This is a work of fiction. All of the characters, organizations, and events portrayed in this novel are either products of the author's imagination or are used fictitiously.

Published in the United States by St. Martin's Paperbacks, an imprint of St. Martin's Publishing Group.

A GARLAND OF BONES

For information, address St. Martin's Publishing Group, 120 Broadway, New York, NY 10271.

www.stmartins.com

Library of Congress Catalog Card Number: 2020030017

ISBN: 978-1-250-25791-8

Our books may be purchased in bulk for promotional, educational, or business use. Please contact your local bookseller or the Macmillan Corporate and Premium Sales Department at 1-800-221-7945, ext. 5442, or by email at MacmillanSpecialMarkets@macmillan.com.

Printed in the United States of America

Minotaur hardcover edition published 2020
St. Martin's Paperbacks edition / October 2021

10 9 8 7 6 5 4 3 2 1

For Aleta and Kathleen—
two of the best friends anyone could ask for

1

December has arrived in the Mississippi Delta, a bitter-sweet time for those of us who miss our loved ones. At times, the holiday gaiety and sparkling decorations heighten loss. The memories of what was contrast sharply with what is. Children grow up and begin their own lives. Relatives and friends move away. My loss is more permanent. I long for those who have gone to the Great Beyond. I miss my family. But Christmas is also a festive time, a time for friends and sharing.

The clear sky, slightly tinged with lavender as dusk approaches, spreads for miles across the barren fields. Winter is a season of death for many plants, but it is also the precursor to spring and rebirth. I love being outdoors on a brisk December day, going about my regular farm chores.

My horses clatter into the barn for an afternoon feeding and their blankets. I scoop the pellets and dump them in the feeders, toss the hay into the stalls, and quickly buckle the waterproof turnout blankets around the animals in preparation for the coming night. There is such satisfaction in caring for my horses. They are healthy and filled with high spirits, but the grain settles them down quickly. I comb their manes and daydream.

I relish the exhilarating rides across the fallow cotton fields on Reveler, Miss Scrapiron, or Diablo this time of year. In the crisp winter air, no bugs bite or annoy us. The wind can cut like a sharp blade across the open spaces, but nothing detracts from the joy of the rhythm of a horse beneath me. No ride would be complete without Sweetie Pie, my loyal red tick hound, coursing beside me. She loves the ride as much as the horses and I do.

But there will be no rides this afternoon. I have my work cut out for me. Each year since I've returned home to Zinnia, Mississippi, I've become more efficient in preparing for Christmas. I have an attic full of ornaments and decorations, and I have holiday joy in my heart. I mentally plan my next attack on hanging garlands and setting up the miniature Christmas crèche that has been in the Delaney family for generations. There's a secretary in the formal parlor that's the perfect site. And while I'm at it, I'll put on some Christmas songs.

I'm almost done in the barn when the horses finish eating and I turn them out. Reveler romps and snorts, eager to be out and free. He is such a boy! He bucks, farts, and gallops away, the others joining him. They're performing that crazy psychic dance that horses do, like synchronized swimmers, all moving in unison. They round the corner of the pasture and disappear, but their hoof-beats still reverberate on the ground. They are healthy and happy, and I am blessed.

Sweetie Pie and I enter Dahlia House, my ancestral home, through the back door. Pluto greets me with a lazy yawn. The cat loves adventure, but he is not de-signed to keep up with a coursing hound or a gallop-ing horse. He has wisely chosen to stay in the warm kitchen, where a pot of gumbo warms on the stove, waiting for me to turn up the heat for dinner. Gumbo is one of Coleman Peters's favorites, and I am looking for-ward to his arrival when he gets off work. Until then—I increase the gas to the gumbo, select a Christmas play-list on my phone, and am ready to vie for the Martha Stewart decorating award.

An hour later, the smell of cedar fills the parlor in Dahlia House as I step back in satisfaction to view the garland of cedar fronds, holly, magnolia leaves, and glistening red ornaments that I've artfully woven around the antique mirror above the magnificent old mantel. Below the mantel, a fire crackles and spits a warm wel-come. "Silver Bells" is playing, and I sing along. All of my friends are hustling and bustling with the fun of buying presents, planning menus, hosting parties, and good-naturedly attempting to outdo one another with decorations and food. This holiday, we have special plans.

My chosen décor comes from nature—the branches and boughs from the evergreen trees that smell so clean and remind me of Christmases past, when I was cod-dled and protected by loving parents. Sometimes the past is a heavy burden to carry, but I thank goodness for stalwart friends and one big burning hunk of lawman love—Coleman Peters. In fact, he should be arriving any minute. He can help me loop the garland down the railing on the gallery. This is how my mother decorated for Christmas, and her mother before her, and my aunt Loulane, who cared for me after my parents died. I cling to some traditions—those that keep my family close, especially during the holidays.

The gumbo smells good, and I have all the ingredients for Dirty Snowmen, one of my favorite winter holiday drinks, complete with chocolate shavings and lots of Baileys. The thought has my mouth watering and my imagination working overtime. There were things I could do with whipped cream—

"Ah-h-h-h-h-h!"

A pale blond woman with curly hair comes running at me with a huge butcher knife. Her white dress is covered in blood.

"Damn!" I dodge her first attempt to attack me, run around the kitchen table, and haul it through the dining room and parlor and out the front door and into the yard. Without benefit of a coat. The night is freezing, but my heart is thudding so hard I don't feel the cold. Who has invaded my home with the intention of slicing me to death?

The crazed woman comes out onto the front porch and screams, "I won't be ignored, Dan!" She glares into the darkness looking for me.

Who the heck is Dan? Even better, who the heck is that crazy woman and how did she get into Dahlia House? I creep around to the side of the porch and peer up at her. She stands, feet apart—bare feet in this bitter cold—in a diaphanous white dress. Therefore she must be freezing, but I'm not seeing any reaction to the cold. My teeth are about to chatter and will be a dead giveaway of my location.

"You play fair with me, I'll play fair with you!" the woman calls out into the night.

She stares as if she's looking for someone to appear in front of her. It occurs to me that it isn't really me she's hoping to see. I creep a little closer until I get a good view of her under the chandelier that lights the front porch. Glenn Close! It's the actress Glenn Close! My first thought is to call Millie Roberts, the owner of Millie's Café here in Zinnia, and the local authority on celebrities and what makes them tick. Why is Glenn Close in my ancestral family home—with a knife in her hand and blood in her eyes?

"Dan, you can't pretend we didn't happen." Her voice is honeyed now, as if she will behave all harmless and playful. The knife blade glints in the light and I know she is deadly.

"Any bunnies in the barn?" she asks.

I knew the reference then. Dan Gallagher. Alex Forrest. The movie was *Fatal Attraction*. Close played a woman whose obsession with a married man ended in tragedy—and a dead bunny. It was a movie scene I'd never forget. And now the crazy woman was in my house. Was she waiting for Coleman?

Now that thought really made me shiver. Was my man up to something I needed to know about? I rejected that idea immediately. Sure, people cheated. People made mistakes. It happened. But the one thing I knew about Coleman Peters was that he would not deceive me. If he found someone he wanted more than me, he would step up to the plate and say so.

So why was a murderous woman on my front porch?

That question troubled me until I snapped out of the Christmas fog and realized that the apparition haunting my porch was Jitty, my nemesis and heirloom haint.

I crept out of the shrubs and put my hands on my hips. "Dammit, Jitty, you nearly scared ten years off my life."

She stepped out of her aggressive stance and sauntered toward me. "Girl, you don't have ten years to squander. Your eggs got a shelf life of"—she consulted a pretty watch on her arm—"maybe ten hours. They don't last forever, you know."

Jitty's primary job at Dahlia House was to aggravate me to the point of near insanity. And also to offer cryptic advice that rarely meant anything to me until it was too late. But this Jitty-incarnation, this cheating and vengeful woman, touched a nerve I thought was long dead.

"Is Coleman cheating on me? Is that what this"—I waved a hand at her—"getup is all about?"

Jitty was slowly morphing from the blond Alex to the mocha Jitty. "Coleman? Heck no. This has nothing to do with Coleman." She made an O with her mouth and popped a hand over it. Jitty was never supposed to give me a straight answer about anything she knew from the Great Beyond. It was part of the rule book of ghosts and spirits.

"Aha!" I was smug. "So Coleman is true blue."

"Any fool would know the answer to that," Jitty grumped. "You don't need a ghost to divine that answer."

I wanted to hear her say it. "So he's loyal?"

"Kind of like that hound dog sleeping on the sofa

and not concerned enough about you to come outside. Maybe that should have been your first tip not to run out of the house without a coat."

She was right. Had Alex Forrest been a real danger, Sweetie Pie would have been on her like a duck on a June bug. Since Sweetie Pie hadn't demonstrated the least amount of concern that a crazy woman with a knife was stalking me, I should have deduced that it was Jitty. After all, Jitty had concocted a thousand different ways to interrupt my life. Now she had me out in the cold winter without a jacket while she indulged her penchant for playacting.

I trudged up the steps and went inside. I slammed the door, but Jitty just faded right through it and followed me into the parlor, where Dean Martin sang "Winter Wonderland." My parents had loved Dino and had slow-danced to his mellow voice, my father steering Mama under the mistletoe to steal a kiss. I made myself a very light Jack and water and plopped before the crackling fire to enjoy the warmth, the music, and my memories. And ignore Jitty. "I'm not going to listen to you," I warned her. "Go away."

"Where's that handsome sheriff?"

"Probably on his way, so you should skedaddle."

I'd been in love before, but Coleman was bigger than love. We'd grown up knowing each other, and he'd been my grade school friend when I lost my parents. He'd been my competitor in horseback riding, sports, driving fast through the cotton fields, and a thousand other things. He had rescued me more than once when my life was on the line.

Coleman and I shared a love of the natural world, and of the Delta in particular. We both fought for justice.

We were children of a particular time and place in the history of a state we both loved and despaired over. And we were also the grown-ups who'd set about to bring change to our home and the people we loved. Change that brought equality for every person, no matter their race, gender, creed, religion, or sexual identification. From the remnants of the old South, a new South was finally being birthed.

"Earth to Sarah Booth!" Jitty was done with Alex Forrest and back to her normal self, wearing my favorite jeans and my new silk blouse. She'd adorned herself with a string of red and green Christmas lights. She felt free to help herself to whatever I had.

"I'm here."

"Just mooning over that man again, aren't you?"

"Maybe." It didn't do any good to lie to Jitty. She could smell the truth like Sweetie Pie could jump the scent of a villain.

Jitty preened a little, and the red and green lights glowed brighter. "You got it bad for that man."

"Maybe."

"Is he going to put a ring on it?"

"Maybe."

"Do you want a ring?"

That question stopped me short. I'd had one engagement ring in my sordid romantic history, and my fiancé had almost broken my heart asunder. "I like things just fine the way they are right now. If it ain't broke, don't fix it." Coleman and I were adults with no dependents and no real family. No one—except Jitty—cared if we lived in sin or not. Most of my friends had engaged in sin and were experts at it. Not a single one of them ever mentioned the *m* word.

"Don't you want what Libby and James Franklin had?"

Jitty could be a downright devil when she set her mind to it, and this was one of those times. "Mama and Daddy came up at a different time. They wanted children. They wanted a legacy."

"And you don't?"

This was sacrilege to Jitty. She had badgered me for months to get pregnant and produce an heir so that Dahlia House would remain in the Delaney family and she would have someone to haunt after I passed on. Watching the effects of pregnancy on Tinkie, I wasn't so certain I wanted to sign up for that experience firsthand. I didn't know a thing about birthing—or raising—babies, and I kind of intended to keep it that way.

"Sarah Booth, you don't want to have a baby girl and give her the gifts Libby gave you?"

Now Jitty was hitting me in my weak spot. "I don't know that I can. I lost too much, Jitty. I don't know that I can risk losing a child."

She stepped back and gave me a long look. "That I can understand."

My jaw almost hit the floor. Jitty was never understanding. This new development made me wary. Did I have a fatal illness? Was something going to happen to Coleman? Or Tinkie? Or one of my pets? "What's wrong with you?"

She laughed. "You can lead a horse to water, but you can't make her drink."

That was one of Aunt Loulane's favorite sayings whenever she thought I was being muleheaded. "I am not being stubborn. I have a right to protect my heart. Smart people do that."

"Uh-huh."

I had to get out of this corner. "Tinkie is cooking up a little trip for all of us to take. I'm going to be gone a few days."

"You're leavin'? At Christmas?"

I had her attention now. "Before Christmas, and only across the state. We're going to stay at an exclusive B and B—we'll have the entire place to ourselves. And we're going to participate in a bunch of Christmas activities."

"Where are you goin'?"

"Columbus, the birthplace of Tennessee Williams and home of the W, where Eudora Welty went to school to get her college degree. It's a beautiful little city."

"You'll be back for Christmas Eve?"

A twinge of guilt bit me like a nasty flea. "Of course I'll be home for Christmas Eve."

"That man goin' with you?"

"Yes, he is. And Tinkie and Oscar, Cece and Jaytee, Harold, and even Millie is going to take some time to go with us. It's Tinkie's Christmas present to all of us." Tinkie Richmond was my partner in the Delaney Detective Agency, and her husband, Oscar, ran the bank in town. Cece was a journalist, Jaytee a hot blues musician, Harold worked at the bank with Oscar and was Zinnia's premier party-giver, and Millie was the best cook in the Southeast and ran the café named for her.

Jitty rolled her eyes. "I see trouble comin' down the road at a fast gallop. You think you can all load up and go somewhere and not get in big trouble?"

"We're going Christmas shopping and to attend a tree lighting and a Wassail Fest. We're celebrating. We don't have a case, so we won't be in any trouble. We're going to be festive."

"That strikes fear in my heart." Jitty dramatically clasped her chest.

I left the sofa and went to the kitchen to stir the gumbo. It was the perfect temperature. I buttered some crispy French bread and turned the oven to preheat. Coleman should be walking in the door.

"What did you get me for Christmas?" Jitty asked.

"You're a ghost. What could I get you for Christmas?"

"I'll make a list. Before you go."

"Be quick, we're heading out in the morning. And I have plans for tonight!"

"You're a wicked girl." Jitty grinned her approval. "Keep that man happy."

"Those are my intentions."

I heard a truck pulling up at the front of the house and Jitty disappeared in a swirl of snowflakes that melted before they hit the floor. Coleman was home and I had a special little gift just for him. It was going to be a long, pleasurable night.

2

Coleman loaded our luggage into the trunk of the honking big limo that Tinkie had insisted on renting. We were the last couple to be picked up. Oscar, Harold, Jaytee, Millie, Tinkie, and Cece were already in the car.

"You're sure DeWayne doesn't mind feeding the animals?" It was hard for me to let go of control when it came to my beloved cats, dogs, and horses. DeWayne Dattilo was Coleman's oldest deputy, and he enjoyed caring for the animals and spending time at Dahlia House. He'd agreed to take care of Chablis, too, for the week we'd be gone. If the little dust-mop pup wasn't with Tinkie or Oscar, she was happiest when she was with Sweetie Pie and Pluto. The little Yorkie was tiny but fiercely loyal to Tinkie, Oscar, and my crew.

"DeWayne is happy to be here with them," Coleman assured me. "We're only a few hours away, Sarah Booth. It's not like we're blasting off to the moon." True enough. It was only a three-hour drive to Columbus, at most.

DeWayne came out of the house with Sweetie Pie and Pluto at his side and Chablis in his arms. They waved goodbye, and we were off.

Tinkie had supplied the limo with champagne, strawberries, and snacks. We were a loud and lively group as we sped through the Delta toward the river town of Columbus. Tinkie and I had gone to the University of Mississippi, better known as Ole Miss, which was northeast of Zinnia. Columbus was slightly southeast, right on the Alabama line. It was an old city with a fascinating history located at the junction of the Tombigbee and Buttahatchee Rivers and Luxapalila Creek. The Tombigbee Waterway was a vital navigation path in current times, and historically it had been a lifeline for supplies to Southern troops during the Civil War. Before that, the original settlers, Native Americans, had also used the river to move people and goods.

"We have something planned for each evening," Tinkie said, listing on her fingers the events she'd arranged for us.

Tinkie was wearing her cruise captain hat, and she had our holiday organized to a fare-thee-well. While I admired and appreciated her wrangling of our schedule, I had hopes of sneaking away from the others for some very private time with Coleman. I had a few Christmas games up my sleeve.

"Sarah Booth isn't thinking about decorating the tree at the Columbus Riverwalk or tossing trinkets on the flotilla on the river." Millie grinned wickedly. "She's got her mind on wrapping holiday garlands around Coleman."

"Guilty as charged," I said as I snuggled closer to Coleman. His hand brushed down my rib cage and I feared electricity would spark across the car. We had a mutual attraction that might ignite.

"So as soon as we get to town, we'll take a little walking tour," Tinkie said.

"I do want to see Tennessee Williams's home." I was a huge fan of the Southern playwright. *Cat on a Hot Tin Roof. Suddenly Last Summer. The Glass Menagerie.* All were plays that spoke to the many varied elements of being a Southerner. Not all were pretty or pleasant.

"Can we tour the W?" Millie asked about the Mississippi University for Women. Once a female-only university, it was now coeducational but still known as the W. "I've always adored Eudora Welty's writing. I want to picture her walking around the campus."

"And that we can do," Tinkie said. "We're keeping the limo the whole week so we can tour wherever we want to go and those who aren't pregnant can sip a little bubbly."

Tinkie was a serious party girl when it came to Christmas and exploring her beloved Mississippi, but impending motherhood had her focused on a healthy baby.

"What a relief not to have to drive," Coleman said as he leaned back. He deftly slid his hand down my thigh and gave a wicked little pinch. To thwart him, I didn't react.

"The Bissonnette House is a boutique B and B on the outskirts of Columbus, and right on the river," Tinkie said. "I've booked all six rooms, so you can spread out any way you like. The owner is something of an authority on Columbus and was very helpful in planning our itinerary. She's something of a character, too. She serves a full breakfast each morning, lunch, and dinner if we make arrangements. Breakfast is the specialty, though. I told her we'd be up and about by eight."

Oscar, Coleman, and Harold groaned loudly. "You don't have to get up every morning and go to work," Oscar pointed out to his wife. "This is a holiday vacation. Operative word is *vacation*! We might want to sleep in."

"Fine. You'll just miss breakfast," Tinkie said, not the least bit perturbed.

Millie only laughed. "I can rustle up anything you need from the kitchen at any time," she said. "I'm just thrilled to have a whole week off. Now no more groaning and complaining."

Harold popped another cork and poured champagne all around. For Tinkie he poured sparkling water.

By the time we got to Columbus, it was time for lunch. We found our rooms—mine and Coleman's was a beautiful suite with a balcony that looked out over the river. I wasn't prepared for the steep bluff, but I should have been. River towns that weren't on a high bluff often didn't last.

I took a moment to watch a few smaller boats and a tug churning down the river. Harold had once owned a sailboat, but Coleman and I were landlubbers. Still, a flotilla would be fun. Tinkie had planned a full itinerary for us, and I was going to enjoy every second of it.

"What are you thinking?" Coleman came up behind me and put his arms around me, pulling me back against him. His chest and abdomen gave me a sense of solidness and security.

"We need to travel to the Gulf and try sailing." Watching the river made me think of traveling slowly on the current. Huck Finn. My childhood obsession had been building a raft, much to my father's amusement, especially since we didn't even have a pond to float it on.

"Really?"

I laughed. Coleman wasn't prepared for my wanderlust. "Maybe not. Riding horses is plenty of work. That's what they say, you know. The two most expensive hobbies in the world are boats and horses."

"I'm good with the horses. Boats just aren't my thing."

"I do love a naughty pirate." I leaned back and tilted my face up so that he could kiss me. For a moment we lingered in the kiss, not wanting to take it further, but just savoring that moment.

Tap, tap, tap. Tap, tap, tap. "Sarah Booth, are you decent?" Tinkie was tap, tap, tapping at my door. I'd forgotten this aggravating habit of hers.

"Come in." Coleman was laughing as he spoke.

"We're ready to go to town and find some lunch. I have a list of places we should eat. We're going to have to eat five times a day to hit all of them."

Tinkie was enjoying pregnancy, and she was like a tapeworm on steroids. "And Darla is down in the parlor. I want everyone to meet her. She's been so helpful in planning our itinerary."

Coleman spun me around, gave me another swift, passionate kiss, and then led me to the door to follow Tinkie down the hallway and staircases to the first floor. An elegant woman in her mid-thirties was waiting for us.

Tinkie made the introductions between Darla Lofton and the Zinnia crew. Darla's hair was as perfectly glitzed and styled as Tinkie's. If they'd been horses, they would have been a matched pair fit for pulling a royal's carriage. They would have been high-steppers, too.

"I'm thrilled to have the Delaney Detective Agency staying in my home," Darla said. "And a representation of law enforcement, banking, and the music world, not to mention one of the finest eateries in the state, and, last but not least, a well-known journalist. I hope you're planning on writing some stories about the Christmas festivities in Columbus," Darla said, winking at Cece.

"I am working—just a little," Cece said. "Zinnia has a parade and storefront window competitions, but we need to up our game. Columbus has given me some ideas."

"There are so many wonderful traditions and customs in the Delta, but here on the other side of the state we have some fun activities, too. Mumming is our latest addition. I do so love to dress up in a costume!"

Darla and Tinkie *were* twins! Sisters by another mother. The only thing missing from Darla was a cute little moppet dog. Chablis was the perfect accoutrement to any of Tinkie's outfits.

The front doorbell chimed, and before anyone could move to answer it, a pretty redhead came in. "Darla, I hope I'm not interrupting. I wanted to meet your Zinnia guests." She held out her hand to each of us. "Kathleen

Beesley, pleased to meet you." Kathleen had pixie features and an impish smile. Her auburn hair was an incredible shade that contrasted beautifully with her pale skin and green eyes.

"I knew you wouldn't last an hour once you knew everyone was here." Darla was chiding her gently, and with a smile. "Kathleen is a busybody," she told us. "She has no malice, but she has to know everything going on. The good thing is she doesn't gossip."

"Columbus is a small town, really. When something is happening, I don't want to miss it." Kathleen was unapologetic about her curiosity bone. "I should write for the newspaper because I am into everything. But it isn't malicious."

It was impossible not to like the two women. They were fun and shameless about their nosiness. Something I understood perfectly.

"Where should we go for lunch?" Tinkie asked.

"The Green Parrot Bar and Grill." Darla checked her watch. "And they're hosting a karaoke Christmas party this afternoon. A lot of the banks and businesses have closed for a half day of shopping for Christmas. And the karaoke competition is always highly competitive and fun. Some of these people make total fools of themselves, but it's for a good cause. They're raising money for an orphanage in town."

"We can't turn that down," Harold said. "Besides, Cece and Jaytee can actually sing." He looked at me. "Sarah Booth, promise us you won't try."

"Hey," Coleman said, my knight in shining armor coming to my rescue. "Let her sing if she wants to. If anyone's ears start bleeding, we can stop her."

So much for a rescue from my man. "I'm going to sing 'Silver Bells' and do all the ting-a-linging by myself!"

Everyone was laughing as we headed out to the limo for a run into Columbus.

3

The downtown area of Columbus was bustling with activity as we made our way to the Green Parrot. The restaurant, which was perfectly set up for karaoke, offered an American menu, great drinks, and rowdy customers packed around tables as they cheered or harassed the singing talent.

We found a table near the stage while a cute young girl sang "Rudolph, the Red-Nosed Reindeer." Because we'd already been drinking champagne, we continued with glasses of bubbly while we waited for our food orders.

Tinkie and Oscar were poring over the karaoke songbook while Coleman was fondling my knee beneath the table. Christmas karaoke obviously made him naughty.

"Santa won't bring you anything unless you straighten up," I cautioned him in a whisper.

"I've already got everything I want," he said, attempting to inch his fingertips up my thigh.

"I'll scream," I said.

He only laughed, but leaned back in his chair. "Why are you looking at the songbook?" he asked with a wary note in his voice.

"I don't really need it. I already know what I'm going to sing." I'd been thinking about this for days.

Coleman deadpanned it. "Let us eat first, so if we have to run out screaming, at least we won't be hungry."

Oscar joined in the teasing. "I thought Tinkie had a signed contract with you guaranteeing you'd never, ever sing in public."

"Keep it up." I grinned.

When the young girl finished, Tinkie grabbed Oscar's hand and dragged him up on the stage. I was impressed with their rendition of "Have Yourself a Merry Little Christmas." It was one of my holiday favorites, and it was clear to see the pleasure they took in each other. And they both could sing.

I was about to go onstage when a slender brunette in a terrific Christmas sweater and leggings jumped on the stage and grabbed the microphone. The emcee introduced her as Tulla Tarbutton. She nodded to the guy working the machine, and the opening music of "Grandma Got Run Over by a Reindeer" came up. She had a pretty good voice, and she knew how to sing to a crowd.

She was about halfway through the song when an arc of electricity moved from the microphone she held to the speakers. There was a loud pop, the lights went out, and Tulla went into a spasm and dropped to the floor like she'd been hit with an ax. Clearly she'd been electrocuted.

Coleman, Harold, and Oscar were on the stage in seconds as they set to work doing CPR. Tinkie called an ambulance, and Cece, ever the reporter, was taking photographs. Pandemonium broke out in the restaurant as the owners and servers rushed over to help. People everywhere were talking, and in the background, I heard a woman say, "Exactly what that ho deserves." When I turned around to try to identify the speaker, I couldn't pinpoint anyone.

"Sounds like someone has a grudge against Ms. Tarbutton," Tinkie said, easing up beside me.

Before I could respond, silence fell over the place. When Tulla Tarbutton shakily sat up—with assistance from Coleman and the men—a cheer broke out and everyone went back to their tables to finish eating.

Coleman helped the woman onto a stretcher when the paramedics arrived. It was then I realized Jaytee was examining the karaoke equipment. He wore a frown, and he was whispering with Cece.

"What's going on?" I asked.

"This equipment was tampered with," Jaytee said. "It was deliberately shorted, or so it appears."

"Why would anyone do that?" I asked.

"Well, you were up next to sing and she jumped your spot. Maybe they've heard you sing before?" Jaytee softened his teasing with a squeeze of my shoulder. "Really, I can't say. But I know this was done deliberately."

"Would someone be able to control who was shocked?" I asked.

"Maybe," Jaytee said. "I'd have to really study this and I don't think that's going to happen."

"Why—" Before I could finish my question, the owner of the Green Parrot took the stage and quickly began unplugging the equipment. A crew of several employees loaded everything up and started hauling it away.

"Hey!" I said.

He looked at me. "This equipment is going to a repair shop. No one touches it again until I make sure it's safe."

I couldn't blame him, but I wondered if we should tell the cops about the short in the microphone.

"Let it go," Jaytee said. "It could have been an accident. I just don't think so. But the police officer there is examining the equipment. I'm sure he'll see exactly what I saw. Remember, Sarah Booth, we're on vacation."

What Jaytee said was true, but I approached the police officer and mentioned what Jaytee had found, just to be sure he was aware.

"You know that was tampering with a crime scene?" the officer asked. "I could arrest you both for that."

I noted his name was Jerry Goode. "We only wanted to be sure no one else was shocked."

"I'm sorry," he apologized, shaking our hands. "I do appreciate the help. It's just that Ms. Tarbutton could have been killed. I can't risk anyone else messing with faulty equipment that might shock them. What brings y'all to Columbus?"

"We're vacationing here. A holiday treat."

He picked up the karaoke planning book—the one the DJ used to cue the next song up. Instead of my name, I noticed that Tulla Tarbutton had been added in just above me. So at least the DJ, an employee of the bar, had known that Tulla was up next.

I pointed that out to the officer. "Look, see, she was on the list, so the shock could have easily been meant for her."

He tapped the logbook. "Thanks for the help. As soon as the doc says it's okay, I'll have a chat with Ms. Tarbutton. If someone means to hurt her, the Columbus police want to be on top of it."

I returned to our table. I'd discuss it with Coleman when we were alone. If he wanted to take Jaytee's information to Officer Goode, he could. It would carry more weight coming from another lawman.

"Well, no karaoke for me and Cece," Jaytee said with a pretend pout. "We might just have to find a stage tonight at a local club and belt out some blues."

"That would be worth watching," I agreed. Cece could really sing. She had the blues in her bones. And Jaytee's harmonica made women swoon.

"No more karaoke, so let's shop!" Tinkie was ready to get on with Christmas. Since she hadn't partaken of any alcohol, she was perky and ready to hit the stores. I, on the other hand, longed for a nap. I knew just the perfect human pillow I wanted to snuggle with. But Tinkie had put her heart into organizing this trip, and if shopping was what she wanted, I was going to shop.

The men split off from us, claiming they needed secrecy to find the perfect gifts. I suspected they were heading to a warm and cozy bar for some darts or pool, but it was good to have my girl posse. It wasn't often that Millie could join us, and she and Cece recounted hysterical stories about celebrity gossip they'd dug up for their new Sunday newspaper column, "The Truth Is Out There," which was a hit. The column had almost doubled the *Zinnia Dispatch*'s readership, and Ed Oakes, Cece's editor, was more than pleased. Cece, the hard-facts journalist, and Millie, who was a devotee of celebrity tabloid news, cooked up just enough scandal and outrageousness to appeal to everyone.

"Speaking of Ed," Cece said, "he was telling me about Friendship Cemetery here in town, where the tradition of Memorial Day began. The women of Columbus selected a day, originally called Decoration Day, to honor the fallen Confederate dead, but when they got to the cemetery, they decided to honor all of the soldiers' graves, even those of the Union soldiers. It became a national holiday to honor the graves of fallen soldiers."

Cece was often chock-full of interesting facts. "I wouldn't mind a spin through the cemetery if we have time."

"Let's focus on shopping. Look at that dress," Tinkie said, pointing to a storefront window, where a red velvet number really was an eye-catcher. "Let's look in there."

So of course we did, laughing and chattering as we selected gifts for others—and one or two for ourselves.

When we'd made it down one whole street, we had more boxes than we could manage, and most of the afternoon had slipped away. "Darla said she was making dinner tonight, so we can relax back at the B and B," Tinkie said. "My feet are tired."

My feet were fine, but I was also ready to give up

the frantic shopping. In the best of conditions I was a terrible shopper. After three hours of it, I was more than done. I had managed to get Coleman an incredible riding jacket. It was warm and lightweight, with plenty of pockets. And it matched his blue eyes. I felt my hard work searching for a perfect gift had paid off handsomely.

As five o'clock rolled around, the shops began to close. During the final days of the season, they would remain open later, and there was a big Wassail Fest event, in which all the downtown shops remained open until ten P.M. conducting business in a final push for those last-minute gifts.

When Tinkie had us herded into the limo, we sailed off to the Bissonnette House and another round of holiday libations as we waited for dinner.

Darla and Kathleen both were there and grilled us on the near electrocution of Tulla Tarbutton.

"Tulla is one of the *nuevo* socialites who's been trying for years to start a Mardi Gras organization here in Columbus. As if we don't have enough of our own heritage to celebrate," Kathleen said as she lit the candles on the long dining room table that accommodated all of us with ease. "We have events all year long. Mardi Gras belongs to Mobile and New Orleans, and that's where it should stay," Kathleen said.

"Columbus has an event every night this week," I agreed. "There's plenty going on."

"It was Darla who brought back the flotilla this year, and I'm glad to see you've booked yourself onto the *Tenn-Tom Queen*. That's the best boat and you'll have a blast." Kathleen was obviously Darla's number one cheerleader. "The flotilla is going to be fabulous."

The *Tenn-Tom Queen* sounded fine to me. Tinkie had made all the arrangements and I gave her a thumbs-up. She'd really put her heart into this trip, the last Christmas before she and Oscar had a child. It was incredibly heartwarming to see my partner aglow with her plans and the love she shared with her husband.

Cece sidled up to me and whispered in my ear. "I got a little scoop on Tulla Tarbutton, the electrocution victim at the Green Parrot. I haven't had a chance to talk to you alone."

I signaled her out on the patio while everyone was busy sipping their drinks and sampling the wonderful hors d'oeuvres that Darla had whipped up. "What's up?"

"I overheard one of the women at the Green Parrot talking about Tulla. She said she was a homewrecker."

"Someone at the bar called her a ho. I couldn't tell who it was, but it was a woman."

"I think Jaytee was correct. The shock was deliberate. I don't think they were trying to kill her. Probably meant to send a message."

"How could they control who was holding the microphone when the shock occurred?"

Cece shook her head. "I'm not saying this was cause and effect. It's just a tidbit of gossip."

"Who is Tulla having an affair with?"

"They didn't say and I could hardly ask, since I was eavesdropping."

She was right about that. "Good thing we're not working." I said it with a grin.

"I know, I know. It's just that the shock could have killed someone. And I heard the very best tidbit."

I could tell by her animated face that this was going to be juicy. "Hit me with it."

"There was a man in town cheating on his girlfriend and she poured Red Devil Lye in his shoes. She told everyone she was going to eat him up from the feet to the top of his head. Because he was cheating on her."

I couldn't help laughing. It was a helluva slow death threat. "Do they even make Red Devil Lye anymore?"

Cece shrugged. "Haven't checked. I haven't tried to dissolve anyone lately."

I had a crazy memory of one of my mother's antique bargain hunts. She'd found a clever little table covered in horrid green paint. She'd taken a bucket of water mixed with Red Devil Lye and a broom and brushed it all over the table. Incredibly enough, the lye mixture ate the paint off and left a beautiful tigerwood oak table that she refinished. But I'd never thought of using Red Devil Lye to dissolve a cheating man.

Cece shivered a little, which caused me to shiver, too. The night was brisk, and we hurried back inside. Harold and Millie were conspiring in a corner, and I wondered what mischief they were up to. I enjoyed a little tormenting of my friends, but Harold could match me prank for prank when he put his mind to it.

Coleman was standing in front of a roaring fire talking to Kathleen. I refilled my glass before I joined them.

"Kathleen was giving me the lowdown on Tulla," Coleman said.

"She's popular in many of the social circles." Kathleen nodded as she talked. "She's invited to the best parties, but there's been talk about some infighting among the women. Tulla likes to . . . flirt." She sighed. "Maybe a little more than flirting. She has a bit of a reputation. People get upset."

Infidelity was a dangerous game, particularly in a small town. Everyone eventually found out, and if the community decided to shun people, they were cut off from all social activities.

"Do you know anyone who would deliberately shock Tulla?" I asked. "Luckily she wasn't hurt, but it could have been serious."

"The shock was deliberate?" Kathleen looked startled.

I shook my head. "Maybe. It's a theory."

"Someone would have to be very angry to electrocute another person." Kathleen's eyes were wide. "I heard that there were some hard feelings, but sending volts of electricity through someone is pretty extreme."

I had to agree. "Was Tulla seeing anyone?"

Kathleen shrugged. "I honestly don't keep up with the activities of Tulla's social circle. I hear things occasionally, but I'm a newcomer to town." She rolled her eyes. "You have to have lived here before the Civil War to be considered a real resident."

"So Tulla and her friends are considered . . . outsiders?"

Kathleen laughed. "They're making inroads because they have money. Maybe my grandchildren will be invited to the high society events. If we had lots of money, we could get there sooner." She walked over and linked her arm through Darla's. "But better than consorting with that crowd, you could have a really good friend who's way more fun than boring high society."

"We like our life working here in the Bissonette House," Darla said. "We live a pretty quiet life. Tulla and that group have stirred up hard feelings, and that never has a happy ending, so we stay clear."

A little warning bell in the back of my brain went off, but I was not working. I was not on a case. And I was *not* going to get dragged into a domestic during my holiday. Every law officer on the planet knew that a domestic was the most dangerous call to get. I smiled brightly. "The town is lovely. The decorations are perfection, and I hear there's a tree lighting tomorrow night at the Riverwalk. We're going to attend, and I hope to find some time to at least do a little walking along the river."

"A perfect plan. Now let me check on the food." Darla excused herself and Kathleen followed.

Coleman put his arm around me and gave me a squeeze. "We all need to burn off some calories. Let's plan a walk tomorrow along the river. Just the two of us."

I leaned into him and whispered, "Let's plan some activities tonight."

"Eat fast," he said. "Santa may come for a visit."

When we all sat down to eat, the meal was delicious. Darla had a light touch with the food and the pasta with butternut squash sauce was incredible. Filling but not too heavy. The salad was crisp and tangy. We finished with lemon squares—one of my favorite desserts—but I gave mine to Harold.

"Darla is going to give us a tour of the moon garden," Harold said. "Are you two coming?"

He knew better, and he was just deviling us. "I'm exhausted. I'm practically asleep on my feet."

"I'll bet," he said. "See you in the morning."

The group headed out, and Coleman and I were finally alone. It didn't take me any time to walk into his arms for the kiss I'd been waiting for all day. I'd met my share of really good kissers, but Coleman was at the top of the league. He was never rushed, always tantalizing, and he hinted at the pleasures to come. With Coleman, the kiss was an end unto itself, not a means to something else. He was a master at building desire.

When I thought my pants would catch fire, he swooped me up in a Rhett Butler moment and carried me up the stairs to our bedroom. Somehow he'd made arrangements with someone—Darla or Kathleen, most likely—to light candles all over the room. They burned on the mantel and on the dresser, beside the bed, on the windowsills, and in the bathroom. A fire burned cheerily in the fireplace, and when Coleman put me on the bed and unbuttoned my blouse, the chill bumps weren't from the cold.

"Are you glad we came on vacation?" I asked.

"Yep." His finger grazed lightly down my skin from my neck to my navel. "Are you?"

"Very." I pulled him to me for another kiss. When we broke apart, I stared up into his eyes. I'd known him forever and loved him for that long. It had just taken both of us awhile to find our way to each other. "I love you."

"I love you back." He smiled. "We're lucky, Sarah Booth. We are. We're lucky in the way we love each other, but we're lucky in our friends, in our circumstances, in this special moment of our life."

There were times both of us might have been killed in our work, but we'd managed to escape death, though we both had a few scars to show for our experiences. "We are lucky. And smart to see how lucky we are."

He kissed my lips and then trailed down my body. "And now it's time to stop talking, unless you want to tell me again how lucky you are."

"Shut up and show me how you love me."

He pulled the comforter over both of us as we laughed like teenagers.

4

Tap, tap, tap. Tap, tap, tap.

I dove under the pillow until Coleman's fingers found my ribs and gently began to tickle me. "Stop it!"

"She's your partner. You open the door."

"Oh-h-h-h." I climbed out of bed and threw on a robe before I opened the door to Tinkie. She held a tray with a pot of coffee and three cups. Obviously, she had plans to "stay awhile," as the old saying went.

"Tinkie, Coleman isn't even up."

"Well, he should be." She sidestepped around me. "I did leave you until the last."

"You've been to every other room and annoyed everyone else out of their sleep?"

"Yep, and no apologies. It's time to get up and get going."

I thought back through the itinerary I'd seen and I couldn't remember anything that was pressing this morning. "What do we have to do?"

"Shopping!"

I sighed. "No shopping. I shopped yesterday. I've had a bait of shopping."

"The girls are going shopping and the guys have some kind of secret mission."

My ears perked up at "secret mission"—especially since it was the holiday season. That could easily mean *they* were shopping. I approved of the men shopping. I'd personally had enough.

"What kind of secret mission?"

"They won't say."

I arched my left eyebrow at Tinkie. "They won't say? As if they had a choice. You can break Oscar any time you choose. Why didn't you worm the info out of him?"

"I tried."

If Oscar was impervious to Tinkie's Daddy's Girl manipulations—tactics that had kept feminine women in control for decades—then it had to be some serious "secret mission."

"I can't believe Oscar has eluded your control."

"Not permanently. Just for right now. Did you ask Coleman?"

"I didn't know about it. But I will." I pointed at the coffeepot. "Let me take him a cup."

Tinkie waved me on as she went to the French doors and stepped out on the balcony. It was a cold December morning, and the air was crystal clear. Below the balcony, the Tombigbee River flowed by. The bluff down to the river was very steep, though. I could see several boats at the dock, and all were wearing tinsel garlands and other holiday decorations. The flotilla was going to be fun.

I took the coffee into the bedroom and closed the door. "Coleman, it's pointless to try to evade Tinkie. You might as well get up."

"Nope."

"What's the secret mission you guys are working on?" I handed him the coffee.

"Nope."

I sighed. "Coleman, don't mess me around. Just tell me."

"Nope." He had that smug look on his face that said *make me*. It was a definite challenge, and if Tinkie hadn't been sitting right outside the bedroom door listening to every squeak of the bedsprings, I would have.

"To be continued," I said.

"I look forward to it." He grinned really big, far too pleased with himself.

"You will pay."

"A high toll, I hope." He laughed and jumped out of bed. "There's no rest for the wicked here. Remind me never to go on vacation with Tinkie again."

It was my turn to laugh. "Maybe I'll send Tinkie in here to extract that information from you."

A flash of worry flitted in his eyes, but then he laughed again. "You wouldn't. You want to settle this by yourself. You don't need help, do you?"

Oh, he was a wicked taunter. "Right now I have to shower. Tinkie is whipping the herd into movement. If you'd been nicer, I would have invited you to shower with me." I put that on the carpet at his feet.

"You're a hard woman, Sarah Booth."

"Thank you." I turned on my heel and went back to the sitting area, where Tinkie was sipping her coffee as if she hadn't been listening at the door. "Do you think Coleman will tell you?"

"Before the evening comes."

"I'm going back to get dressed. See you in the lobby in forty minutes."

"Yes, Field Marshal Tinkie."

"Tease me all you like. I get things done."

That wasn't an exaggeration.

Tinkie had roused us all for our shopping ordeal, but she relented on allowing time for a hearty breakfast when Darla appeared with an egg, cheese, and asparagus casserole that smelled like five delicious pounds of extra weight. Homemade biscuits, scuppernong jelly, and vegetarian sausage completed the meal. We were a full and jolly crowd as we parted at the front porch, the men going their way and the women heading to town.

"Be sure and go by the Wooden Spoon," Darla called out to us as we loaded in the limo. "They're having a big sale today. I'll be there later to pick up some kitchen supplies."

Safely in the car, we watched the men cluster on the front porch to make plans. The limo driver would return for them and take them to their secret destination.

Tinkie nodded at the limo driver. "If push comes to shove, we can force him into telling us where they went."

Rex was the driver, and he'd been nothing but professional. I had a moment of pity for Rex. He would never withstand the onslaught of Tinkie's charms, should she choose to unleash them on him.

"Let's hope it doesn't come to that." I was curious, but willing to put it on hold for the day. Whatever the men were up to, it was going to be fun for us girls. Or that was the theory I was going with. "Now what's on the shopping hit list?"

"Shoes!" They all three answered at once.

I sighed. Resistance was futile.

Cece and Millie were in great spirits, eager to hit some of the shops we'd missed the day before. It was beyond me how shopping could provide entertainment for two days, but I was the minority vote, and since Tinkie was in charge, my vote didn't count anyway.

Though the men were responding to texts, they refused to tell us where they were or what they were doing. I could tell it niggled at Tinkie. Millie and Cece were oblivious. The men would never tell us now that they knew we were dying of curiosity. They had gotten our goats with their boys' club secretive behaviors, and they would not relent. Not until they were good and ready.

We walked the sidewalks gazing at expertly decorated storefronts that could have won awards back in the day when awards were given for such things. When I was about ten years old, my mother had taken me to Memphis to see the window dressings at the big department stores. It wasn't Fifth Avenue, but it was better for me, because it was within a close drive of home. I had fallen in love with the way the best window dressers could tell an entire story with a couple of mannequins, clothes, and a few props.

At Catfish Alley, where a wonderful mural depicted the African American history of the town, we heard the stories of how local vendors would catch catfish in the river and fry them up in the parking lots near the alley, and how the delicious smell of the frying fish wafted down the alley, drawing merchants and shoppers for a plate lunch of fish, slaw, and hush puppies. I loved that the local merchants had such pride in the history of their town.

We lunched at a little bistro on a corner, and I noticed that Tulla Tarbutton was at a table alone. She looked none the worse for wear after her shocking episode. When a gentleman arrived and she stood up to kiss him with passion, I realized she was completely healed from her experience. Cece saw it, too.

"Who's the guy?" she asked me.

I shook my head. "I'm not yet programmed for facial recognition in Columbus."

She poked me gently in the ribs. "Wiseacre."

I started to say something else, but the door of the bistro blew open and a darkly beautiful woman walked in. She cast a glare at the man with such malice, I thought he would be turned into a toad on the spot. He stood up abruptly, almost upsetting his chair.

"Sunny, what are you doing in town?" he asked.

"I got a call," she said, walking over to the table. "About you. And what you're up to." She drew back her hand and slapped the handsome man hard. Before anyone could react, she turned on her heel and left the restaurant.

"Now that was a statement she made without saying a word," Millie said. She'd captured the drama with her cell phone. "This would make *Variety* if either of those two were celebrities. Too bad they're just local citizens." Millie had jumped into her new career with both feet.

"This town is chock-full of drama," Tinkie said. "It's beginning to wear on me."

The waitress came around with a dessert tray, saving me from having to answer my partner.

"Have the chocolate doberge cake. It's to die for," Millie said. "And keep in mind every town has people who behave badly. Columbus is no exception."

"True," Tinkie said, "but it's tiresome."

I ordered a cup of coffee and kept an eye on Tulla and the man at the table. They were leaning in, whispering. When they abruptly got up and left, I heaved a sigh of relief. I was on vacation. Tinkie was right—we didn't need drama of any kind. Shopping was bad enough. Drama was out of the question.

We finished our meal and continued with our shop-by-shop tour of the town. The wares in the Columbus stores were beautiful and unique, but by five o'clock, I was footsore and weary. I stepped out on the sidewalk and almost ran into Tulla Tarbutton and another pretty woman. They were the nuevo social elite—thin, perfectly coiffed, clothes fitted and without wrinkles. I didn't know if Columbus had Daddy's Girls, but these ladies were kissing cousins to that breed.

"How are you feeling, Tulla?" I asked.

"Fine. The shock didn't leave any permanent damage. No twitches or spells of spitting." She pulled a face to let me know she was teasing. "Thank you and your friends for all you did." She looked past me. "Where are the men you were with?"

"Busy," Tinkie said quickly.

"Tulla, you said you were going to clean up your act," the other woman said with a wicked glint in her eye. Turning to us, she added, "Tulla is a great admirer of men who belong to other women." She held out her hand. "Bricey Presley."

"Maybe you're the one who has an act to clean up, Bricey," Tulla said, but without malice. "Where'd you get that brand-new Cadillac convertible you're driving?" The two women were laughing at each other.

"At the getting place," Bricey said. She gave a saucy shake of her head. "Tulla can't stand it because men give me expensive gifts all the time."

"Probably because she's blackmailing them," Tulla said.

"If I was blackmailing them, I'd have a lot more than a new car," Bricey said with a sniff. They both burst into laughter.

"Are you coming down to the Riverwalk for the tree lighting?" Tulla asked us.

"We're headed there now."

"See you there. Bring those handsome men!" She gave a wave as she and her friend left.

"I'll bring a slap upside her head," Tinkie said darkly as they walked away.

5

We met the men at the Riverwalk, where they were waiting for us, looking as innocent as Attila the Hun at a pillaged Roman village. Harold had arranged delivery of champagne and strawberries dipped in chocolate. Tinkie had her own thermos of hot chocolate, made by our host, Darla, just for her. We sipped the bubbly and ate the strawberries while we milled around the twenty-foot Christmas tree and the food tables.

A woman dressed as Mother Goose was hosting stories for a group of enthralled children who were hanging on her every word. Elves and Santa's helpers were mingling in the crowd, offering canapés for adults and cookies for the children.

Darla had brought beautiful punch bowls filled with

nonalcoholic drinks for all the attendees, and I noticed several of the participants spiking their cups. It was the holidays, and the night was cold. A little nip was part of the celebration.

Coleman had thought to bring my heavier coat, which I was glad to slip into. But I was even more glad for his arms around me, holding me close against him.

A crowd of about two thousand had gathered to watch the tree lighting, and I caught Tinkie gazing at several children staring up at the live magnolia tree in awe, waiting for that magic moment when the multicolored lights would be turned on. Cece snapped photos and I gave her a thumbs-up. Soon Tinkie would have a baby of her own. The one thing she'd wanted more than anything else was going to be hers. Good things did happen to good people. Right now I would not contemplate if this pregnancy was due to the three Harrington sisters, self-proclaimed witches, who'd given Tinkie a potion to get pregnant. The witchy sisters had given me a gris-gris bag to bring a man to my bed. Coleman had showed up, but I wasn't going to think about that, either. Nope. Not thinking about *any* of that.

Across the beautiful park area, Darla and Harold were carrying on like old friends, and I wondered if a spark of romance might have been lit there. She was a woman who would complement his life. She had all the social graces, and it was obvious she enjoyed hosting parties and events. Harold threw the best parties in Zinnia. Even if they just remained friends, Darla was a nice connection for him.

Cece and Jaytee moved out of the circle around the tree to the fringes of the park, where they found a bench and snuggled up close together. My friend had been through a lot of hardship in her life. She was the bravest person I knew, and this Christmas she had found someone to love, someone who loved her back. I took a photo of them with my cell phone for a great memory. If they ever wanted to make Christmas cards with photos, this could be the one they'd use.

Millie was helping a toddler who'd gotten tangled in a Christmas garland. They were both laughing. Millie looked younger and happier than I'd seen her in months. Watching my extraordinary friends, I had a lot to be grateful for.

"You look pensive." Coleman snuggled up the collar of my coat to keep the cold wind from slipping in.

"I was thinking how happy my friends are. It only magnifies my happiness."

"They do look happy. Harold has snagged him a fancy fish. Darla looks very interested in him."

"For today, anyway." I saw Tulla and Bricey coming out of the crowd making a beeline for Harold. "Uh-oh, the piranhas are on the move."

Coleman leaned forward. "Should I go save Harold? They'll gobble him up in two minutes."

"Oh, no." I was looking forward to watching this unfold. "Harold can hold his own. *If* he wants to. That's a big if."

The women made a fuss over Harold, and I wasn't certain but I thought I saw a bit of jealousy on Darla's face. That wasn't good. Harold wasn't a man who liked to be fought over. He enjoyed women. He was handsome, wealthy, and known as the best catch in the Delta—and therefore he liked to chase, not be chased.

Coleman leaned over to whisper, "Pack of hounds with a ham bone. They're licking it now. Soon they'll go to chomping."

Coleman did entertain me. "If Harold screams, we'll save him. He looks like he's enjoying it, as far as I can tell." Harold seemed to be at his courtliest best. The women were all attractive, and while they might suck his soul out of his ear while he slept, they were good for his ego.

"Let's explore the Riverwalk," Coleman suggested.

I jumped to my feet, hoping for a kiss. I had to hand it to Tinkie for booking a very romantic holiday trip for us. Coleman and I had found more time to be together than we normally did. We were both away from work, relaxed and playful.

We walked down to the river and I glanced into the dark water flowing by. Of all the bodies of water, rivers and streams pleased me the most. Cece was a Gulf girl, and Tinkie had grown up in pools, but I loved the slow, gentle movement of the rivers.

"Look, a shooting star," Coleman said, pointing up and across the river.

I looked up at the starry night. Coleman's lips found mine. We were making up for lost time. Coleman's kisses just melted my bones. I lingered in the kiss, relishing the intimacy. When at last we broke apart, I said, "This is wonderful. I'm so glad Tinkie thought of this trip."

"Me, too." Coleman tipped my chin up for another kiss, but alas, Tinkie was onto us. She'd bird-dogged us successfully down to the river.

"We're about to start the caroling," she said.

"Are you sure you want Sarah Booth to participate?" Coleman asked. "I thought I'd keep her occupied here until the singing was over."

I jabbed him in the ribs and Tinkie grabbed his hand. "Nice try. Not going to work. Come participate." We had little choice but to follow her.

We made it through the singing of three carols, a speech by the mayor of the town, and the actual lighting of the tree, which was truly beautiful. It was worth waiting for.

Just as the applause was dying, I heard the sound of heavy equipment in the parking lot up the hill above us. The beep, beep, beep of a machine backing up, and then what sounded like a crash.

Coleman signaled me and we took off to check it out, our group following behind us at a more leisurely pace.

Under a bright light in the parking lot was a huge pile of cement. It took me a moment to realize that under the fresh cement was a beautiful new Cadillac convertible. "Oh, my." I didn't know what else to say.

Luckily I didn't have to say anything. Bricey, Tulla's friend, came caterwauling across the parking lot. "My car! My brand-new car! My car! Look what someone did to my car! Call the police. I want them arrested."

Tinkie sidled up beside me. "Someone is playing a dangerous game in this town," she said.

"Cheating is always dangerous." The warm and relaxed feeling of the evening was slipping away. Tinkie was right. Someone was eventually going to get seriously hurt if this kept up.

"Someone is out for revenge," Tinkie said. "Tulla's shock at karaoke. The destruction of a $70,000 car. This is getting more and more lethal."

"And more and more public," Cece chimed in. She and Jaytee had sauntered up. "Millie and I are taking notes in case we can use them in the Sunday column. I mean, seriously, dumping a load of cement into a car is pretty out there, but it's a great image for the paper."

I couldn't disagree with her. People did a lot of crazy things for love or revenge. Even murder. "Let's just be glad this isn't Zinnia and we don't know these people. We don't have to get involved in this."

"Good thinking." Tinkie said. "Let's head back to the B and B. I think we should play charades tonight!"

Coleman and I looked at each other. We'd play charades for a while, but then we had other business to attend to.

6

I'd cracked the balcony door open just a little so I could hear the wind soughing in the trees and drink in the clean, fresh smell of winter. I didn't know what had awakened me, but I was restless, and Coleman was sound asleep. The room was a little too cold, so I slipped out of bed, found my slippers and warm robe, and stepped out on the balcony for a moment to glance up at the clear sky dotted with a zillion pinpricks of light. The wide-open nocturnal Delta vista was incomparable, but Columbus, with this view across the wide black river, had a pretty good nightscape, too. My room on the third floor of the B and B put me above the treetops.

I heard the door creak open behind me. I'd tried to be quiet, but obviously I'd awakened Coleman. "Come sit by me and keep me warm." I patted the extra-wide chaise I'd curled up on.

"I don't ever remember feeling this awake."

I whipped around because the voice was female, not Coleman. The woman standing in front of me lifted up a pair of cat's-eye dark sunglasses to reveal deep blue eye shadow. She wore red lipstick and capris. Her brown hair was windblown. She wasn't anyone I knew.

"Who are you? Why are you in my room?"

"You said you'n'me was gonna get out of town and for once just really let our hair down. Well, darlin', look out, 'cause my hair is comin' down."

Maybe it was the sweetness of her voice that gave her away. A woman-child finally on the brink of adulthood. I knew her then. Thelma stood in front of me, waiting for me to pick up on the role of her sidekick and friend Louise. They were a movie duo that had burned into celluloid history. Thelma was a fictional character, but she was being played by a ghost.

"Nice job with the makeup, but Jitty, you need to go home to Dahlia House. Sweetie Pie and Pluto are missing you."

"I'm not a dog you can order around." Jitty was still in her Thelma persona. She put her hands on her hips and stared me down.

"I'm not ordering, I'm asking reasonably. You have to get out of here. You're going to wake up Coleman. Then what am I going to do? What if he sees you? You could be banished from ever going back to Dahlia House." The thought made me really sad. My home wouldn't be my home without Jitty. She was so much a part of Dahlia House now that I couldn't do without her.

"You gonna have to tell him about me sooner or later."

"Later. Once I know what the end result will be." I motioned her to come sit beside me. "I can't do without you, Jitty." Tinkie was my partner and best friend. Cece owned a hunk of my heart, as did Millie. But Jitty— she was the key to my past, and like it or not, my past haunted me the way Jitty haunted Dahlia House.

Jitty put on a pout that almost broke my heart. "I can't ever go back."

I recognized the line from the movie, when Thelma finally understands she can't ever return to the abusive life she'd finally escaped. "Are you talking about Dahlia House or something else?"

"I'm trying to speak my lines." Jitty's impatience relieved me. She was merely playing her role.

"Didn't you kill a man in that movie?"

"Maybe."

There was something dangerous in her lovely Geena Davis face. Thelma was a woman who'd reached her limit. Driving off a cliff was preferable to going back to a life she could no longer tolerate. "What are you up to, Jitty?"

She grinned, and slowly my beautiful ghost began to show through the Geena Davis actress playing Thelma. "Life tests us, Sarah Booth. You know that better than most."

"Why are you showing up as women who murder people? Or at least who *want* to murder people."

She shook her head. "Not sure even I know. I just like the sunglasses and convertible."

And that would have to do for an answer as she spun

in a circle and sparks of red and green shot out from her. Another moment and she was gone, leaving only the smell of pumpkin spice and cedar. Jitty knew how to make an exit.

I went back inside and slipped under the covers, trying hard not to disturb Coleman. I thought I'd spend some time thinking about Jitty and her strange appearances, but instead, I was out like a light in under thirty seconds.

I awoke the next morning to an empty bed and sun streaming through the open balcony doors. Coleman was sitting out on the chaise. "Wake up, sleepyhead. Tinkie has been up here twice, and I told her if she woke you up, I was going to withhold her Christmas present this year."

My watch showed eight-forty, and I sat up and stretched. The bedroom was chilly with the door open, but it felt good. At least while I was under the covers.

Coleman came into the bedroom with a steaming cup of coffee for me. "Darla made a tray with a carafe," he said. "She's a superior hostess. She made some cheese Danish for breakfast, so it's kind of eat when you're hungry."

"I'm hungry." I yawned, remembering Jitty's appearance as Thelma. "Did Darla say anything about the incident of the Cadillac buried in cement?"

Coleman sat on the edge of the bed. "She said Columbus was a conservative town, but that there were people here, like everywhere else, who got caught up in passion. She said Tulla and Bricey had both been rumored to have affairs with married men. Darla kind of felt like the wives had decided not to take it lying down anymore."

"Revenge." It was the theory I'd already gone to. And a messy motive at best, especially in the world of infidelities. Revenge was the step that came after a total loss of hope that the relationship could be salvaged. Once the card of revenge had been thrown on the table, there was no going back. At least not for normal people.

"What's on Tinkie's agenda for today?" I didn't want to think about cheaters and losers. If someone was lucky enough to have love and then too stupid to appreciate it, I was happy walking on by. Not people I wanted in my life.

"You're touring the Waverley Mansion estate and heading over to West Point today to see that town. Tonight is the Columbus Christmas pilgrimage of homes."

"This sounds more fun than shopping, but what is this *your* business? You make it sound like you're not coming to Waverley."

"Oscar, Jaytee, Harold, and I have some work to do."

"What?" I sat up. "You really aren't going with us?"

"I think you can tour a mansion on your own, and I've been to West Point a number of times. Oscar has, too. We really have to finish up some stuff."

"Finish up some stuff? On your secret mission?"

"Exactly," Coleman said. He stood up and refilled my coffee cup. He was already dressed for the day, and I realized too late that he was making a break for freedom. "See you tonight for dinner before the pilgrimage."

He was out the door and I heard his footsteps in the hall. Whatever those men were up to, I was going to find out. All this secret-schmeecret business was getting under my skin.

I showered, dressed, and met "the secret mission widows" in the front parlor. The limo was back from delivering the men to whatever destination they had picked.

Rex was as silent as the grave. Oscar and Harold had either bribed him well or threatened him into zipping his lip. No matter what we asked, we got stonewalled. When Tinkie asked him if he'd like to tour Waverley with us, he declined, saying he'd stay in the car.

"So much for wheedling information out of him," Millie said with a laugh. "Few men can stand the onslaught of Zinnia's Queen Bee Daddy's Girl. You have to give the devil his due, Rex is loyal to Oscar and Harold."

"We could withhold sex from the men," Cece said as we walked up the brick walk to the beautiful old house with a unique design. The place was surrounded by forest. Not far away was the Tombigbee River, which had been crucial in the selling of goods and development of Waverley plantation, as it was originally known.

"No! We are *not* withholding sex," I said with more force than I'd intended, and my friends laughed out loud. I calmed my voice. "We don't have to do anything rash. We can just follow them tomorrow," I said.

"True enough," Tinkie agreed. "Now on with the tour. This place has a fascinating history."

Two hours later, filled with stories of tragedy and joy centered around Waverley, we were on the way to West Point. The city, one of the three in the "golden triangle," was decorated with tinsel and lights for the holiday season. Shoppers were out in force, and the town literally bustled. I'd suggest to Tinkie that we make a trip to West Point next Christmas. We could make a tradition of visiting a Mississippi town every year just before Christmas.

7

After lunch and more shopping, we headed back to Columbus. Per our plan, we met up with the men for dinner and then went on to Rook's Nest, one of the oldest homes in Columbus. It was a three-story gingerbread beauty with all of the Gothic architectural twists of the finest pre–Civil War homes in the South.

People were coming and going, oohing and aahing over the twinkling lights and the beautiful décor. We entered and accepted a glass of wine as a server passed by. The people of Columbus had retained the grace and social niceties of a time gone by. On this one magical night when local residents opened their homes to strangers for some holiday cheer, I was reminded of a period when grace and manners marked the character of a town. I was in awe of the elaborate decorations in Rook's Nest. To be honest, I had no idea who our hosts were—I hadn't read the detailed itinerary Tinkie had mailed out. But I was glad that Tinkie had bullied me into taking the pilgrimage. This was something my parents would have enjoyed. They were small-scale party-givers. Except at Christmas. My mother had adored Christmas, and I knew she would have loved the huge fir tree with the hand-carved and -painted figures of rocking horses, toy soldiers, angels, elves, and other Christmas creatures. The fir smelled wonderful, and I inhaled the delicate odor, taking in all the memories that came with it. I'd come to realize that almost everything I loved was bittersweet. I felt the joy of the holidays and of being with the ones I loved, but also a tinge of sadness for the ones I had lost.

"Sarah Booth, are you okay?" Millie had sidled up to me. She was an astute judge of character and mood. She, too, had suffered loss.

"I am. This is a beautiful house. Would you say Victorian?"

"Queen Anne, I think. I'm not an authority on architecture," Millie said. "I can attest to the fact it's beautiful and lends itself to all this decadent decoration."

Harold had joined us. "In the days when this house was built, you could actually order pattern books to show you how to add the recognized Queen Anne flourishes like the turrets and wraparound porches. Another identifying characteristic is that the houses are asymmetrical."

My home, Dahlia House, with its wide sweeping front porch and huge columns, was more formal and less fanciful. "This is just pretty. And did you see the staircase?

It almost floats!" I was also a big fan of the cantilevered staircases. The one in Waverley Mansion had been astounding, and this one, on a less grand scale, was just as lovely in its own way. The staircase curved up to the second floor and then on to the third.

"Where did Coleman, Oscar, and Jaytee get off to?" Harold asked. The men had all been with us, but now three of them had disappeared.

"Maybe doing secret mission work," I said wickedly. "Why don't you tell us what's going on?"

"Not going to happen, Sarah Booth." He shook his head. "But I'd like for you to try to make me talk. Maybe a few threats? I love it when you talk brash."

Harold was incorrigible. He would never spill the beans. It was a waste of my time, but we both enjoyed the challenge. "Tinkie might be more effective at wringing the truth out of you. After all, her daddy owns the bank." Harold worked with Oscar at Zinnia National Bank. They were both, technically, employees of Tinkie's father, but Avery Bellcase left the running of the bank to Oscar, and Oscar relied heavily on Harold. Avery never interfered and Harold knew that.

"Ah, threatening my livelihood. That is a new low, Sarah Booth."

"Maybe I'll just get some compromising photographs of you and . . . what is her name? Tulla? Bricey? Or . . ."—I pointed at the beautiful blond woman who was making a beeline for us—"maybe her."

"Watch out for her," Coleman whispered to me, his breath tickling my ear and neck. He'd reappeared out of nowhere. "She's a barracuda."

"How do you know that?" I asked.

"Years of experience with dangerous women."

Coleman was teasing me, up to a point. I could tell by his expression that he was genuinely wary of the woman who came up and introduced herself.

"Hello, I'm Clarissa Olson. Welcome to Rook's Nest. This is my home. I'm intrigued to have private investigators here"—she stared at Coleman a moment too long—"and an official member of Mississippi's finest."

"What about bankers and musicians?" I asked.

"Oh, them, too. But Sheriff Peters isn't wearing a ring. There's a flock of women who've noticed already. The same for the banker and the musician." She eyed Jaytee and I wondered if she would actually drool. "I hear he blows a hot harmonica."

It was impossible to tell if she was being serious or coy. I decided to go with the latter. Some women had been raised to be the coquette; it was the only behavior they knew.

We all offered compliments on her house and decorating skills.

"Thank you. I'm just fortunate to have a house that allows me to indulge in these excesses of Christmas." She waved a hand to include the tree, the garlands of greenery draped everywhere, and even the mistletoe hanging from a chandelier. She grabbed Coleman's hand and tugged him under the batch of greenery. She stood on tiptoe, intending to plant a big kiss on my guy. I slid between them with the subtlety of an elephant stampede, pushing Clarissa backward with a bit too much verve. She was lucky Harold caught her when she stumbled and almost fell off her high heels.

"I don't recommend messing with Sarah Booth's fella," Harold said loudly enough for several bystanders to hear. A little twitter broke out among the females.

"Oh, honestly," Clarissa said, straightening the emerald shantung jacket she wore. "People in this town are so uptight about a little Christmas buss."

Before our encounter could escalate, my attention was drawn to the top of the beautiful staircase. All around me laughter and conversation bubbled, but for me, the room had gone suddenly silent. At the top of the stairs, a man teetered on the soles of his feet as his arms windmilled. Events unfolded in silent slow motion. I watched in horror as he hurtled down the steps, tumbling in a topsy-turvy heap so that I couldn't identify who it was, only that it was a male. Sound returned with full intensity when several women screamed, and then all conversation stopped as the man made the curve in the staircase, heels over head, and sprawled to a stop right at my feet.

The entire room drew in a collective breath. The man bleeding on the expensive Oriental carpet was George Clooney handsome and definitely injured—and one I'd seen before with Tulla Tarbutton in a restaurant. He of the angry wife. I knelt down to feel for a pulse. "He's alive! Call an ambulance now!"

Panic broke out as several people came over to assist with first aid. A dark-haired woman broke through the crowd and dropped to her knees beside him. "Bart! Bart!" She tried to get a response. "Tell me you're okay." It was the wife—the same one who'd slapped his face in the restaurant.

But Bart wasn't talking—and might never again. I had no idea how serious his injuries were or what had happened. As people with medical ability took over, I stepped back to the fringes of the crowd, watching as Coleman took command of the scene. He was clearing everyone away while Harold and Jaytee knelt by Bart, who was moaning and starting to show signs of wanting to get up. The woman on the floor kneeling at his head looked up into the faces of the guests. From an expression of fear, her face went to full-blown rage. She pointed at Tulla Tarbutton. "This is on you! This is your fault."

"I didn't push him," Tulla said. "I wasn't upstairs. I was over in the corner with some others. Maybe you did it, Sunny. He's your husband. You're the one with a motive to kill him."

Sunny came off her knees like she was powered by a nuclear reactor. "How dare you! I'm going to pull every hair out of your head." She lunged across her husband's prone body, but Coleman captured her and held her.

"Calm down. Just calm down. Let's get some help for your husband before you do anything rash." Coleman had a tiger by the tail. Sunny was almost foaming at the mouth.

Movement at the top of the stairs caught my eye. I saw Bricey Presley dart down the hallway and into a bedroom. A door closed silently. My attention was drawn back to the injured man.

"The paramedics are on their way," Cece said, and I was glad to see she'd had the presence of mind to make the call and was now videoing everyone at the crime scene. That would prove valuable to the police when they began investigating, if an investigation was warranted.

"Did you get any video of Bart falling?" I asked Cece, who'd come up beside me.

"Most of it." She leaned a little closer to me. "Rumor has it that Bart and Sunny are always at each other's throats. He's a notorious womanizer, and Sunny probably pushed him down the stairs. Or maybe one of his mistresses did it."

"You think he was pushed?" I asked. "That's terrible. Thank goodness Tinkie and I haven't been deeply involved in domestic cases," I said. "Those are just the worst. They're a no-win situation for a PI."

Clarissa Olson appeared at my side. "May I have a word?"

"Sure." I stepped away and followed Clarissa to where Tinkie was standing, a stricken look on her face.

"This is terrible. What an awful accident," Tinkie said.

"I want to hire your detective agency," Clarissa said before I could ask any questions.

"For what?" Tinkie asked.

"Someone is pulling a bunch of dirty tricks around here. The dump truck load of cement on Bricey's new car. The shock to Tulla. Now Bart has been pushed down the stairs. Someone is going to be seriously hurt—if Bart isn't already. Or even killed. I need to know who is doing this and stop it."

"Was Bricey Presley involved with Bart?" I asked. I'd seen her at the top of the stairs.

Clarissa shrugged one shoulder. "That's for you to find out. I'll drop by the B and B later and bring a check."

"I'm not certain we want to be involved in this case," I said. "We're here on holiday and we have to leave in a few days."

"You don't live on the other side of the ocean," Clarissa said, waving a hand with a diamond ring the size of a walnut. "Surely you can manage a case in Columbus even if you live in the metropolis of Zinnia."

Her sarcasm wasn't making me eager to work for her, but I had my eye on a new saddle for Coleman's Christmas gift. A paying case would give me the extra cash for year-end expenses at Dahlia House *and* the saddle. "We could manage it if we wanted to," I said. "I'm just not sure I want to get embroiled in what looks to be a cluster of serial cheaters. That's a thankless task. Besides, no one is going to be happy with what we find out."

"You could save a life." Clarissa was done with sarcasm. "This has gone from nasty warnings to dangerous pranks and now to potentially fatal attacks. Maybe you think these people don't deserve to be saved, but that's pretty judgy of you, Sarah Booth Delaney."

"Sarah Booth isn't judging them," Tinkie said. "She's just making a point that she might not be keen to associate with them. This kind of case is like stepping in a cesspool. Nobody comes out of it clean."

"I'm sure there are other private investigators in Columbus who could do a fine job," I said. Tinkie was right. We seldom turned down cases, but this one had the reek of bad trouble.

"I'm not going to beg you," Clarissa said. "If you're afraid of a little domestic kerfuffle, then you're afraid."

"We're not afraid." Tinkie took the bait before I could stop her. "We'll take your case. But we need an honest answer from you."

"About what?" Clarissa asked.

"Are you involved with Bart Crenshaw?"

Clarissa chuckled. "I danced with that monkey years ago." She swiveled her hips, "Cha, cha, cha! Bart and I burned hot and fast. Now there's not even a glowing ember left. But I don't want to see him murdered. He's selling my property for me, and he's the best real estate agent around. I've made a killing since we teamed up professionally."

"What do you know about Bricey Presley?" I asked. If Bricey had pushed Bart, and she was there with him on the second floor, it would be a simple case. Tinkie and I could collect our fee and call it a day.

"She's been involved with Bart, but that's in the past. He paid her off with that Cadillac that got filled up with cement."

That was interesting. "So maybe Bart decided she didn't deserve a fancy car."

Clarissa shook her head. "No, Bart gave her the Cadillac as a parting gift. Bart never leaves a lady with a frown on her face. This is something else."

"Was Tulla Tarbutton involved with Bart?" I was going to need a scorecard to keep all of these entanglements straight.

"No clue."

"Was Tulla involved with anyone else?" Tinkie asked.

Clarissa played the dumb blonde. "That's your job to find out. I just want you to figure out who's angry enough to nearly kill a man and then I want you to stop them. Leave me out of this completely. No one should know I've hired you."

"Why not?" I asked. What was Clarissa trying to hide?

She put her hands on her hips. "Look, this kind of cheating thing goes on everywhere. In a small town, it's just easier to spot. There are happily married couples and there are swingers. By day, no one knows the difference, but at night, some folks grow old in front of a television and others stay young by . . . scratching an itch."

"Are you cheating with someone?" Tinkie asked, getting right to the point. "Maybe you're afraid someone is coming after you."

Clarissa laughed, and it was almost as tinkling and bell-like as Tinkie's own signature laugh. "Tulla is my best friend. I know she's inserted herself into more than one marriage around here. She doesn't mean any harm— it's just that she's a predator. She sees a man she wants and she goes for him. When she's done, she walks away. No harm, no foul. The problem is, someone put a water moccasin in her mailbox last week. The snake was dead, but the message was clear."

"That's pretty drastic, but cheating isn't just a game. People get hurt. Lives are ruined." Tinkie was not a fan of deceit or lies.

Clarissa shrugged one shoulder. "This is the real world, ladies. It happens. Spouses and fiancés stray. Women and men sleep with their boss or employees. Young girls hone their skills chasing older men. These are all passing stages. None of them should be taken seriously by any party involved."

Her philosophy of life wasn't appealing to me, but what she said was at least partially true. It took all kinds to make a community.

"Are you kidding me?" Millie had walked up for the tail end of the conversation. "That kind of crap can kill a marriage and put a person's life in danger. It's not just a passing moment of great sex with no cost. It has a cost. Sometimes a high one."

Clarissa grabbed a glass of wine from a passing server and swallowed most of it. "Perhaps in your plebeian world, but those of us with some sophistication understand that man is just an animal. We have animal urges. Once you own up to it, then it frees you to enjoy life."

"People get hurt when someone they love cheats. Most people don't like to be hurt. Sometimes they lash back." Millie held her ground.

"Sex has nothing to do with love," Clarissa insisted. "Only a naïve fool would confuse the two."

I put a hand on Millie's shoulder but spoke to Clarissa. "Maybe you should rent the movie *Fatal Attraction*. Oh, and if you have any rabbits, it may be best to rehome them."

"Pish posh," Clarissa said, shaking her head. "I don't care if you are judgmental about us. Your view of what we do is neither here nor there. Will you take the case?"

"What do you want us to prove?" I asked.

"Find out who's behind this series of accidents and let's get them the mental help they need. Someone is going to get hurt. I can agree with you on that. Poor Bart came down those stairs like he was a sack of potatoes. He could have easily broken his neck."

"Our retainer is fifteen large," Tinkie said, upping our normal fee and also attempting to sound like a gangster. I loved it when she got her back up.

"I'll have the money. Now I must see to my guests." She walked toward the bar. "Everyone, please, refill your glasses. This has been a terrible accident, but Bart is on the way to the hospital to get the care he needs. There's nothing else we can do for him. Please drink up."

"You think we can solve this before we leave Columbus?" Tinkie asked. Around us the sound of hushed talk continued. Clarissa turned the Christmas music louder.

"If this was going on in Zinnia, it would be a snap because we would know exactly the right people to ask." Every town had a couple of people who were up to speed on all the gossip. We just didn't know who that might be in Columbus.

8

It took some effort on Clarissa's part, but she finally got the party revved up. I wanted to leave, but the beautiful old Queen Anne house was jam-packed with potential suspects, so Tinkie and I split up to cover more ground. Cece and Millie were also helping: they walked up to groups of women and inserted themselves into conversations, eventually leading the talk back to the cement-buried Caddy and Tulla's shocking karaoke experience. I was also interested in Sunny Crenshaw, wife of the tumbling Realtor. She hadn't gone to the hospital with her husband but instead had remained at the party, drinking pretty hard. I also had an eye out for Bricey Presley. She was my number one suspect in Bart Crenshaw's unfortunate "accident."

A group of laughing women clustered around Darla, who was recounting stories about bad B and B guests from holidays past.

"And then there was the man who would get up in the middle of the night, sneak into the kitchen, and eat every single Christmas cookie I'd baked."

"How many cookies?" someone asked.

"One night it had to be three dozen. I was terrified he'd go into a diabetic coma or have a heart attack." Darla was an engaging storyteller. Everyone was laughing. I hadn't really considered how awful it might be to have people in her home all the time, wandering around at night, looking for snacks, going to the bathroom, or playing musical bedrooms. It wasn't a situation I wanted to deal with. As one of those guests at Bissonnette House, I would be on my best behavior.

I skirted the group listening to Darla and went to an alcove off the formal dining room, where an incredible mahogany table caught my eye. When I went to examine it, I found a woman sitting alone in a dim corner of the room. Her back was to me, but I recognized Kathleen.

"Are you okay?" I asked.

"I'm fine. It's just a shock to think someone almost died at a Christmas party."

"That whole business with Bart Crenshaw was just awful. The way he tumbled down the stairs. I keep seeing it in slow motion in my brain," I agreed.

"Have you heard if he's going to be okay?"

I hadn't, but Coleman could check for me. "I can find out."

"Would you?"

"Why not? Come with me." We left the dim corner

and went outside where Coleman, Jaytee, Harold, and Oscar had escaped the buzz saw of gossip in the house. When I asked Coleman to make the call to check on Bart, he didn't even ask why.

A moment later, he had an update. "Bart is in a room. No broken bones. A concussion, but they don't think it's serious. They're going to watch him, though."

"What about a brain bleed?" Kathleen went right to the darkest place possible.

"From what the local police officer who is in the room with him said, it looks pretty good that there's no serious injury. They're anticipating a full recovery."

Kathleen blew out a breath. "Thank you. Now I should go help our hostess." She turned away from the group.

"Kathleen, got a minute?" I asked.

She looked toward the doorway and actually edged in that direction, but I followed her. "Tell me about Sunny Crenshaw."

"Oh, Sunny comes from money. Big money. She was fabulously wealthy before she married Bart. Once his real estate business got going, they were set. They're just wallowing in greenbacks. Everything Bart touches turns to gold."

"I've heard he's got the magic touch with real estate." I just wanted to keep the conversation going. The quicker I got my bearings in Columbus society, the sooner I would solve this case. "Clarissa Olson said she worked with him and he'd been very helpful to her."

Kathleen rolled her eyes. "She thought she was going to break up Bart and Sunny's marriage, but Bart gave her the heave-ho. That whole real estate thing she goes on and on and on about is just to save face."

"So Clarissa was really into him? She made it seem like a long-ago fling."

"She plays it off like it was just a game of the beast with two backs, but he knew how to light her rockets, and she couldn't get enough of him. She was reckless, forcing public displays on him. She wasn't smart enough to keep the details to herself."

"How did Sunny take that . . . affair?"

Kathleen slowed to a stop. She frowned. "I never really thought about it. She never let on like she knew anything was happening between them, but she had to know. Like I said, Clarissa couldn't keep her lip zipped. She did ridiculous things like show up at his real estate office dressed as a gift box and naked as the day she was born inside the box. Everyone in town knew about it."

"Did Sunny retaliate with her own affair?" I wanted more than anything to make some notes, but I knew if pulled out a pad and started writing, Kathleen would flee as if her hair were on fire. Around Darla, Kathleen had a certain bravado, but she was timid alone.

"Sunny would extract her pound of flesh, and there was talk that she had had an affair not long after they were married. You can believe that or not. But she made Bart pay, I'm sure. I don't know how she did it, though. She may have had an affair and just been more discreet. Or she may have a nice offshore bank account plumped up by condo sales in Oxford, Mississippi. Now that's a hot real estate market."

"Did Sunny go to Ole Miss?"

"Vanderbilt. Her family is related to the Vanderbilts and she always felt she was a bit superior to all of us here in Columbus. She rubbed Bart's nose in her aristocracy."

Kathleen had regained some of her pluck and was more comfortable talking to me. "I don't blame him for looking for affection somewhere else. She's a cold fish."

"Is she capable of attempted murder?" I was curious what she'd say.

"I think so. In my opinion, the only thing that would hold Sunny back from committing a felony would be fear of getting caught. If she thought she could pull off a murder and get away with it, she wouldn't blink."

"Tell me about Bricey Presley." If I had a gushing fountain of information, I was going to stay awhile and drink.

"Bricey runs around with Tulla and a few others. They're minor-league homewreckers compared to Sunny or Clarissa."

"Is everyone in town having an affair?"

She thought a minute. "Probably not. Just the ones with time on their hands."

I thought about that. It did take a lot of time and energy to sneak around. Women with children and jobs could do it, but it would put a crimp in their style to have to juggle schedules and free times. "Who dumped that cement in Bricey's car, do you know?"

"I thought it might be Bart. I heard they had a nasty breakup, and Bart knows a lot of guys with heavy equipment because he develops subdivisions and such. But so does Sunny. And Clarissa. It could be anyone."

"Only someone who hated Bricey."

"That means it could be anyone," Kathleen repeated. "Now I have to go. I'm tired of this Christmas foolishness. I'm ready for this week to be over. Most days, Darla and I take care of her guests and we meet new and interesting people and don't give a thought to what's happening in Columbus. It's just at Christmas that we kind of have to dive in headfirst."

"I'll see you back at Darla's," I said as she took her leave.

Tinkie was still chatting with a group of men, and from a distance I watched her work them. Tinkie had them eating out of her hand. When she saw me, she gave them a flirtatious wave and joined me. "Let's go to the hospital to check on Bart," she said.

This was really the first time I'd had a chance to chat with Tinkie alone. "I saw Bricey Presley on the second floor just seconds after Bart took that tumble. He gave her the Cadillac when he broke off his affair with her."

Tinkie's eyebrows hit her hairline. "Whew!" Tinkie motioned Oscar over to join us. "We've got a new case."

When Oscar started to protest, Tinkie merely kissed him. "It's a domestic about to go bad. We'll finish before it's time to go home to Zinnia. No murders, no guns, no danger. Just a bunch of foolish people determined to trash their own lives."

"Tinkie, you're in a delicate way," he reminded her.

"I'm pregnant. I haven't turned into glass. This is a simple case, really. Nothing to worry about. The baby is my first priority, and you're my second."

I took note of her gentle response to Oscar and her quick moves to alleviate his fears. Tinkie was compassionate, and she was also very smart.

"We were just headed over to the hospital to check on Bart Crenshaw," Tinkie said to Oscar. We waved over the rest of the crew. "Cece, when you get a minute I'd like to look through the footage of Bart's tumble down the stairs."

"Sure thing. In fact, I'll come to the hospital with you."

"Me, too," Millie chimed in. "That leaves the boys to finish their secret mission stuff."

It chafed me to let the guys get away with the he-man woman-haters club business, but I didn't have a choice. Money over curiosity, as Tinkie had pointed out. Money won.

The boys said they didn't need the limo because they had other means of transportation—a statement that concerned me. But we loaded up and headed to the Columbus hospital. Bart had been taken to a room, and Millie occupied the floor nurses while we slipped unnoticed into his room. He was propped up in bed watching TV and looked none too pleased to see us.

"You were at the party." He said it as an accusation.

"True," I said. "We were having a fine time until you decided to see if you could bounce."

He moaned as he shifted positions. "Get out of here. I don't want to talk to anyone."

"We've been hired to find out who's attacking members of the Columbus social scene."

"Hired by whom?" He tried to sit up in bed and his monitors went haywire.

Cece pressed him gently back into the pillows. "It doesn't matter who hired Delaney Detective Agency, and you hold still." She kept one finger on his chest.

"Our client is afraid someone is going to get hurt, if not killed. And you're a central player in what's going on. We'll leave as soon as you tell me who pushed you."

"Nobody. I wasn't pushed!"

"I saw you fall. And I saw Bricey Presley on the second floor not ten seconds after your spectacular tumble."

He looked from me to Tinkie to Cece. When Millie

came in the room, he realized she wasn't going to save him, either.

"This is none of your business."

"I saw Bricey run off like a criminal."

"She was upset about her Cadillac getting destroyed. She thought maybe Sunny had dumped the cement in the car. She wanted me to make it good."

"Make it good?" I asked.

"Get her a new car."

"And?" I said.

"And I told her I would. Look, sometimes it's better to write the check. Bricey isn't all that smart, but she's relentless. She would never give up, so I decided I'd just buy her another car." He sighed. "She went to hug me, but I saw Sunny watching us from downstairs and I stepped back. I didn't realize I was standing so close to the edge of the stairs. I lost my balance and that was it."

"You weren't pushed?" I watched his face carefully.

He swallowed. "No."

"I thought maybe Bricey Presley helped you take flight," I said softly. "You could get her off your back if you pressed charges."

His eyes were bleak. "Bricey had nothing to do with it."

"You gave her the original Cadillac." I leaned in a little closer. "To soften the blow of the fact you'd grown tired of her?"

Tinkie stepped in. "A Cadillac that someone filled up with cement. Someone must have been pretty pissed at your gesture of parting."

"This really is none of your business." He tried to sit up again, but Cece put her finger back on his chest. It was just enough to keep him prone.

"We've been hired to prevent a tragedy," I said. "Our

client feels that things are getting out of hand here. She thinks someone may want you dead."

"Me?" He finally looked me fully in the face. "Why just me? And if anyone wanted me dead, it would be—"

"Yes, who would it be?" Cece was on it.

Bart realized he'd stepped in quicksand. His eyes narrowed. "Clarissa hired you, didn't she? She's the one stirring this pot. Listen to me, you should check into Clarissa's past. Back when she lived in Oxford. Make a few phone calls. She's been involved in suspicion of murder before. Maybe that's why she hired you. To throw the blame on someone else. She pretends to be all worried about other people when she's really trying to game the system. Typical Clarissa."

"Didn't you have an affair with her?"

My question pulled him up short. "Who told you that?"

"Doesn't matter," Tinkie said.

"Okay, so Clarissa and I had a fling. It's in the past. She's a passionate woman with a bit of kink in her. It was fun for a while, but then she got out of control. I had to end it before she ruined me all over town. Columbus is a town with solid values. Most people don't care what you do in your private life, but they don't like having their nose rubbed in things they find . . . inappropriate. I had to end it or I was going to lose all my business."

"Not to mention your wealthy wife," Millie said with a bit of heat.

Bart waved a hand. "Sunny got the ring and the marriage license. That's what she was after. She's happy as long as I'm there to escort her to social events. On occasion she gets her back up if I embarrass her."

Millie leaned in. "Are you sure about that? No woman likes to be made a fool. I don't suppose you'd care for it if she flaunted her lovers all over town."

"One thing about Sunny, she's discreet. I value that about her."

"Look, Crenshaw, you could have been killed. Tulla Tarbutton could have died from a lethal shock. Whoever unloaded that cement on Bricey's Cadillac destroyed property valued at seventy grand. This is not just an aggravated lover slashing a few car tires. This has crossed a line. You may think this is all fun and games, but I'm not seeing it that way. But hey, you're the biggest target so far. If you aren't worried, why should I be?" I shrugged.

"Look, I had an accident. I'm going to be fine. Just drop it, okay? Someone's on a warpath. It will settle down if you don't keep poking it with a stick."

Tinkie sat on the side of his bed and smiled sweetly. "You need to watch your back. You were lucky this time. Luck only takes a man so far. And yeah, maybe you should keep it in your pants."

9

"Have Yourself a Merry Little Christmas" played softly as we gave our drink orders to the waitress and settled into a dim corner of Players' Bar. The men were out and about with their "secret" business, and we'd decided to grab a drink and chat before we went back to the Bissonnette House.

"Let's see that video of Bart falling," Tinkie suggested as we all had our drinks. Tinkie sipped a cup of hot tea. She was a model of baby production.

Cece found the video on her phone and began to play back the recording as we all hung over her shoulder.

"There's Bart at the top of the stairs. And look! He's stumbling backward. Wait." Cece started the video over. "Do you see any hands pushing him?"

We replayed the video several times, but we couldn't find definitive proof that Bart was pushed. It was clear he'd lost his balance and stumbled back, but we couldn't determine why he'd stumbled. It just wasn't shown in the video.

But I had noticed something interesting. As Cece had panned her phone to follow Bart down the winding staircase, she'd also captured the faces of everyone in the crowd. Most were horrified or at least shocked.

Tinkie leaned down and took off her shoes. "Ladies, I need to head back to the B and B. Maybe the men will be there."

That sounded like a plan to me, too. Tomorrow I had some legwork to do. And no matter how Tinkie pressed to go shopping, I was going to resist.

On the way to the limo, Tinkie linked her arm through mine. "If we don't resolve this before we leave, we aren't giving her her money back."

I laughed. "We can finish up on this case after Christmas. Trust me, if they're cheating now, they'll be cheating on December 26."

Tinkie sighed. "You're right about that. I'm just tired and cranky. You'll find out when you get pregnant."

"Not on a dare." I laughed out loud. Tinkie wanted that baby more than she'd ever wanted anything. "It isn't just the pregnancy. My feet hurt, too. A bed sounds wonderful."

The morning came in with a brisk wind and storm clouds. I snuggled against Coleman and decided staying in bed was the perfect answer to a cold December day. Yes, I had a case to work, but it was a case I didn't much like. Not a single person involved inspired me to want to put out a big effort for justice.

Tap, tap, tap! Tap, tap, tap!

Dang it, Tinkie was at the door. The goblins could not be pecking with more persistence. I got up, hoping to save Coleman, but it was too late. His blue eyes were wide open. "She is a morning menace," he said.

"Tell me about it." I closed the bedroom door before I opened the door of the suite. "What is it?"

"Up and at 'em."

"What is *wrong* with you? Why aren't you and Oscar in bed, doing what married people do?"

"Been there, done that, got the baby prize to prove it." Tinkie grinned. "We've had more practice than you, Sarah Booth."

I couldn't help laughing. "What's set your tailfeathers on fire this morning?"

"We need to work on our case. I want to clear it up before we leave. I don't want to be driving back and forth over here. Besides, I was thinking, how hard can it be to find out which cheating person has it in for all the others? There's a logical answer. It's the woman—or man—who has no one. The one who got dumped or left out. Simple."

She was a lot better at math than I was, but somehow I wasn't sure that motive and deed added up to that end result in this situation. "How do you propose we find out the winners and losers in the cheating game? You think if we just ask, someone will tell us all the dirty little secrets of Columbus society?"

"No, but I'm thinking we can do a little legwork and see what turns up."

"What? No shopping?"

"Millie and Cece need to write something for their Sunday column, so they've begged off shopping this morning. I know you hate shopping. I thought we could put this case to bed."

I decided to tease her a little. "I thought we were going to follow the men today. To find out what their secret mission is." I realized *I* wanted to snoop and follow Coleman around. Coleman and I had our share of fun wherever we were, but in Zinnia, I couldn't bird-dog him or play pranks. He was the sheriff, and if the citizens didn't respect him, it could be costly. Here in Columbus, no one knew us or cared what we did.

Tinkie was staring at me like I'd grown a second head. "Are we getting paid to follow the men?" she asked.

She had a point. "Okay. Let me shower. I'll be down in fifteen minutes."

"I'll have your coffee waiting."

I took an extra two minutes to snuggle with Coleman before I forced myself into the shower and a clean pair of black jeans, my boots, a turtleneck, and a hoodie. I picked up a scarf and gloves. The day would be pleasant, but if we were anywhere in the shade it would be chilly.

"You're really going to interview cheaters this early in the morning?" Coleman asked when I had my hand on the doorknob to leave.

"Yep."

"I know you don't like this case."

"Nope, but cheating money spends just like honest money." I grabbed his big toe and twisted.

"Stop it!" He snatched his foot away. "Do that again and you won't be able to go anywhere with Tinkie."

"As tempting as that sounds, I'll see you later."

I bounced down the stairs. Despite the chore ahead of me, I was in a great mood. And so was Darla and the ever-present Kathleen. I wondered if Darla's friend lived on the grounds or if she simply had abdicated her life to Darla's. Tinkie and I had become very close since I'd returned to Zinnia, but she had a husband and a life. All of my friends had commitments that kept them busy. I wondered what it would be like to have a friend who could completely blend her life into what I was doing.

"Frosty the Snowman" was playing on a speaker in the kitchen when I joined Tinkie at the counter for a beautiful omelet, biscuits, grits, and coffee. "Darla, if I don't stop eating, I'm going to explode." Tinkie truly had a reason to eat, but I had lost all restraint. There would be wardrobe repercussions.

"It's the holidays. Enjoy. There'll be time to diet after the first of the year."

"I can't even think about that," I admitted.

"Diet is just another four-letter word," Tinkie said. "I'm pregnant, so I can pretty much eat whatever I want."

I rolled my eyes and Darla laughed out loud. "You two are like sisters more than partners in a PI agency."

I liked the sound of that. "We are close."

"I saw Clarissa had you buttonholed at the pilgrimage."

She didn't ask, but it was clear she was dying to know what was up, and I figured Darla would be able to help us. "We're on a case," I said.

"A case we don't want," Tinkie threw in.

"Clarissa hired you?" Darla was a little taken aback. "She's usually the cause of scandal and disruption. I can't believe she's really interested in finding out who pushed Bart down the stairs."

"So you, too, think he was pushed?" Tinkie asked.

"Of course. Bart was up there with Bricey arguing about that damn Caddy. Bricey doesn't have the sense of a roly-poly. She wanted Bart to give her another new car because that one got destroyed and she was too busy flitting around town to get insurance for it."

"Oh, dear," I said. "That's a heavy financial loss, then."

"As it was obviously meant to be." Darla refilled our coffee cups and I inhaled the wonderful aroma. "Bricey has no one to blame but herself, but of course she'll end up blaming everyone. I got a call this morning from the committee that handles the Christmas tree lighting. She was trying to intimidate them into buying her a new car."

"Seriously?" Tinkie said. "She feels the tree decorating committee is liable for the damage?"

Darla nodded. "Bricey believes she is owed that car. She doesn't care who pays for it. She made the case that since it happened on city property, the Christmas tree committee should pay for the car out of the city coffers. She is just a prostitute."

"How so?" I took note of Darla's prickly anger.

"She slept with Bart and she has the prostitute mentality. She wants to be paid for her work. It's all transactional to her."

"That car's a cool seventy grand. She must think she's thrilling in the sack," Tinkie muttered.

Darla and Kathleen laughed out loud. "Oh, she thinks

she's better than a ballerina on a trapeze," Kathleen said. "I heard Bart was so bored with her he'd rather go to the neighborhood association meetings than spend time with her."

That was a charge of serious brain-numbing boring— I'd been to some of those meetings at Tinkie's behest. I'd rather go to the dentist than endure another one. "Maybe she wasn't all that, but once upon a time Bart Crenshaw willingly jumped in the sack with Bricey."

"Some men are after the conquest. Some like a little strange. Some are morons. I put Bart in all three categories. He can sell the hell out of property, but his real focus in life is chasing women."

I did my best to study Darla without being obvious. "Who do you think dumped the cement?"

She shrugged. "It could be half a dozen people. Bricey's made some enemies."

"Because she sleeps with married or affianced men?"

"That and . . ." She turned away and went to the sink, where she rattled dishes. Kathleen started to clear our empty plates off the counter.

"Hey, don't leave us hanging," Tinkie said. "We have to dig into this, and it would be a big help if you could give us a head start."

Darla faced us and nodded. "Bricey plays cutthroat with her business deals, too. She's a take-no-prisoners kind of woman. She runs a private nursing business where she supplies in-home nurses to sick people, the elderly, people in hospitals that require constant monitoring. She's had . . . issues. Accusations."

"What kind?"

"You'd need to check that for yourself. Bricey doesn't

strike me as what I'd call an angel of mercy for sick folks." Darla brought the coffeepot over for one last refill.

"Bricey seriously has her own business?" I wondered how she found time to hold down a job—or what kind of job could be done from a prone position, which seemed to be her favorite pose.

"Like I said, she owns and runs a home health nursing service. There was some talk a few months back about a client who died . . . from neglect."

This put a whole new angle on the case. "Patient's name?"

Darla shook her head. "I'm not comfortable going any further. I feel that I'm painting her black when I don't know what happened. I've only heard gossip, not facts."

"We'll look into it," Tinkie said gently. "No one is accusing her of anything, and we will check it out. You can just save us some time if you gave us the basic details."

"It was Jerry Goode's grandmother. He's a city police officer. He was at the karaoke event when Tulla was shocked. Anyway, his granny was at Supporting Arms Care Center and Jerry had paid Bricey to send a private nurse over every day to check on her and make sure she was clean and ate a good lunch. Only Bricey didn't send anyone. I guess she figured the old woman was in a care facility and she was getting proper care."

"This is going to be very interesting." Tinkie slid off the barstool, ready to rumble. She was very protective of the elderly and babies, and the slight flush in her cheeks told me she was now gunning for Bricey. "We should get busy, Sarah Booth. Thank you, Darla, Kathleen. You've been a big help."

I thanked Darla and Kathleen for breakfast, grabbed my purse, and we were out the door. "Let's walk," I suggested. I noticed Tinkie had on sensible flats, and we'd both eaten enough food for a football team. Some exercise—the vertical kind—would be good for us.

The day was overcast and gray, a little foreboding. But we had three solid leads to pursue, and I discussed them with Tinkie as we walked down the sidewalk.

"We need to check into the heavy equipment angle. Someone had to hire that cement mixer. The driver had to be paid. That shouldn't be hard to track down." Even as I said it, I realized that few drivers were going to admit to destroying an expensive car. It was going to be harder than I thought.

"And we have the nursing home angle to check out," Tinkie said. "Killing a person's granny is a lot more serious than a car."

"To you," I pointed out. "I'm not so sure Bricey feels the same way. She's a bit on the shallow side. I think the car may be more important than one old lady."

Tinkie laughed out loud and I was rewarded for my snark.

"And don't forget we need to look into our client's background. Bart all but called Clarissa a murderer."

"He did indeed. We should have brought our laptops to Columbus," Tinkie said.

"We didn't plan on working," I reminded her. "We can always borrow Cece's. Darla has one in her office. Or we can stop in at the public library and do some online research."

"The library is just up the street, right?"

"Yep."

"Let's hit that coffee shop and get two cups to go. Then look up what we can find on Clarissa Olson's past."

"It's a plan."

10

Twenty minutes later, we were at the library door when they opened. We stepped inside, and I inhaled the odor of books. It was a smell that made me feel smart. We found the computers, and while we didn't have some of the apps we used for research, we were able to do some basic background checks on Clarissa Olson.

What we discovered was eye-opening. Clarissa was a real estate mogul. She held property in downtown Columbus, and there were a dozen local newspaper stories about her "kingdom" and her influence on the city zoning board. One of the members of the board was none other than Bart Crenshaw.

"Don't you think it's a bit *conflicted* that a real estate developer is on the zoning board?" Tinkie asked.

"More than a bit. And check this out." I'd found another story where Clarissa had developed a row of high-end condos in Oxford, Mississippi. They were luxury condos within walking distance of the stadium where the Ole Miss Rebels played. "The owner of the land says he was cheated out of his money by Clarissa."

"And no charges against her were filed, right?"

I kept checking. "It doesn't appear charges were filed."

"Then it could just be sour grapes. Someone sold land and then realized they could have asked more for it." Tinkie was more pragmatic about land deals than I was.

"Or it could be a reason for mischief."

Tinkie considered. "How would the things happening in Columbus reflect back on Clarissa?"

"Why is she so interested in stopping them?" I countered. "It's possible she knows who is doing this and wants it stopped before something about her is revealed."

"Good point. See if you can dig anything else up. Bart said something about murder in her past."

I kept going back through the months and the last few years before I finally hit pay dirt: "Realtor Questioned in Hunting Death of Oxford Businessman." The story made me think of Jitty's appearance as Alex Forrest back in Sunflower County.

"I can't read the story. You're hogging the screen," Tinkie said. "What does it say?"

She was sitting across from me and wasn't even attempting to read the story. She just wanted to complain. "It says Clarissa was picked up, questioned, and then released. It involved an Oxford man, Johnny Bresland, who died in a hunting accident."

I did a search on Bresland and found his obituary. "Bresland died on a hunting trip at Hell Creek Wildlife Management Area. He was accidentally shot—or that was the ruling." I kept scanning the story and reporting to Tinkie. "He was out by himself at dawn, and when he didn't come back in at dusk, the other hunters went looking for him. Found him shot in the back. The assumption was that it was accidental and the person who shot him probably wasn't even aware they had killed anyone."

"Right." Tinkie was as skeptical as I was. "That sounds like a *really* plausible story."

"The local sheriff bought it. No charges were brought against anyone."

"Do you think Clarissa shot a man in the back?"

I had to think about that. "I honestly don't know. What about you?"

"It could happen." She stretched. We'd been sitting doing research for almost an hour. "Clarissa is focused on what she wants. I think she views everything between where she is and where she wants to go as just an obstacle to overcome. And she strikes me as the kind of person who would use the most expedient path to get there."

"Ambition, I agree. She has that in spades. And she loves money and nice things. That's clear by her house. But this would be a revenge killing. That's kind of a distraction from true ambition."

"Not if she gained in the settlement." Tinkie picked up her cell phone and dialed Harold. When he answered, she put the question to him. "Do you know anyone in the Lafayette County Chancery Clerk's office who might look up a will for me?"

I couldn't tell what Harold said, but I watched Tinkie's expression shift. "I will make it up to you." She was grinning. "Oscar is going to be very, very nice to you in the new year."

"Watch out, Harold!" I yelled at the phone, causing the librarian at the desk to glare at me. I clapped a hand over my face and then mimed *I'm sorry*. I had forgotten where I was.

Tinkie scribbled down a number, and signaled me to come outside with her. We stood on the brown winter lawn of the library as she made a call to chancery clerk Deeter Odom in Oxford. Not ten minutes later we had the man with all the answers about Johnny Bresland's last will and testament.

Tinkie listened for a moment before she turned to me. "Clarissa might have a very big reason to want Johnny Bresland dead," she said.

"Who inherited his money?" I asked.

Tinkie put the question to the clerk, who was still on the line. I watched her eyebrows rise almost to her hairline. "Thanks," she said before she hung up.

"What?"

"Johnny Bresland's wife, Aurora, died a month before Bresland was shot in the back. Clarissa was the only heir. There was an outright financial gift of three million dollars to her, and Clarissa was the real estate agent in charge of selling the Bresland property, which was extensive, and which means she got huge fat commissions from that."

We returned to the library and continued to search. The wildlife preserve where Bresland had died was in another county and we couldn't find anything. We could find no details on the death of Aurora Bresland or what she had so conveniently died of. It was time to move on to our other leads.

After we left the library, I wanted to run by the Supporting Arms Care Center to check on health inspection records and how involved Bricey Presley was in the business. I knew Bricey provided home health care services for shut-ins, the elderly, and those in hospice care, but I wasn't certain if she was a stakeholder in the nursing home itself. But Tinkie had other plans. I was about to call an Uber when Tinkie linked her arm through mine and propelled me down the sidewalk.

"Let's walk," she said.

The day was overcast, but it wasn't bitter cold and the wind had calmed. Walking was a good idea. My pants said so, too. In fact, I'd had a few long conversations with my pants and they were giving me the dickens about a lot of my recent bad habits.

Downtown Columbus was a beehive of shopping as Christmas approached. While we were near the bank, I deposited Clarissa's check and called the tack shop to order Coleman's new saddle. It would be delivered Christmas Eve. I'd done most of the rest of my shopping. Since it was only Coleman and my friends, I had an easier time buying gifts than a lot of people did.

We walked slowly and enjoyed the window displays and downtown decorations. A children's toy store had worked *The Nutcracker* theme into the presentation, and I had a moment of nostalgia for last Christmas and Jitty's spectacular rendition of that wonderful ballet— even though I had almost frozen to death in the process of witnessing it.

Before I could stop her, Tinkie darted into the toy store. I knew her credit card would be smoking hot when she came out. Toys would be bought for the forthcoming child—lots of toys.

A boutique window across the street featuring mannequins dressed for the outdoors caught my eye. I admired the display—a snowy scene complete with fir trees and even a fake reindeer wearing a knit cap and leg warmers. But it was the human clothing that caught my eye. The denim leggings, lace-up knee boots, and oversize embroidered sweater with a snowman scene were exactly the kinds of clothes I loved. With time to kill, I crossed the street to check out the display. Tinkie would likely spend an hour shopping for toys, and I'd have plenty of time to try on some outfits if I found something I just had to have.

Up close, my eyes were drawn to the mannequin's features. With her upswept red hair, she bore a strange resemblance to Bette Midler, one of my favorite actresses. I loved her in so many films, but *The Rose,* based loosely on the life of Janis Joplin, had struck a chord with me. Bette Midler had a great set of pipes and amazing comedic timing.

For a long time I stared at the mannequin, remembering that bittersweet movie. But when I turned to go into the shop, I saw one of the mannequin's hands move. Just a tad. I turned back to study the plastic figure. She stood perfectly still again. Perfectly. I had to laugh at myself. Then as I stepped away, the mannequin winked at me—an impossibility, since it didn't have any eyelids.

Back to the window I went. I almost pressed my face against the glass to get a closer view. But the mannequin was just that—a molded plastic figure with a few hinged joints. Creepy as hell. I pulled up the hood on my jacket and wrapped my scarf more tightly to ward off the chill that had suddenly seeped into my bones. This was ridiculous. I was being played for a fool by a storefront dummy.

I started toward the front door one more time, but I couldn't stop myself from glancing back. With a jolt, I saw Bette pressed against the glass of the window, eyeing me. She waved. I thought my heart would stop until I caught on to the wickedness at work. Yes, it was a haunted mannequin—haunted by my personal haint. It was Jitty. And I was going to kill her.

I motioned her out of the window, and she simply faded through the glass to land on the sidewalk beside me. When I looked back in the window, the display showed two ladies in evening attire in a ballroom setting. No snow. No reindeer. Nada. Jitty still wore the outfit I'd been interested in. The tags hung on the clothes.

I looked all around. So far we hadn't drawn attention to ourselves and Tinkie was still inside the toy shop. "What are you doing? We're on a busy street in broad daylight."

"And you're the one acting like a crazy person," she said. "You goin' all googly-eyed at a dressmaker's form, talking to yourself in the middle of the sidewalk. Folks can't see me, but they sure can see you."

She had a point—a damn good one. "Why do you look like Bette Midler and what movie are you from?" I couldn't quite place this Bette. The coiffed hair was a clue, but I couldn't figure out exactly what my haint was up to.

Jitty flicked her hand at the display window on the

other side of the shop's front door. This one featured two extremely thin mannequins in red corselets that laced up the back, red fishnet stockings, and a big bow tied around each of their waists. Like they were some kind of Christmas gift for someone who loved skinny women. They both wore Santa hats and vapid expressions.

"So some people have a thing for tarted-up mannequins that make a whippet look fat," I said. "At least they know enough to stay put in the display. Unlike someone I know." I pointed at her.

Jitty struck a pose and her facial expression shifted to comic outrage. Her voice was all Bette. "Who's supposed to eat that? Some anorexic teenager? Some fetus? It's a conspiracy, I know it is! I've had enough. I'm leading a protest. I'm not buying another article of clothing until these designers come to their senses!"

"Brenda!" I knew her instantly. She was one of the wives whose husband was a cheater in the 1996 movie *The First Wives Club.* As I recalled the movie, she'd found her husband, Mort, with a younger model. His financial impropriety had yielded the turf she needed for revenge, meaning she turned him in to the IRS. The movie had also featured two other wives whose husbands had strayed. Goldie Hawn, another longtime acting favorite of mine, and Diane Keaton starred in the film. I could put two and two together—cheating spouses in the movie corresponded to cheating spouses in Columbus. "You're not helping, Jitty."

"Maybe you're not listening." She started to waver, her image gradually beginning to fade.

"Come back here. Do they sell those clothes in that store?" I pointed in the window before I realized a clerk inside the store was staring at me. She had her phone in her hand, as if she was going to report me as some kind of mental patient. I waved at her and smiled, which only made her step behind a dress rack and hide.

"Dammit it, Jitty. Now look what you've done."

"Better get in there before she dials 911 and says there's a crazy woman roaming the streets. Just remember, a shopping spree always helps a heartache." She grinned.

I was done with Jitty, but I really liked that outfit. "Give me those clothes. In my size. I want to buy them."

"Too late! Tinkie's headed this way."

Jitty did a single turn to a blare of angelic horns, and she was gone. I prepared myself to meet my partner. Tinkie had caught me several times talking to "myself." I couldn't tell her about Jitty, and I didn't want to start that tired old conversation again. I had to pull myself together.

I faced her with a big smile. "I was just admiring the displays."

"Find something you like?" Tinkie asked, staring at the shop widow with a puzzled expression. "That?" She pointed at the very thin models in evening gowns. Tinkie knew me well enough to know that was not anything I'd normally be interested in.

"They are lovely dresses, if I had a place to wear them." I'd been royally tricked by Jitty, who was just making sure I knew she was still in Columbus. It was Jitty's mission in life to pester me no matter where I went.

"And if you'd starved yourself for the past nine months." Tinkie rolled her eyes. "What's really going on?"

The store clerk had come out from behind the rack

of dresses and was now filming me with her cell phone. Proof for the cops she would call any second if she hadn't already.

"Let's get moving," I suggested.

"If you like that dress, why not try it on?" Tinkie grabbed my elbow to propel me into the store.

"The dress is beautiful, but not for me. What about Cece?"

Tinkie pondered it. "I'll tell her. It would look marvelous on her with her slender hips."

"Excellent idea. Let's finish up our work so we can get her down here to try it on." I was literally pushing her down the street. The clerk had edged out of the doorway and was still filming us. I tugged Tinkie around the corner with a huge sigh of relief.

"Is something wrong?" Tinkie asked.

"Not a thing. Ready to get to work."

"Are you ready to look up the heavy equipment dealers?"

"I am." I was more than ready to get busy and relieved to be getting off so lightly. Tinkie apparently hadn't witnessed my sidewalk debate with an empty space or the distressed salesclerk. Whew! I tucked her arm through mine and set off at a brisk walk. Tinkie let me get about a block before she said anything.

"I watched you at that store window."

I felt the rush of blood to my cheeks.

"What were you doing? It looked like you were having an argument with yourself. Sarah Booth, you looked a little nutty. That clerk in the store was about to call the police. So just tell me the truth, please."

"Okay." I drew in a breath. "I thought one of the mannequins looked like Bette Midler and I was imagining her playing Brenda in *The First Wives Club*. I guess I got carried away having a conversation with Brenda about cheating husbands. You know, because of our case."

I kept on walking to put more distance between me and the store, just in case the clerk called the law. Tinkie kept pace with me. "That has to be the truth. No one could make up something that far-fetched."

"It's the truth."

"Why are you . . . daydreaming about that movie? That was the nineties. The fashion was horrible then." Tinkie shuddered at the thought of heavily padded shoulders and permed hair. She was barely five feet, and she said those huge shoulder pads made her look like a linebacker for a tiny tots team.

I shook my head. "I think it has something to do with this case and all the cheating husbands, cheating wives, and people set on revenge."

"O-o-o-kay."

Tinkie wasn't convinced, but she was going to let it go. Or so I hoped. I picked up a little speed. If I set a fast-enough pace, Tinkie would have to step double time to keep up with me and she wouldn't have breath to ask questions. "So where are we off to?"

"We need to run back to the local newspaper."

"Okay, right. To check the heavy equipment rentals in the area. If we can find out who paid the cement truck driver to dump that load, we'll have a name."

"The way I figure it, the newspaper will know which truck drivers would destroy a car. Could save us a lot of legwork." She grabbed my arm and pulled me to a halt. "Slow down. You can't outrun my questions."

"You're right about that." I used my phone to find the newspaper office and was delighted to discover we were only three blocks away. The *Columbus Packet* was within our strike zone.

"Do you know anyone at the newspaper?" Now would have been a good time to have Cece with us. Journalists could almost always find common ground.

"Cece called ahead for us." Tinkie grinned. "She's paved the way. Should be a piece of cake. Ask for Debbie Harris."

"Hurray. We're going to a journalist to ask about the sleazy side of town." I had a sudden drop in enthusiasm for this case. "We really shouldn't have taken this on."

Tinkie sighed. "I know. But we did, and now we have to finish it. We have a standard to live up to, Sarah Booth. We have always given our clients our best effort. We can't do less here."

She was right about that and I had sudden clarity. "I think Clarissa is behind this and she's hired us as a beard for her activities." I'd finally found the words to say what was troubling me. "I think we're being used and I don't like it."

"The same thing occurred to me," Tinkie admitted as she reached for the door handle to the newspaper office. "But if that turns out to be the case, think how much fun it's going to be to nail her. *And* we'll get paid to do it."

I thought about it for a few seconds and brightened. Tinkie was right. We could put it to Clarissa—if she was the one behind these nefarious deeds—and get paid for it. "I just wish she hadn't picked Christmastime for all of this. What kind of people cheat and deliberately damage others at Christmastime?"

Tinkie shrugged. "The holidays bring out a lot of extreme emotions in people. Sometimes people just flip.

Let's hope she's smart enough to cease and desist with these crazy episodes."

"Or let's hope we catch her in the act before she harms someone else."

We stepped into the chaos and clatter of a working newsroom.

11

Debbie Harris was a brunette with ivory skin and bright red lipstick. She ran the lifestyle section and was a long-time friend of Cece's. "Sorry Cece isn't with us," I said once we were seated. Her office was almost an exact replica of Cece's madness. Papers, books, cameras, and scraps of paper with writing on them seemed to have exploded in the room. There wasn't a chair to sit on because everything was covered with piles of paper.

"I'll catch up with her at the flotilla tonight," Debbie said. "I just love that new column she and Millie Roberts are doing." She held up her hand and moved it across the room in front of her as if she were reading a marquee. "'*The Truth Is Out There.*' That's genius. And those celebrity stories. Where in the world do they come up with those? When I read the one about Oprah being pregnant with Elvis's baby, I thought I'd die." She arched one eyebrow. "But wouldn't that be kind of wonderful? Two Mississippi icons. Man."

I'd actually loved that story, too. "Millie is a huge fan of celebrities and Cece is a great researcher."

"Tell me the truth. Where do they come up with that stuff? It's not research, it's inspired!"

"We have a psychic friend, Madame Tomeeka, who helps out." It was true, but I suspected Debbie Harris wouldn't believe a word of it.

"You crack me up. But that's a great angle, too. I've read a couple of those columns and I love it when they consult the psychic."

"I'll pass your compliments along to Madame Tomeeka," Tinkie said. "Now what can you tell us about the heavy equipment owners who might have dumped a load of cement in Bricey Presley's car?"

Debbie tapped a pencil on her desk. "I suspect it was a man named Colton Horn. He runs a foundation business, mostly fill dirt and cement for foundations, driveways, and pools. Occasionally sand deliveries. Nice guy. And easy on the eyes."

"If he's the one who unloaded on that car, he destroyed some expensive property." He didn't sound very nice to me.

"You don't know what he was told, now do you?" Debbie asked. She had a "cat that ate the canary" grin. No matter what she said, she sounded like she was a wiseacre. It made me like her a bunch. And she had a point.

"Do *you* know what he was told that convinced him to do that much property damage?"

She nodded. "The owner of the car paid him to do it."

That was a stunner. "Bricey paid him?" Tinkie and I said together.

"Yep." She grinned wider, pleased with the shock she'd delivered. "Bricey Presley herself. She showed him the bill of sale that the car was hers and she paid him in cash to dump the cement in it. She said she wanted it crushed. Colton came to me when he first heard there was a furor over the incident."

"But why would she do that to her new car?" Tinkie and I chorused together.

"Not certain about that," Debbie said. "I'm digging into it, but Colton seemed to think she was getting even with someone."

"Even with herself?" Tinkie asked. "That makes no sense at all."

"Are you going to run this story?" I asked.

Debbie frowned. "That's tougher to decide than you might think. I know Colton. He's pretty upset about this because Bricey is pretending that she wasn't in on the dump. He said she's threatening to sue him for the value of the car—she's claiming she didn't know anything about the load of cement. She's hired a lawyer. Colton got a letter asking him to fork up the dough to replace the car."

"But he has a signed contract, right?" Tinkie asked.

"Not exactly." Debbie sighed. "Folks around here don't always dot all the *i*'s and cross all the *t*'s. They operate on a handshake and a gentleman's agreement."

Folks in Zinnia were sometimes the same. It wasn't smart, but it was how deals were struck in small-town Mississippi. "What's Mr. Horn going to do?"

"Hire a lawyer. Try to defend himself. Bricey's a cagey

one. She hired him, paid in cash, never signed a contract or anything. Now it looks like he destroyed that car and is lying about why. And Bricey gets to play the victim, and it looks like she might get a new car on top of it."

"Where could we find Mr. Horn?" I asked.

She gave us the address for his business on the outskirts of down. "He may not talk to you, but I'll let him know you're only looking for the truth."

"Thanks, that would be helpful." I did appreciate Debbie's help.

Debbie picked up her notepad and pulled her glasses into place. She was ready to get to work. "Maybe I'll see you later tonight at the flotilla. It's going to be a lot of fun."

"Great. We're looking forward to it," I said. "I've heard it's a very gala affair."

"Those boat owners have been decorating for over a week. It was a great competition for many years, until it was canceled back in the early 2000s."

I was suddenly very interested in a history lesson. "Was there a reason it was canceled?" I asked.

Debbie shrugged one shoulder. "It takes a bunch of effort to keep all these events going. The Columbus downtown merchants manage to keep things going in town, but the flotilla involves a lot of work: someone has to coordinate the boats and make sure they're decorated and in the proper order. Boating people sometimes like to tipple a bit, and boats and alcohol can be a dangerous combo. Darla had to get every boat captain to sign an oath not to drink." She rolled her back and I heard several vertebrae snap. "And folks just get tired of putting in the time. It seemed like the same people were providing all the elbow grease every year. The younger folks weren't stepping up to take on some of the work, so the flotilla was put on hold."

"But they're bringing it back this year," Tinkie pointed out.

"Some new blood moved into town. Your hostess, Darla, has been instrumental in reviving the flotilla. It's perfect for her, what with her B and B right on the river. She has a dock right there and her own boat. She knows the boat people, and they like and respond to her. You're going to love it, and it's great advertising for her!"

I was looking forward to being in a boat on the water on a brisk pre-Christmas night with Coleman. There was something romantic about the gentle rocking of a boat, especially one decorated with Christmas lights and garlands. "I'm eager to experience it."

"Wait until you see the decorations. Folks go all out. Best to wear something warm, though," she cautioned. "It gets cold on the water."

"Will do. Thanks for the tip, and also thanks for calling Mr. Horn and laying the groundwork for us."

"He's a good guy in a tight spot. I hope you can clear him of any malicious intentions. And I'll bet he never takes another job like that without a signed contract and photo documentation."

I nodded as we left her office and headed back to the street.

Colton Horn was a good-looking man comfortable in his own skin. He nodded at both of us when we entered his office on the outskirts of town—a walk that was just long enough for Tinkie and me to develop a plan. It wasn't exactly original. Per usual, she was the good cop and I was the bad cop.

In contrast to Debbie's office, Colton's was spartan and immaculately clean. I literally could have eaten off the floor, it was so spic-and-span. The top of his desk had one folder, open in front of him.

"Mr. Horn, did you fill the car in the parking lot at the Riverwalk with cement?" I started out bold and strong. That was what bad cops did.

He leaned back in his chair and assessed us.

"Don't pay any attention to her," Tinkie said, pointing at me. "She's always a crank when she hasn't had lunch. We're just trying to get to the bottom of what's going on in Columbus, and we heard a rumor that you'd been hornswoggled."

"I get that you're PIs. Debbie said you were looking for the truth, but I'm not so sure about that." Once burned, twice shy, as the old saying went. Colton Horn wasn't going to trust anyone who just walked in off the street. "Who are you working for?"

He was smarter than I'd hoped. "Doesn't matter. You're the one on the hook for a top-dollar car. We're looking for information. What we find may help you, or it may not." I moved closer and leaned in. "What person in his right mind would fill a new car with cement?"

"The person who was hired to do that specific job and got paid to do it." He looked down at his desk. "The person who is feeling more and more like a dupe and a fool."

At least he wasn't going to pretend he was innocent.

"Lord, Mr. Horn, that's a wild story." Tinkie was shaking her head in sorrowful sympathy. "I don't know if a lot of people will believe you were hired and paid to do that by the very woman who owns the car. It would be better for you if you told us the truth about who is behind such an expensive bit of vandalism."

"I'm telling you the truth. The car's owner, Bricey Presley, was sitting in that very chair where you're sitting. She showed me the title to the car and she hired me to destroy it. She even told me the mix. She insisted on crack resistant." He shrugged. "It didn't make a lot of sense to me, but these rich women come up with crazy things all the time."

"Wait, Bricey isn't rich," I said. "She's well kept, but she isn't rich."

He leaned forward, elbows on his desk. "This woman was rich. Expensive clothes. Expensive jewelry. She had the title to the car. I saw it. Ms. Presley said she wanted the cement *in* the car, the full load of it dumped all at once. She wanted the car demolished. She said it was payback. And she also told me where she'd leave it parked, with the top down. She parked away from the other cars so I had easy access with the truck and chute. It was just as she said. I delivered the load exactly at the time she wanted it there, did my job, and left."

"You didn't find it strange she wanted to destroy her beautiful car?" Tinkie asked in that mesmerizing voice she used to lure men into thinking they were safe. Tinkie was partial to Caddies and I knew the brutal destruction of the car struck a nerve with her, but she was playing it smooth with Colton.

"I thought it was damn strange," he said. "But hell, it was her car. What if she wanted to destroy a car or a perfectly good swimming pool? People with money do things I wouldn't do." He rubbed his lower face with one hand. "They just don't want something anymore, so they call me to fill it in with dirt or cement or bury it. No skin off my teeth as long as their check clears."

"Did she say she didn't want the car anymore?" I asked.

He frowned. "Not in those exact words. But why else would she demolish it? Look, women do crazy things all the time. I guess you may not have noticed that while *you* were busy doing crazy things. The female gender isn't all that fond of rational thought."

I had to turn away to hide my grin. It was clear that Colton Horn had tangled a few times with women who were on the left side of sane. Those were the exciting ones, the wild ones with no limits. The ones who turned dangerous when the fun was over. Alex Forrest, as Jitty would point out.

"It's going to be fine, Mr. Horn. I'm sure you got all of that in writing," Tinkie said, as sweet as syrup. "Like, you have a signed contract to destroy the car? If we could just see that contract, we could move you out of the suspect list and go about our business."

Colton palmed his forehead. "No, you can't see it. I mean, I didn't get Ms. Presley to sign the contract. She said it was her car, she had the title, it was a simple onetime delivery. I just did as I was hired to do." He watched both of us. "And that is going to be a big problem, isn't it?"

Tinkie shook her head. "Not with me, sugar, but it may be with Bricey. I think she may be one of those crazy women you know so much about. I don't know what really happened, but looks to me like this plan sounded all crazy and just a little exciting when she thought it up. Then she got you to go along, but it was still just a fantasy in her mind. Bricey overlooked the fact she hadn't bothered to insure the car, so . . ."

"This is terrible. She hired me. That's the truth. Why would she change her mind and deny that?"

"I can only guess at the woman's motive," Tinkie said. "It looks like she had this idea of a grand, dramatic gesture that would put her in the limelight. In reality, the game wasn't as much fun as she thought it was going to be. I mean, dumping a load of cement right on top of a convertible may have been a momentary thrill, but when you realize you're going to have to walk home after work, the excitement is gone."

He moaned. "I was so stupid."

"Maybe it's not that bad," Tinkie said, and signaled me closer. "My partner and I aren't interested in the car. We just want to be sure that this was the woman who hired you."

She pulled up some photos on her phone that Cece had shared with her. "Is this her?"

He looked at the phone and the color drained from his face. "No, I've never seen that woman before in my life."

Tinkie and I both sat forward. She searched the phone for another photo of Bricey. "How about this one?"

He shook his head. "That's not the woman who hired me." He swallowed. "Is that the woman who truly owns the car?"

"That's Bricey Presley," Tinkie said. "I'm sorry."

"Not as sorry as I am. I've been had." Colton stood up. "I'm going to find the woman who set me up. I acted in good faith, and unless I find the woman who paid me to do that, I'm going to be held accountable for a lot of destruction."

He was basically right, since he didn't have a signed contract. "Hold on," I said. "Tinkie, show him more photos. Maybe he can pick her out of the crowd." Tinkie had photos from all of the Christmas festivities. She'd taken pictures of almost everyone in town.

"Great idea." Tinkie handed him the phone. "Just keep swiping until you recognize someone."

He went through several photos he studied carefully. "I do a lot of work around the region, but I mostly deal with men. I've built some foundations for women in the area, brought in fill dirt for projects, mixed the concrete for some driveways." He went through more of the party photos. "I mostly date women from out of town, and these women aren't my social set. None of these women are her." He inhaled and blew it out. "I'm not familiar with a lot of the leading ladies of Columbus."

"And you're lucky there in some instances," I said under my breath.

He'd recovered his equilibrium and gave me a wry grin. "I'll say. I do my best to stay out of the way of people with a wire loose and enough money to make really bad decisions. I messed up this time. The woman who hired me just walked in the door. She was a looker and she had an imp on her shoulder, all filled with this idea of making mischief. She seemed so confident, so sure of what she was doing. She sucked me right in. I never considered she was using me to commit a crime."

"Didn't you wonder why she wanted to destroy her car?" Tinkie asked, motioning him back into his seat.

"I've had clients who want to knock down beautiful houses or bulldoze incredible groves of trees. I don't ask questions. I do the work. And this time I had the cash in hand."

He had a valid point. People often did a lot of things that didn't make sense and seemed to be against their self-interest. "Keep flipping through the photos. Maybe you'll get lucky and we can find the woman who hired you."

"Forgive me if I'm a bit wary of taking a second bite of that apple. Why would you want to help me?"

"Because that woman may hold the answers to a bunch of other stuff that's been going on around Columbus."

"What kind of stuff?" He was justifiably cautious.

"Cheating, cheating, home wrecking, and cheating," Tinkie said.

"Got it." He studied the phone screen. When he got to the end of the photos Tinkie had taken in Columbus, he handed the phone back. "I didn't see her."

"Can you describe her?" I asked.

"Average size. Brunette. She wore sunglasses." He sighed. "That should have been a clue, I guess. She never took those sunglasses off."

"Any characteristic you remember?" Tinkie asked.

He shook his head slowly and suddenly stopped. "She kept tucking her hair behind her ear. It was like an unconscious thing. And her hair was really glossy. Maybe too glossy. I think she was wearing a wig."

"You think?" I asked, impressed that the female car-killer had possibly gone to such lengths to hide her identity. The wig observation might prove helpful in finding her.

"Maybe. She was fussing with that area right behind her ear." He rubbed his eye. "Or maybe she had an itch or something else. I don't know. I was in a hurry and she put cash on my desk." He closed his eyes. "And the cash is yet another clue that something was off, right? I've been really stupid."

I felt sorry enough for him not to rub salt in the wound. "It's hard for honest people to perceive dishonesty sometimes. Cut yourself some slack."

"You might want to call your insurance agent," Tinkie said. "See how you're covered for this kind of damage."

He nodded. "I could lose my business because of this."

I had a sudden thought. "Have you ever been caught cheating on your girlfriend or spouse?"

The instant he looked down, I had my answer.

"It could be you were targeted, Mr. Horn."

He started to object. "No, my ex-girlfriend wouldn't ruin me. She wouldn't. She was upset with me when she found out, and she left me, but she isn't vindictive like this. She knows I live with the reality that my cheating was the stupidest thing I've ever done in my life. Stupider even than dumping cement in a car. She's not the kind of woman to ruin my business. I told you, I don't date crazy."

"Maybe she didn't start out crazy, but maybe you made her that way," I said.

He sat back in his chair with a huff. "I don't believe that."

Tinkie put her phone away and snapped her purse shut. "It could be that your ex has nothing to do with this, but that someone you know was aware of your infidelity and decided to take action against you."

He went white at that prospect.

"Now we need to head to the Supporting Arms Care Center. Do you know anything about that place or a healthcare service that offers extra care to those who need it?"

"Not a thing."

His answer seemed sincere. I doubted he knew that the real Bricey Presley owned that very business. "Thanks for your help." We walked to the door.

"If you find out anything, will you let me know?" he asked.

"Sure thing."

12

Supporting Arms was a redbrick manor house set in a grove of oak trees. The outward appearance was serene. The whole idea of a facility where old people waited to die really jangled my nerves, though. Tinkie and I walked abreast down a sidewalk flanked by lit-up candy canes. The front porch was decorated with poinsettias, and when we entered, the foyer had a huge live Christmas tree that filled the area with the clean scent of spruce.

There was a dayroom to the left and the administrative offices were to the right. Tinkie and I headed to the right to speak with someone in charge. It was not going to be a pleasant exchange, but it had to happen.

Mal Provent was the administrator, and once he heard

why we were there, he was eager to see us out. "What happened with Mrs. Goode was a tragedy, but we're not liable in any way. If Jerry Goode hired you to investigate us, then you can just get out now."

Tinkie shook her head. Irate bureaucrats were her specialty. "We're here to *help* you, Mr. Provent." She could lie with the best of them when necessary.

"Help me? How?"

"A lot of strange and . . . untoward things have been happening in Columbus. It's possible Mrs. Goode's death is somehow linked."

"Things outside the home here? Is there a connection to Mrs. Goode?" He was definitely interested. If he was a rat, he was sniffing the cheese.

"That's right, things outside the home. And there could be a link. We're examining it. Look on us as your advocates." She smiled and held him firmly in her blue gaze.

That was stretching a point. I saved him from her mesmerizing stare. "We're more interested in the sitter who was supposed to be attending Mrs. Goode. I understand that her grandson had contracted with an outside nursing service to provide daily visits and professional care. Does the care center have an arrangement with Bricey Presley for additional care, such as when a patient needs a private sitter?"

"Not an arrangement so much as an accommodation. As you're undoubtedly aware, no care facility can provide full-time nursing to seriously ill patients, and Mrs. Goode was a very sick woman. We have a ratio of four patients per nurse, but if a patient is critically sick, it's incumbent on the patient's family to make arrangements for private nursing. To that end, we allow Ms. Presley to send nurses into Supporting Arms to supplement the care we normally give. Ms. Presley was responsible for hiring, vetting, and managing the nurses she sent in here." He wanted to go on, but he stopped himself.

"What happened with Mrs. Goode?" I knew he wouldn't answer, but it was worth a try.

"She was old and sick. That's what happens to people in their eighties. Death is a natural result of old age."

"I'm afraid we need more specifics." I pressed for details.

"She was prone to throw blood clots. One hit her lungs and killed her."

"She was supposed to have a private nurse with her." Tinkie said.

"Her grandson had made arrangements with Ms. Presley's care service. Yes, Mr. Goode had hired someone to be at his grandmother's bedside."

"But no one was there," Tinkie said gently.

"That's accurate. Since the arrangement for private nursing is between the patient, the patient's family, and Ms. Presley's service, Supporting Arms was not involved in any way."

Easy to say, but perhaps not so supportable in court. "Mr. Goode is upset." I put that out there. "Is Jerry Goode suing the care center?"

Provent's cheeks had reddened. "No, the last I heard, he's thinking about suing Ms. Presley." He was clearly uncomfortable. "Now I have work to do."

"Do all of the old and sick patients hire special sitters?" Tinkie asked. "I would think that folks here pay, what? Maybe three grand a month for care?"

"Please leave." He was done even pretending to be helpful.

"We'll be in touch," I said as we left. When we were

outside, I couldn't shake the feeling that I needed a drink. A stiff one. Death waited for all of us, that was a fact. But it was hard to look it in the face.

"Places like that upset me," Tinkie said.

"Me, too. Nothing looked wrong. Everything looked very clean and all. It's just that we have a society where folks don't have time to stay home to care for the elderly. Old people end up in a facility being cared for by strangers. It's the best solution sometimes, I know that." I had not been home to tend to Aunt Loulane when she fell ill. She hadn't told me she was sick, and I was trying for a stage career in New York. She was dying before I even knew something was wrong. It still bothered me that I hadn't been there for her until the very last. "Everyone works all the time to make ends meet."

Tinkie sighed. "You know my mother and I aren't close."

That was an understatement. Tinkie's parents traveled all the time. It was my understanding they were in Rome at the moment. Or maybe it was Paris, for the Christmas holidays. They were never in Mississippi, and that suited Tinkie and Oscar just fine.

"Your mother has a very active life. She's lucky to be able to travel so much," I said, struggling to find something to say that didn't sound mean. I didn't really know Tinkie's mother. I didn't know the dynamics of that relationship. I knew Tink was much closer to her father, but that was about the sum of my knowledge. And I didn't want to step on anyone's feelings.

"I've thought about this." Tinkie wasn't going to let it go. "I have the luxury of the option of in-home care for my folks, when that time comes." Her forehead was drawn in thought. "But I know I should care for them myself."

"You have a big home and money for private nurses. They will not be neglected." I agreed with her. "But that decision is a long time off, Tinkie. Let's not borrow trouble."

"I guess with the baby coming and all, I just want to cocoon myself in with Oscar and my friends. I know that sounds selfish."

"Not in the least." Whatever Tinkie decided when the time came, I had no doubt that Mr. and Mrs. Bellcase would have the best of care, with Tinkie at their side as much as possible.

"Where to next?" she asked.

I had my phone out and was getting ready to call for another Uber. "Jerry Goode. We need to talk to him."

It took only five minutes to get to the police station. Normally Tinkie and I would have walked, but she tired more easily than usual. We enjoyed the Christmas decorations as we drove through town. At the municipal complex, the driver let us out with a wish for happy holidays.

Jerry Goode was on call and in the station. We'd lucked out, though he didn't appear all that happy to see us.

"We need to talk to you about Bricey Presley," I said.

"I'd help you if I could, but I can't. My lawyer told me to keep my lip zipped."

"Good advice, but it isn't about your granny. And I'm sorry to hear about your loss."

"Not nearly as sorry as Bricey Presley is going to be."

"You should know making threats isn't smart."

He signaled us into an interview room. "Look, she

took my money and failed to provide the service I was paying for. My grandmother died because she wasn't being watched."

"I am sorry," Tinkie said. "That's unforgivable. But we're here to talk about the Cadillac now pretending to be a giant cement block."

He tried not to grin, but he couldn't help himself. "Sometimes good things happen to bad people."

"You know anything about the woman who ordered that cement?"

He shook his head. "Colton said Bricey ordered it herself. He thought she was nuts, but he did what he was paid to do. I hope you're not trying to make trouble for him."

"No, *I'm* not, but there's a big complication. It wasn't Bricey who ordered the job."

Goode whistled softly. "Wow. Bad news for Colton. Do you know who put the order in?"

"That's what we need to find out."

"And you were wondering if the woman who showed up with cash to pay for a load of cement was somehow tied to me?"

He'd put it together pretty quickly. "The death of a grandmother is a pretty good motive for revenge," I said.

"Nope, not involved in this. I'm a lawman and I settle my disputes in the courtroom, not in a parking lot."

"What have you discovered about Tulla Tarbutton's shock at the karaoke event?" Tinkie asked.

"There's no proof that it was deliberate," he said. "That musician fellow, Jaytee, talked with me. He's pretty certain it wasn't an accident, but we both went over the equipment and the events, and we couldn't find a way to prove it was deliberate."

"And what about Bart Crenshaw's tumble down the stairs?" I asked.

"He insists that he stumbled and fell. We have to take him at his word."

"And what about the convertible?" Tinkie pressed. "Someone ordered that done, and it was someone who meant to inflict damage."

"That's still under investigation." He didn't flinch. "I had nothing to do with it, but we'll find out who ordered it."

I gave him a business card. "Would you call us when you figure it out?"

He took the card and put it in the pocket of his shirt. "Sure."

"By the way, I think there's something hinky about the way Bart Crenshaw 'lost his balance.'"

The faintest grin touched his lips. "I tend to agree with you, but there's little we can do if he doesn't say who pushed him." He shrugged. "Some men love the danger. They're as bad as the local drama queens who stir up trouble because they have to be center stage. But I'm aware of this, and I'm investigating. Now I have work to do."

It was clear we'd been dismissed, and I, for one, was eager to move on down the list of things we needed to check.

Lunchtime arrived, and the motto of Delaney Detective Agency was "never miss a meal." To that end, we called Cece and Millie to see if they'd finished their newspaper work and could join us at the Green Parrot. The karaoke machine was back up and the locals were belting out the words to every Christmas song ever written. I wasn't there to sing, but to ask questions.

Cece and Millie joined us, and we found a table in the corner where we could watch the room. I didn't recognize any of the patrons, but we kept our voices low anyway. As we hashed over the case, I realized we had too many suspects and too many weak motives.

But the one fact Tinkie and I had discovered made a big hit. Cece and Millie were all over the news about an impostor posing as Bricey Presley.

"That's . . . genius," Cece said. "I mean if you really hated Bricey, that would be a masterful play."

"She's not exactly beloved," Millie threw in. "From the gossip at Rook's Nest, it seemed pretty clear that Bricey has dipped her toe in way too many people's monkey business."

"True. Destroying the car is one thing. But nearly electrocuting a woman and pushing a man down a flight of stairs? Both of those could have ended in a fatality."

"Which makes me think there's more to all of this than just jealousy or revenge for cheating." I had nothing more than a gut feeling—no evidence.

"What are you thinking?" Millie asked.

"We have a man whose grandmother died because Bricey didn't uphold a contract for professional care. We have a cheating man with a lot of business entanglements who almost died falling downstairs. And we have a known homewrecker who could have gotten a fatal shock. Add this to what we discovered about Clarissa in Oxford."

"Do you think she really killed that Bresland man?" Tinkie asked.

"I think she's capable. Don't you?"

All around the table my friends nodded.

"She's a shark," Millie said.

"I think I need to go to this Hell Creek Wildlife Management Area and check out the location where Johnny Bresland died." Somewhere we had to find some physical evidence that would support my theory or crash it. I honestly didn't care which. But if we were to make headway with this case, we needed more than hunches.

"I'm game," Tinkie said. "We can get Rex to drive us."

"Let's just rent a car," Cece suggested. "We'll have more flexibility and Rex can keep an eye on the guys for us."

I wondered if Tinkie had finally co-opted Rex as a spy, but I didn't ask. Some things were better left alone—at least until I had time to poke into them.

The rental agency delivered the car to the restaurant by the time we were finished paying our bill, and we were off for a pretty drive through the Mississippi woods. I didn't know what I hoped to find, but at least we weren't shopping. That in itself was a miracle. I'd googled Johnny Bresland's death notice and discovered that Tippah County had been in charge of the investigation. On the way, I telephoned the Tippah County sheriff's department and asked to speak with the officer who'd worked the Johnny Bresland accidental shooting.

Deputy Len Ford sounded to be an experienced lawman who put the facts on the line. He freely gave us the details of the shooting. Bresland was found in a cluster of trees and he wasn't wearing hunter's orange. There were deer tracks near his body. The deputy pointed out that hunting fatalities weren't uncommon, especially when buck fever was running high.

"It was a simple accident," Ford said. "We investigated.

The shot came from an area where several other hunters had set up. As you probably know, we can't trace buckshot to a particular gun, and those guys aren't going to talk if they even know who's responsible, so there's no real way to identify the shooter. It's had a tragic impact. The guys Bresland was hunting with, this has pretty much ruined their lives. They all feel guilty."

"You knew Bresland's wife died only a month before he was shot?" I asked.

"That was up in Lafayette County. I heard the talk, read the official report. Suicide. That's why his buddies took him hunting. He was drinking too much and spending too much time alone. His friends said he seemed overwhelmed with guilt and remorse at his wife's death. They thought getting out in the woods, some time with his friends, would put him on a better path."

I wasn't a fan of hunting as grief therapy, but I didn't say it. "Are you sure Aurora Bresland's death was a suicide?"

"She died at her home just outside Oxford. Lafayette County investigated that one. We weren't involved, but I did check into the basic details. Seemed a little odd that she'd die and then her husband would get shot to death. But I couldn't find anything to hang my suspicions on. From what I was told, it was pretty open-and-shut. Mrs. Bresland was depressed—she'd been seeing a therapist—and she took a bottle of sleeping pills. She left a note that said if suicide was good enough for Marilyn, it was good enough for her."

Chill bumps raced over my body. That didn't sound like any suicide note I'd ever read. It was flippant. And depressed people seldom achieved flippancy no matter how hard they tried.

"In our investigation did you hear any rumors that Johnny Bresland was cheating on his wife?"

"His wife was dead *before* Bresland was shot. It occurred to me that something was wrong in the marriage for the wife to kill herself, but she wasn't a suspect in the shooting. Dead people make poor murder suspects. Juries don't tend to believe in revenge from a spirit." There was a hint of humor in his voice. "Men cheat all the time, but few women kill themselves because of a cheater."

"Cheating may have been the cause of Mrs. Breland's suicide, but I'm really interested in how the Bresland estate was handled. The man was wealthy—extremely so. No children. His wife should have been his sole heir, except she was dead. That left the door open for a stranger to benefit from his death." I let that sink in. "I'm headed to the Hell Creek area. Care to meet me?"

"I'm about ten minutes from there anyway. I'll wait for you on the North Trace road."

This was better than I'd hoped. "Thanks, Deputy Ford." I hung up and nodded at my friends. "The deputy that worked the case is going to meet us there."

13

Deputy Ford was a big, strapping man with keen gray eyes that didn't miss a lot. He was middle-aged but without the excess padding that a lot of men in their late forties or early fifties tended to pack on. He eyed the four of us with no emotion, waiting to see what we'd reveal. He was alert but nonconfrontational, and I realized he'd agreed to meet us out of curiosity to see what we might be up to.

He was standing, leaned against the back of his patrol vehicle, when we stopped behind him and got out of the car. The woods around us were dense, a lovely mixture of hardwoods on land that rolled and sloped, sometimes sharply. I looked on the north side of the road, where the terrain slanted down to the gurgle of a fast-running creek.

"Thanks for meeting us," I said.

"I wasn't expecting a posse," he said at last.

I gave him a business card. "We're on vacation," I explained. "It just so happens that we were asked to look into some strange events in Columbus, and the trail has led us here."

"To the middle of a wildlife preserve where a man was shot to death." He watched me closely. It was clear that now he'd caught sight of us in the flesh, he thought we had some ulterior motive.

"It's a long shot," I said, "but the woman who hired us, something doesn't click with her. As private detectives, we like to know if we're being sandbagged by a client."

Millie approached the deputy and handed him her business card. "Ms. Falcon and I are newspaper reporters. We work for the *Zinnia Dispatch* and we're consultants with the Delaney Detective Agency."

I turned away to hide my grin. Millie liked what she saw in Deputy Ford. My hardworking friend had had one fling with a man she met at a Cupid's party, but distance had stymied that romance. It was good to see her strut her stuff at a man.

"Millie runs the best café in the Southeast," I said. "If you ever happen through Zinnia, you should stop for some coffee and apple cobbler."

He looked at me, then glanced at Millie and grinned. "Apple pie is my favorite."

"With the way sparks are flying, y'all could set the woods on fire," Cece said drolly. "Now where was the body found?"

"Prepare for a hike," Ford said. He led the way and Millie joined him, chatting as we entered the woods.

Cece and Tinkie were as proud as if they'd negotiated a Middle East peace treaty. "They're hitting it off," Tinkie said.

"This will do Millie a world of good," Cece answered. "And right at Christmas, the perfect time for a romance."

I spoke up. "What if he's married?"

"Simple," Tinkie said. "We kill him."

I glanced down at her and I couldn't tell for certain if she was kidding or not.

We came to a clearing surrounded on all sides by trees and dense undergrowth. "There's a tree stand over there." The deputy pointed north. "And the other hunters were on either side of the stand. Bresland's body was right over here in that clump of elderberries and Johnson grass. It seems obvious he was staring down that slope to that thicket. He must have been watching a deer himself, calculating a shot. But then someone up the slope saw him moving about in that tall grass and just thought it was a deer."

His assessment made perfect sense. Except for one thing. "Wouldn't a hunter have come down to check and see if he had a kill?"

"My guess is that there actually was a deer here and the hunter missed. When the deer took off into the woods, the hunter just assumed his shot was bad."

"How many men were in the hunting party with Mr. Bresland?" Tinkie asked.

"Four, counting Bresland. They'd hunted together for years. Bresland wasn't known to be an early riser, so they were a little surprised when he got up earlier than they did and headed out on his own."

I nodded, looking around the scene. The story fit the terrain. Hunting accidents happened. Sometimes people walking in the wrong place got blasted. "Thanks for showing us."

"It did seem pretty open-and-shut to me," Ford said, completely at ease. "I just couldn't tie any two things together solid enough to come up with a motive and a suspect."

"Thanks again," I said. "We really appreciate your time."

"As it turned out, my time was well spent." He smiled at Millie and started back the way we'd come.

"Deputy Ford," Tinkie called out, "are you married?"

He stopped and turned back. "No, why?"

"Because if you were, I was telling Sarah Booth that we'd have to kill you." Tinkie smiled really big. "No one messes with our friends."

He laughed. "You got a set of them." He offered Millie his arm and they strolled ahead of us.

We returned the car to the rental agency and then went back to the B and B. Darla let us use her computer. The men were still conspicuously absent, but they'd return soon. We were due to set off for the flotilla at six o'clock. Darla would prepare a light dinner for us at five so we didn't end up on the water drinking on an empty stomach in the cold. She was really good at taking care of us.

Millie was holed up in her room talking to Deputy Len on the phone, and Cece was doing her best to eavesdrop. I tried to shame her into stopping, but she was having way too much fun. Tinkie and I left them to their own devices while we dug deeper into the death of Aurora Bresland. Coleman would have been a big help here, but he wasn't around, so we had to persuade the

Lafayette County authorities to give us as many details as they would.

We found out what we could online and then we called the Lafayette County sheriff's office.

The deputy we spoke with wasn't exactly forthcoming, but he did pull the file and read the case notes to us. It was exactly as Deputy Len had said. Aurora was found in her bed, empty pill bottle and the suicide note on the end table, typed but signed. Her husband had verified that it was her signature and had broken down in the sheriff's office proclaiming that his cheating had killed his wife.

"The guy was truly broken up," the law officer I was talking with said. "I took his statement and I felt sorry for him."

"He was cheating on his wife," Tinkie said with some heat. "How about feeling sorry for her?"

"Well, you know what I mean," he blustered. "We interviewed some of her friends and they said she was distraught by what she viewed as the end of her marriage. Her husband had found a younger, more attractive model, and she felt her world was ending."

"Any indication Bresland intended to divorce her?" I asked.

"None. And he denied a divorce was in the works. In fact, he said he'd decided to end his affair."

"Why?"

"He said something about the woman he was involved with being a little . . . unbalanced."

"Unbalanced enough to kill his wife and make it look like a suicide?" Tinkie asked.

The question didn't catch the deputy off guard. "We thought of that," he said, "but there was no evidence that anyone else was in the house with Mrs. Bresland when she died. And there was the note."

Tinkie rolled her eyes, but I put a finger to my lips to shush her. "Did you interview Clarissa Olson?" I asked.

"Why would I interview her? She wasn't romantically involved with Bresland. She was a business partner and nothing more."

"She's the other woman," Tinkie explained rather tartly.

"No, she was Mr. Bresland's real estate partner. He was involved with someone else."

"Who?" I asked.

"He refused to say. He denied any involvement with the Olson woman except financial. She was making money hand over fist with Bresland's contacts and managing his real estate. There was one complaint about her business ethics filed in our office, but we investigated and her actions were perfectly legal. If not ethical, they were legal."

"Are you positive Bresland was no longer involved with Olson?" I pressed.

"That's what the man said, and he was pretty torn up about his wife's suicide, so I think he was telling the truth. The coroner believed him, too."

Coleman would never have left a loose end like that, but I wasn't going to say it. We'd pursue this at a later date. We just had time to get ready for the flotilla.

14

My thick jacket, layers of sweaters, double socks, boots, scarves, and gloves made me feel like a Goodyear blimp as I waddled down the dock toward the waiting boat. Luckily, Coleman gripped my hand so I didn't float away on the brisk wind. And I couldn't help but express sincere pleasure at seeing the boat—decorated with garlands of lights and tinsel and bows. The *Tenn-Tom Queen* looked like Santa's sleigh packed with sparkly lights, toys, people, and gaiety.

"Rockin' Around the Christmas Tree" came over the speaker system, and I looked up to find Coleman watching me with amusement. "You're afraid I'm going to sing, aren't you?"

"Only a little," he said, then brushed a kiss across my

lips. "Sing if it makes you happy, Sarah Booth. I only want you to be happy."

Because he had such a generous heart, I decided to restain myself. "Let's get a drink," I said as he handed me onto the bow of the big party boat, which was ready for the holiday cruise.

"All aboard!" Darla called out. Her faithful friend Kathleen was at her side, handing out cosmopolitans, the perfect color for the season, as we boarded. Kathleen was even more layered up than I was, if that was possible. And she had the cutest stocking cap with a snowman on the top. Darla took us around and introduced us to people we didn't know. The boat was really a floating party. Just before we were ready to cast off, Clarissa jumped aboard. I had to admire her catlike grace and her sleek fitted skiwear.

Darla cast the boat off from the dock and jumped aboard and we were slowly drifting downriver to join up with twenty other vessels that were floating decorations. When the boats drifted close to the docks where people cheered us on, we threw Christmas necklaces, candies, garlands, and novelties that Darla had generously provided for all of us. It was one of the best parades I'd ever been in.

"Are you having fun?" Coleman asked as he pulled me back against his chest.

"I am. This was a genius idea that Tinkie had."

"Yes, it was. I haven't been this relaxed in a long, long time."

"And I don't get any credit for that?" I teased him. "Seems to me I've worked some of those kinks out."

"And there are more that need your attention tonight," he said.

The rest of the gang joined us at the rail as we whooped and hollered and sang Christmas carols to the spectators on the banks of the river. The music was loud enough to drown out my voice, but I still had the pleasure of singing—a perfect combination.

When I saw Clarissa standing alone near the wheelhouse, I signaled Tinkie to follow me. It was time to confront her about Johnny Bresland. We approached just as she stopped Kathleen for a fresh drink.

"You're going to ask me about Johnny Bresland, aren't you?" She sipped the cosmopolitan she had taken from Kathleen's tray without even a thank-you. "I wondered how long it would take you to get to that bone. Not long. I'm impressed that I've hired professionals."

Kathleen darted a disapproving look at her before she said, "Excuse me. I need to refill my tray."

"Stop back by when you replenish the tray," Clarissa said. "I'll be ready for another, I'm sure. And could you chill my glass a bit?"

"Clarissa, maybe you could ask politely?" I really disliked the woman I worked for.

"Don't you worry about Kathleen. Waitress is the perfect occupation. Half the town knows she's been mooning over another woman's husband, and I intend to make sure the other half of the population hears the story. You shouldn't come to play in Columbus with a pocketful of secrets."

"Do you have secrets, Kathleen?" I figured Clarissa was just getting in another dig.

"Not me. Clarissa has plenty, though." She turned to the woman. "You have your own secrets you'd rather keep hidden. Keep that in mind." Kathleen walked off, back stiff, shoulders rigid. She was just too polite to throw a drink in Clarissa's face, which is what should have been done.

For a brief moment, Clarissa's lips thinned, but the expression was gone almost before I could register it. She smiled. "Now ask your questions. I have gossip to spread. What do you want to know about Johnny? By the way, I didn't kill Aurora or Johnny. But I did benefit from their deaths." She shrugged and drained her cosmopolitan. "That's how real estate works sometimes."

"You benefited more than a few commissions. You inherited."

"There was no one else." She shrugged. "I was a good partner to Johnny. We both made a lot of money. After Aurora died, he was . . . not himself. He wrote a new will, left it all to me, and then went hunting. That's it. End of story."

"You had an affair with him?"

"At one point, yes. But that was over long before things went bad with Aurora."

"The deputy investigating Mr. Bresland's death denied there was an affair with you. Did you pay him off?"

"Goodness no. What happened between Johnny and me was ancient history. It had no bearing on anything. Johnny and I agreed never to admit to it, so that deputy never knew about it. Look, Johnny and I had a good time for a while, but he had such guilt about betraying his wife. It was intolerable. Sniveling is a turnoff, don't you think?"

"It would be for someone completely amoral," Tinkie said. She gave her best party-girl smile.

"That's not an insult from where I sit," Clarissa noted. "Morality is a seat belt for those terrified by their own animalistic nature. Those of us who embrace our complete right to seek pleasure—well, we don't need a seat belt. We find it constricting."

Who in the heck were we working for? The best thing to do was finish the case as quickly as possible and put the barracuda who'd hired us far behind.

I eased closer to her. "Why *did* you hire us, Clarissa?"

She looked around for another waitress with fresh drinks, and when she didn't see one, she sighed. All around us smiling people were singing and laughing and enjoying the Christmas spirit. Not Clarissa. She was like a big spider, waiting for a fly in her web. At last she looked at me. "I enjoy life. A lot. I take what I want and I don't make apologies. Someone is trying to punish those of us who live life to the fullest. They haven't targeted me—yet. But they will in time. I don't want to take a tumble or have a snake put in my bed. So find out who is doing this and put a stop to it before someone is really hurt. That's what I'm paying you for. There's no ulterior motive. I just want my normal life to resume. You've been paid, make it happen."

And we had deposited her check. There was no way around that fact. So much for the efficiency of modern banking and our cynical decision to make sure the check cleared. Now we were obligated to dance with the devil.

"Who do you think is behind the karaoke shocking and Bart's fall?" Tinkie asked Clarissa. "It would help if we had a direction, and since you're all up in this, who's been talking?"

"I gave you all the tips I had. It isn't me. I'm not responsible. So who is?"

"Is there anyone who lost a spouse or fiancé to cheating recently?" Tinkie asked.

Clarissa considered. "Sunny Crenshaw is at the top of that list. She hasn't lost Bart, but he views her as an old shoe. You know, something to wear when the yard is full of mud. That must cut her to the quick, though I have no illusions that she truly loves him. He pursued her hot and heavy, with all the charm and romance any woman could want. She brought the money to that marriage. She set him up in business. He gave her the royal treatment until the marriage license was signed, and then he was tired of her."

"We do need to talk to Sunny," I said. "Thanks." We'd been remiss in not getting to Sunny Crenshaw before now, but I'd hoped to have more facts when I did talk to her. Her husband might be a serial cheater, but she remained married to him.

"She isn't on Darla's boat, but Darla will know which boat she's on. Darla has the passenger list."

"Where can we disembark?"

"Downriver there's a marina."

I looked downriver and saw the glittering lights of the boat parade. The river was broad and slow-moving in this stretch. The night was calm, with no wind. The multicolored lights reflected on the water, creating a fairy-tale illusion. A burst of brilliant fireworks flared from the bank, and spangles of color illuminated the night. Any minute now Tinker Bell might appear.

Coleman came up behind me, and his arms captured me for a kiss. With the fireworks and the lights and the gentle motion of the boat, I closed my eyes to drink in the experience. Coleman held me safely against him. Just then there was a cry from the wheelhouse and the boat lurched hard to the left. Coleman grabbed the railing and held me safely upright as passengers tumbled in all directions. Women and men stumbled around the deck, grasping for anything to hold on to as the boat rolled slightly. Those who couldn't find something to grab hit the deck and slipped toward the side. Bodies slid toward the rail.

A cry arose from the bow. "Man overboard!"

"Tinkie! Cece! Millie!" I called out, immediately concerned that they'd accidentally gone over the side. To my relief, my friends answered. Jaytee, Harold, and Oscar were also safe. We helped other passengers to their feet as a flustered Darla held a clipboard with the names of all her passengers, trying to take an inventory.

"What happened?" I asked.

"I don't know. The skipper thinks we hit a log or something in the water. At least that's his best guess right now, without having a chance to really examine anything. The motor is gone. He thinks the propellers are broken."

"Did someone really go overboard?"

Darla was clearly upset. "I'm trying to check off the passengers against my boarding list now. If someone fell in the river, they could freeze." She hailed a man I'd seen working in the wheelhouse. "Get all the lights you can. Radio the other boats. We have to start searching."

"Shouldn't you check the list?" I suggested gently. "Maybe no one went over."

"You could be right. I just think of someone in that cold water. Even a strong swimmer might not last long."

Coleman approached Darla. "What can we do to help?"

"Check belowdecks. No one should be down there, but people are curious, and a lot of people have been drinking heavily, which is another concern if they went in the river. Since the motors are locked up, I've put in a call for someone to come tow us." She looked up from the list. "Have you seen Kathleen?"

Tinkie had also joined us. "No. Nor Clarissa."

"Oh, dear." Darla put a hand on Coleman's arm. "There's a high-beam light in the wheelhouse. Can you get it and scan the water?"

"Sure thing." Coleman was gone in an instant.

I went belowdecks to the small living quarters, hoping to find the two missing passengers, but the living space was empty, as was the head and galley. With the motors quieted, the only sound was the gentle creaking of the boat. Cece joined me. "Do you have any idea what happened?" she asked.

"None. Darla thinks we hit something in the river. The boat's motor isn't running. It could have been something mechanical."

"That water is cold. We have to find whoever went over."

"I know," I said. "There's no one down here."

"Let's go back above and see if we can help search the waters."

When we arrived back on the deck, I saw that the other boats in the flotilla were circling around us. All had high-beam searchlights, which were panning over the water. I noticed Tinkie was talking to a woman who was near hysterics. Cece and I joined her.

"It was awful," the woman said. "I saw that blond woman standing near the railing. It was like she saw something in the water and leaned over. Then the boat lurched, and someone—I think it was another woman— came out of nowhere, just hurtling along. It looked like she intended to push Clarissa Olson into the river, but maybe she just lost her balance. They both went over the rail."

"You should go into the cabin and sit down. I'm sure we're going to find whoever it is," Tinkie assured her. She pointed the woman in the direction of the cabin door, where at least she would be out of the night and somewhere warm.

Millie joined us. "Clarissa Olson *is* missing."

"You're serious?" I couldn't help it. Clarissa was like a force of nature. She didn't have accidents or clumsy moments. And she'd also been afraid someone was out to get her.

"Darla has checked everywhere," Millie said. "Clarissa isn't on deck. Unless she was below."

"Not down there," I said. "I wish I could do something more."

"There's nothing—"

"Kathleen!" Darla's cry was like a stab in my heart. It was filled with anguish and fear. "I can't find Kathleen!"

From the side of the boat a man called out. "There's something in the water. Hey, over here. Bring a life preserver. Hurry! Hurry! She's sinking!"

Harold grabbed a life preserver off the wall and rushed over to the side, where he flung it out into the river. "Grab hold!" Harold said. "Hold on." The men began to pull the rope, dragging someone toward the safety of the boat.

When I went to the side and looked over, I saw Clarissa Olson clinging to the life preserver. She was drenched and obviously nearly freezing to death. "Help me," she said, and her voice was weak.

Before I could stop him, Coleman shucked off his coat and boots and went over the side. He caught her and held her as a small motorboat came over and began hauling both of them into it. Three minutes later, the boat was racing toward the nearest dock, where the red lights of an ambulance spun.

"What about Kathleen?" Tinkie asked softly.

Darla was leaning against the boat, crying hard. "Are we certain she went over the side? Couldn't there be a mistake?"

Tinkie shook her head. "She's not on board now. We've looked everywhere."

"Let's keep looking. I'm not willing to give up."

We joined the others at the railing, and as the high-beam lights swept across the water, we prayed that we'd find Kathleen bobbing in the river. But two hours later, we had to concede defeat. The boats on the river began to break up as professional search-and-rescue vessels headed downstream in case the current had caught her and transported her from our search area.

Darla was distraught, and Tinkie went to comfort her. She was far better at that than I was. Cece and Millie hung back with me.

"Do you think she's still alive?" Millie asked.

"I don't know. If she's a strong swimmer, she may have made it to shore. If she went to the other side . . ." Cece was holding out hope.

"Let's get off this tub and search along the shore," I said. "I'm sure we can find some good flashlights. Maybe she did swim."

It was better than abject despair, and we waited mutely as the towboat hauled us slowly to the dock. Once we were on land, we split up to find flashlights. I didn't know where we were, exactly, and doing a search of a river-bank in unfamiliar terrain in the dark was not going to be easy. But it was better than sitting around doing nothing.

15

Some Columbus residents came down from their homes to the river with heavy-duty lights, blankets, thermoses of coffee, and sandwiches. The town pulled together to search for a missing woman. The residents silently handed out supplies to the searchers, or else brought small motorboats and joined in the search on the water. A breeze on the river whipped the marshy grasses into a low hum as we spread along the shore, looking for any sign of Kathleen. The black night and dark river seemed to have swallowed her whole.

Darla had reluctantly left the search and gone to the hospital to check on Clarissa. The deputies were talking among themselves, but I was too far away to hear an update. I knew better than to ask because they didn't know me and wouldn't share information. Besides, I was worried about Coleman. He was plenty self-sufficient—I knew that with all my heart. He'd get dry clothes and either rejoin us here or return to the B and B. The best thing we could do was help with the search.

Cece and I took an area that bordered on marsh. The footing was treacherous, and I couldn't stop my brain from turning every floating log or pile of debris into a waiting alligator. "Too cold for snakes. Too cold for snakes." I kept repeating that mantra to myself as I stepped onto soggy patches of ground and moved the beam of my light all around, hoping to see Kathleen on the shore, maybe freezing but alive. In the distance I could hear Tinkie and Oscar. Millie was searching with Harold, and Jaytee was helping Jerry Goode and some other deputies set up a bank of floodlights. His electrical expertise was sorely needed.

"Kathleen!" I called for her, knowing it was likely futile, but there was always a chance. "Kathleen!" The cry moved down the bank of the river, echoing hollowly into nothing. On the other side, several searchlights came on as volunteers crossed the river and began to search the other side.

"Do you think the boat hit a log?" Cece asked when we stopped for a moment to catch our breath. The mud was thick and heavy and sucked at our feet, making the going rough.

"I don't know what happened. It felt as if the propeller hit something. I'm not really a boat person, so I'm not sure. It could have been part of the motor freezing up."

"They'll check it out and know more tomorrow," Cece said. Something was obviously troubling her.

"What are you thinking?"

"I think Clarissa deliberately pulled Kathleen over the rail. She was treating Kathleen badly all evening. Like she was a servant or something. I noticed it and so did Darla and several others. And Kathleen threatened to reveal some secrets."

"What secrets?"

"I don't know. Yet."

"And you think Clarissa was the aggressor? But the eyewitness said—"

"You know how unreliable eyewitnesses are. And Clarissa is well known in Columbus as a member of the elite class. Kathleen isn't well known. She's much quieter. You know people often *see* what their expectations train them to see. I'm just saying it's *possible* that it happened the other way around. Or that they both lurched over the rail without touching each other. The boat took a pretty big jolt and a lot of people lost their feet."

"If Clarissa did this as a deliberate act . . . If Kathleen isn't found, that's murder."

"Yes, it is." Cece was speaking quietly, but her accusation was powerful. "Think about it. Clarissa is your best suspect. She has the money to make all of this happen. And how smart to be the one to hire you to dig into this. Throws all the blame off her."

"Maybe." She had a point, but Clarissa had nothing to do with Tulla's shock, as far as I could tell. And we had no proof she was involved in the destruction of Bricey's car. Or Bart Crenshaw's tumble down the stairs. Or even Kathleen's disappearance, for that matter. My friend really disliked my client, and I shared her sentiments. But we couldn't let emotion get ahead of evidence and logic, no matter how pleasurable that might be.

Some unusual marks in the weeds by the edge of the river caught my eye. "Look at this." I eased closer, careful to avoid the pools of water and mud that were all about us. The swamp grass, normally very resilient, had been crushed down. There were ruts in the mud.

"Looks like something heavy was dragged up on the shore," Cece said. She shone her flashlight all around. "I can't tell what. It could have been a log or a person."

From behind Cece came a harsh barking sound, followed by a terrifying hiss.

"Or an alligator!" we said in unison as we turned toward the bank.

Forgetting water and mud, we slogged toward firm land as fast as we could churn. My legs were virtual eggbeaters, whipping the muddy water to a froth.

"Gators are slower in the winter," I said, hoping to give us both confidence in a fact I wasn't certain was true.

"They only have six-inch legs, but they can run sixty miles an hour for a short distance," Cece said. "We're doomed!"

I grabbed her hand and tugged. "Run! Just shut up and run!"

"I'm running!" she called out as she put everything she had into making for the dock.

Somehow we managed to push through the unfriendly terrain without falling—or getting eaten by a gator. When we finally got to firm ground, I stopped and swung the light behind us. Nothing. Not even eyes reflected back at us.

"Was that really an alligator? Maybe it was a bird." Cece gave a nervous laugh. "I'm going to feel like such a dolt if I let a bird chase me up the riverbank."

"Don't know. Not going back to find out." I started toward the dock where people were still milling about.

"Wait! What if it was where Kathleen crawled out? What if that was her trying to get our attention to help her?"

"I don't believe Kathleen would hiss and bark." I wasn't going to let Cece make me regret my hasty retreat to civilization.

"We have to go back."

I turned to face her. "No, I'm not. Not without a gun." I didn't know if I could shoot an alligator. After all, the gator was just living its life. It wouldn't be like shooting a criminal, someone who deserved a bullet. "Kathleen isn't in that area, Cece. You know it and I know it. It's crazy to risk getting ourselves hurt." The truth was, we had searched our area very thoroughly. Other than the sliding marks in the mud and grass, there had been nothing that would indicate anything came out of the water and up onto the bank. "We'll tell the police officers what we saw. Tomorrow, in the daylight, they can do a more thorough search."

"If she's along the shore, she'll likely freeze to death before daybreak," Cece said.

It was an ugly reality. One I had to accept, too. "Okay. Okay, let's get a guy with a gun to go with us."

Ten minutes later we were headed back to the Land of Alligators with Jerry Goode. He was about as pleased as we were to go clambering through backwater, mud, and slime with the possibility of meeting an alligator face-to-face. But he had a Q-Beam light and an automatic pistol. He was better equipped than we were.

We made it to the river's edge without encountering anything—alive or dead. Jerry studied the marks in the mud and pulled out his phone to take photos. "You could have done this and shown them to me and I would have told you someone pulled a boat from the bank into the river. Strange place for a boat to be left, but it's clear the boat had been resting here for a while. See how the grass is crushed and dying?"

"Can you tell what kind of boat?" I asked.

"I'd say something like a canoe or small aluminum fishing boat, but I can't be certain until I take some molds of these tracks and do a comparison. That looks like some footprints, too." He pointed out something we'd overlooked with our weaker flashlights. He lifted his foot and the mud gave a loud, sucking noise that was slightly embarrassing. "Next time, though, just take photos."

Great. The man was pointing out the obvious and making me feel even more a fool because he was correct. Cece and I had panicked at the thought of an alligator slithering up on us. We could have taken photographs— if we'd been thinking instead of panicking.

"They dragged a boat *into* the river?" I asked, focusing on the more important elements.

"Looks that way to me," Jerry said. "Good work on finding this, and I can see why you thought it might be an alligator." I couldn't see his face in the dark, but I knew he was grinning at us. In a friendly way.

"We did overreact," Cece said. "But we also came back and brought you."

"I don't see any indication of anyone swimming to shore here." He moved along the water's edge more quickly than Cece and I could navigate it. "I'd say this is unrelated to the disappearance of Ms. Beesley, but I'll check it out. Likely some boaters pulled up here to take a break or repair something. You two should go back to the dock. I'll look around here a little more, just to be on the safe side."

Those were sweet words to my ears. "You sure you don't need us?"

"Go ahead. Tell the police chief that we'll need a forensic team down here first thing in the morning. I'll mark the area for them. But you might want to take a look at this before you go." He shone the light about thirty yards away where there was a slight rise in the bank. Two golden eyes stared back at us from a hidey-hole. "Now *there's* your alligator. But he's not interested in you or me," he said.

"See you at the dock!" I was already moving toward safety.

"You take care now," Jerry said. And to his credit, he didn't laugh.

When we were almost to the dock, I stopped. I thought I'd wait for the lawman to come out of the swamps. I didn't trust that alligator. "Cece, would you see if you can find Tinkie and maybe check on Coleman for me, please? I have a question to ask Jerry."

"Will do. I'm going to catch a ride back to the B and B. Someone needs to be with Darla, and I reek of river mud. I smell like something dead."

We were both pretty odiferous. "Good plan. Can you find a ride?"

"I don't want Oscar to call the limo for me because I'm filthy, but maybe I can hitch a ride in the back of a pickup truck."

That was illegal, but it would be wasted breath to try

convincing Cece of that. She did exactly as she pleased almost all the time. "You go right ahead. I'll poke around this area a little more." I was on firm dry land, and if I saw a gator or anything else I didn't like, I could make tracks.

Cece headed to the docks, where a bank of lights suddenly came on, illuminating the search area. Boats on the river signaled back and forth, but there seemed to be no sign of Kathleen.

For a moment, I was alone, and I could take a deep breath and acknowledge that someone I knew most likely had died. It was an upsetting fact. As long as I could hide in activity and busyness, I didn't have to think about loss. Now, though, I had time to confront what may have happened. One eyewitness had claimed to see someone—presumably Kathleen—knock Clarissa over the side of the boat. I didn't buy that. Kathleen was a passive person, but Clarissa was the take-action kind. I could believe it had happened the other way around. Kathleen had hinted at revenge against Clarissa by spilling her secrets. In truth, both women had threatened to do that. Was that enough to provoke murder?

The crack of a stick came from behind me, and I whipped around to find a large black woman with a huge bosom standing only inches away. She was at least six feet tall, with gray "church" hair, a frumpy dress, sensible shoes—and a gun! She brandished the gun like a sheriff in a saloon brawl. I had a suspicion who this might be, but I just didn't want to believe it.

"Whatchu lookin' at?" she asked, eyes narrowed in suspicion.

"Where did you come from?" As big and awkward as she was, I should have heard her come up.

"Does it matter? I got things to say to you."

That sounded distinctly ominous. And very much like Jitty. "You don't even know me. What could you have to tell me?"

She waved the gun. "I got the power of the Lordt on my side and a little help from my friend right chere."

I knew the figure standing in front of me. It was Madea, the Tyler Perry character. I knew he filmed in the South, but I didn't believe he was in Columbus. Mr. Perry was not in a swampy part of the river looking for a woman who'd fallen off a ship. And he would not be talking to me. But Jitty would. I realized it didn't matter *why* Jitty was here as Madea—I could use her help. Madea was hell on wheels when it came to cheaters!

"I need to turn you lose on a whole bunch of people in this town," I said.

She shook the gun. "Say heller to my peacemaker! This can clear up a lot of issues. And just so you know, hanging around this town, I see what's goin' on and I'm about to violate my parole!"

I loved every inch of her. "I need your wisdom."

"Yeah, you do. Women might be able to fake orgasms, but men can fake whole relationships. That's the problem in a nutshell. Ever'body fakin' somethin'."

I wanted to hug her, but she started striding around and her bosoms were bouncing so ferociously that I didn't risk getting too close. "Can you help me?" I asked.

"This is what I learned in all these years on this earth.

If someone wants to walk out of your life, let them go. Deliver that message, please."

That was sound advice, but not particularly helpful. "Jitty, get rid of those big ta-tas before you put my eye out." She was jumping around and I feared for the safety of my vision.

She whipped a knife out of the folds of her dress. "I will shank you, fool! Back away!" she said. "Just back away."

I couldn't help it. I had to laugh. I loved Madea, and in this terrible moment in time, I so needed a good laugh. "Jitty, cut it out."

"You know I only go to church for two reasons, weddings and funerals. Which one we gonna have today?"

Even though I didn't want to, I laughed. "Stop it, Jitty. Folks will think I'm out here in the swamp laughing about a drowned woman. They'll put me in an institution."

"When you go off in a dangerous swamp looking for people, remember this. Stop editing your pictures on that ridiculous Facebook. What if you go missing? How you expect us to find you if you look like Beyoncé on Facebook and like Linda Blair playing Regan in real life?"

"Please stop!" I had to control myself because Jitty was going to get me in a world of hurt. "Do you know where Kathleen is?"

Madea slowly started to fade, and in her place was a beautiful woman with dark curls and a wistful expression. "I don't know where she is," Jitty said. "And if I did, I couldn't tell you."

"Has she crossed over?" I pressed. I was genuinely

worried about Kathleen, and the idea of her stuck somewhere on the riverbank, dying of hypothermia—thanks for that image, Cece—was more than I could bear thinking about.

Jitty shook her head. "Not sayin'."

"Would you tell me if you could?" I was curious if some of this was Jitty's obstinacy or if the rules were that rigid in the Great Beyond.

"It is what it is, Sarah Booth. No amount of askin' and whinin' is going to change anything."

"So what prompted your appearance as Madea?"

"Your chin was draggin' the ground, and any minute you were gonna step on it. I had to make you laugh."

And she had done that. "I have to get up to the docks. I'm concerned about Coleman, too. He went in that river to save Clarissa. I need to find him and make sure he isn't hurt."

"Warm that man up, Sarah Booth. You know how to do it, don't you?" Slowly she began to return to her Madea form and her body was doing things that might make me go blind if I kept looking.

"Stop!"

"You lock those legs around your man and you hang on like you a cowgirl! Hallelujer! Ride that bronco!"

With the jinglejangle of some spurs, Jitty disappeared. I heaved a sigh of relief. Sometimes she just wore me out.

I trudged back to the dock. There was no sign of Kathleen from any of the other searchers. Cece texted me that she had caught a ride back to the B and B. She'd checked on Coleman, who said he was fine and would meet me soon. There was nothing else we could do in the dark. Tomorrow, we'd volunteer to search more.

Good ole Rex was there waiting to whisk us back to the B and B. I had to leave my clothes in the trunk and wrap up in a blanket before I was allowed in the car, which I actually found reasonable. I stank. Oscar, Tinkie, Millie, Harold, and Jaytee were pretty glum as we loaded into the limo. This was not going to be a lot of fun with Darla.

16

The evening at the B and B was a sad affair. While Darla insisted on making a late supper for us, no one really had an appetite to appreciate her efforts. But working in the kitchen kept her hands busy and thoughts of Kathleen in the background. Worry for her friend was clear on her face.

Tinkie signaled me out of the parlor and onto a side porch. "Do you think Kathleen is dead?" she asked. "I didn't want to ask in front of the others. I don't want to crush their hope."

"She probably is." I told her about the boat tracks in the mud. "But Jerry said it was a boat going *into* the water, not coming back to shore. As far as I know, that's the only thing anyone found. If she's still in the water, hypothermia will probably get her." I didn't mention the alligator that I'd seen. Tinkie didn't need those gruesome images. "Did Darla say if Kathleen was a strong swimmer?"

Tinkie sat on the balustrade and slumped. "I heard her tell the deputies that Kathleen could swim, but that she wasn't a great swimmer." She inhaled sharply. "Clarissa managed to stay afloat until Coleman got her out. Why couldn't it have been Kathleen instead?"

I felt the same way. "Speaking of Coleman, he texted and said he was on the way from the hospital." I was eager to see him. "Maybe he has new information for us."

Tinkie shivered, whether from the cold or her own thoughts, I didn't know. We returned inside. Everyone had huddled in the parlor, where Darla had a roaring fire going. She did her best to play the perfect hostess, but her red-rimmed eyes and sniffles let us all know she was in distress over her friend.

"Why don't I make a pitcher of martinis?" I suggested. I, too, needed something to do to keep my hands and mind busy. Waiting was the hardest work on the planet. I took a vote on gin or vodka and got the Grey Goose from the bar. In no time I was serving the drinks. "Shaken, not stirred," I said, imitating James Bond as best I could. I got a few weak smiles. Everyone was physically and emotionally exhausted.

We sipped our drinks as the fire crackled. When the front door opened, I was up like a shot and hurled myself into Coleman's arms. "Thank goodness you're okay." He gave me a kiss that left no doubt how glad he was to see me.

When I stepped back, he accepted the drink Cece

offered. Coleman was dressed in something far more preppy than he normally wore. But he was dry and warm and smelled great. He'd also had a shower. Something I needed to take care of. "Any word on Kathleen?"

He swallowed and shook his head. "No sign of her. They're still searching." He gave Darla his full attention. "I'm so sorry."

"Clarissa?" Darla asked.

"As far as I know, she was checked out and released."

"Did she say what happened?" I asked.

"No." He sounded exhausted.

Cece, Tinkie, and Oscar decided to make another round of martinis, but I was done and worried about Coleman. "I'm going to take a shower and go to bed." I turned to our hostess. "If we can help in any way or if you hear anything at all, don't hesitate to wake us up."

She blinked back tears and nodded. "Thank you."

I gave Coleman a kiss and whispered for him to come up when he was ready. I had to wash the river smell out of my hair and skin. The minute I stepped under the hot spray I felt better. I'd been so tense my shoulders were rigid, but the pounding of the water helped a lot. I braced against the shower wall and gave in to the pleasure.

From somewhere in the bedroom I heard the sound of bells jingling. "Oh, no." Jitty was back. She was determined to get me in trouble in this town. I shut off the water, grabbed a towel, and headed into the bedroom to have it out with her. As much I enjoyed her forays into drama, comedy, and aggravation, now wasn't the time.

I opened the bedroom door and said, "You have to stop this."

Coleman, wearing nothing but a grin and a necklace of jingle bells, said, "I don't think I want to stop."

I was taken aback, but I hid it behind a daring smile. "Then you'll just have to get what you deserve." I went to him, still wet, and put my arms around his neck for a kiss. The towel hit the floor and I hit the light switch as he picked me up and lifted me onto the bed.

The next morning I stretched and snuggled against Coleman's warm body as the events of the evening replayed in my mind. I was a lucky woman. And Coleman was a lucky man. By the grace of persistence, we'd found each other.

I was about to drift back to sleep when I heard the infernal noise. Tap, tap, tap. A pause. Tap, tap, tap. Tinkie was at it again. I knew ignoring her wouldn't work. There was only one solution. I got up, grabbed a robe, and went to open the door.

She was waiting with a tray of coffee and some news. "Let's go out on your balcony," she said.

"Coleman is still asleep."

"Then put on some clothes and let's go outside on the terrace."

Tinkie was worse than a dog with a bone. There would be no shaking her. Best to do as she asked and be done with it. I slipped back into the bedroom, found jeans, socks, a T-shirt, and a heavy sweater. The morning was brisk, and I knew before it was over I'd be down at the river, hoping for good news about Kathleen.

When I found Tinkie on the terrace, she had coffee, condiments, and a basket of homemade biscuits with

Darla's dewberry jam. I discovered I was starving, and I matched Tinkie bite for bite.

"You should slow up," she told me. "I'm eating for two. You're not!"

"I'm twice as tall as you are and need double the calories." It was a stupid rationalization, and we both laughed.

"How is Darla?" I asked.

"She's cleaning her cabinets."

That pretty much said it. No one cleaned cabinets unless they were desperate for something to do. "Maybe we should check with Tulla and Bricey."

Tinkie nodded. "We don't really have any leads, except the mystery woman who hired Colton to murder the car."

"We could go down to the river."

Tinkie brightened. "I'd kind of rather spend time with an alligator than those two homewreckers."

"We can leave a note for the men." I was tempted to rush upstairs to tell Coleman in person, but I knew the power of his seductive skills. I might not make it out of the bedroom for several hours.

We settled on a generic note saying merely that we were down at the river where the search party had set up. Tinkie decided to call an Uber instead of rousting Rex out of bed. He'd been up as late as we had.

In only a few minutes the driver was there and we headed to the search site. The driver was a woman our age and a chatty one at that.

"Terrible about Ms. Beesley," she said. "Such a nice woman."

"Yes, we're hoping she'll be found safe," Tinkie said.

As the Queen Bee Daddy's Girl of the Delta, Tinkie felt it necessary to *almost* always employ good manners.

"I heard the boat hit something."

The driver was pumping us, but I didn't mind. "Maybe. The police were examining it to determine what actually happened."

"I heard some of the society dames were opposed to bringing back the flotilla."

Tinkie and I sat forward. "That's a shame," Tinkie said. "Who would oppose a flotilla? It was so beautiful last night on the river, and the people at each dock seemed to have a great time. The voices echoing off the water singing all the old carols and then the fireworks. It was just wonderful fun. Until the accident."

"A handful of grande dames have run the whole Christmas celebration until recently. Now a few people are bucking the dragons and coming up with new and interesting ideas. The return of the flotilla met a lot of resistance because those biddies had killed it back in the 1990s. They didn't care whether it was a good idea or a bad one. It wasn't *their* idea. Kathleen was telling me about it in the beauty parlor just last week."

"Did she name names?" I asked with as much subtly as I could muster.

"Clarissa Olson, for one. She's opposed to anything that doesn't up the value of her many properties, and as far as I know, she doesn't own anything on the river. Ironic that Clarissa went in the river with Kathleen."

The driver was right about that. "Do you know Clarissa Olson?" I asked.

"Nope, and I don't want to. Nothing stands in the way of her getting what she wants, or at least that's the word on the street. I steer clear of bulldozers when I see one coming."

We were approaching the rescue site and soon our talkative driver would be gone. "Did you hear about Bart Crenshaw's tumble down the stairs at Clarissa's house?" I asked.

She chuckled. "I did. I won a three-hundred-dollar pot that Clarissa would get even with Bart before Christmas was over. It was all over town that he dumped her."

"I was at the house and Clarissa was nowhere close to the stairs when he took a header down them." I had to be honest.

"Doesn't mean she wasn't involved. When we made our bets, I was smart enough to make the distinction that Clarissa would be *nearby* or *implicated* if Bart was hurt. That's the premise I won the bet on." She laughed. "I wouldn't be surprised if she didn't do something to the stairs to guarantee he'd tumble. I would have won more if he'd broken his neck."

Tinkie and I exchanged horrified looks. Betting on someone's death was unseemly. Amusing but unseemly.

"What about the other accidents around town?" Tinkie asked. "Is Clarissa involved?"

The driver shrugged. "Who knows. Tulla Tarbutton and Bricey Presley aren't even in the same category of cougar that Clarissa is. I find it hard to believe she'd waste her time in revenge on them. But you never know."

She pulled up to the parking lot. "That'll be five dollars."

Tinkie gave her a twenty. "Keep the change. Could we have your number in case we need another ride?"

"Sure."

Tinkie programmed it into her phone. Dallas Swee-ney, our driver, was a valuable asset to have.

We watched her pull away. "That girl knows more about what's going on in Columbus than anyone else," Tinkie said. "We'll call her again."

"Roger that," I said as we were hailed from the dock area by Jerry Goode.

17

"Ladies, I have some questions," Goode called out.

"And so do we," Tinkie sang back to him, earning a smile.

We met in the middle of the dock, and Jerry graciously gave us an update right off the bat. "Tell Sheriff Peters that Clarissa and Bart Crenshaw are both out of the hospital."

"Any sign of Kathleen?" Tinkie asked. She tried not to sound hopeful, but I could read it in her expression.

Jerry shook his head. "She simply disappeared. She should have washed up right around here on the shore where you gals were looking yesterday. The current pulls everything from the river to the right and deposits it along the west bank there where you were looking."

"Why would she sink so fast?" I asked. "Clarissa was able to stay afloat for a few minutes at least." It hadn't taken Coleman long to leap in and grab her.

"Maybe the clothes she was wearing. Some things absorb water more quickly. The weight then would drag her down."

"She had on a poly-filled vest and a cotton sweater." I recalled because I liked the snowman on her red sweater and her hat. They had been happy garments. "Blue jeans and what looked like hiking boots."

"That could have sunk her," Jerry said with a frown. "They're going to drag the river to see if they can find the body."

"Has her next of kin been notified?" I asked.

"She doesn't have anyone. Kathleen came to Columbus awhile back. She's made friends, but there was no next of kin listed on her medical forms. Just Darla Lofton, who had her medical power of attorney."

So Darla was both Kathleen's friend and adopted family. No wonder Kathleen was there all the time.

"I can't believe she's dead." Tinkie stared out at the river where the sun had just begun to sparkle on the water. "This is just wrong."

"Believe me, I'm hoping she turns up," Goode said. "Maybe she was bumped in the head and floated in to land somewhere and can't remember who she is."

Jerry Goode was weaving a complicated fairy tale, but it was one with potentially a happy ending, so I didn't say a word.

"Do you really think that's possible?" Tinkie was grasping at straws.

"Maybe," Goode said. "Let's focus on that. Better to expect a good outcome than a sad one."

I glanced at him. I would never have taken him for a Pollyanna type, but he seemed genuinely saddened by Kathleen's fate. "Jerry, has anyone ascertained what went wrong with the boat or how the accident happened?"

"We had a diver inspect the bottom of the boat and the propeller was badly bent. Looks like the boat hit a partially sunken log."

"So it was an accident." I sighed. That was a load off my mind. "And what about how both Kathleen and Clarissa went over the rail?"

Jerry shook his head. "Mixed bag. Some say Clarissa stumbled and took Kathleen, and some say Kathleen was knocked off-balance when the boat lurched and bumped into Clarissa."

"And what does Clarissa say?" I asked.

"That Kathleen is a clumsy ox and knocked her over the railing."

"I doubt Clarissa would ever accept responsibility for anything," Tinkie said baldly. "She's not keen on Kathleen anyway."

Jerry scoffed. "The woman has a serious issue with what she considers to be her elite class status. There's her and then the rest of us who were born to serve her. A couple of nurses in the hospital were ready to put her in a straitjacket for a psych eval."

"Why?" I had to ask. My gossip bone was itching.

"She wanted them to go to town and buy her a latte at Starbucks. She said the hospital coffee was giving her a migraine."

Hospital coffee was pretty gruesome, but to ask a nurse to play servant was a little too ballsy. "So she's at home?"

"She is, and singing the praises of Sheriff Peters." He grinned. "That snake will bite, Sarah Booth. Keep an eye on it."

"Oh, just let that vixen make a play for Coleman. I will snatch her bald-headed," Tinkie said. "I'll beat her butt with an ugly stick. I'll smack her in the mouth so hard her teeth will march out her ass like little white soldiers. I'll—"

I clapped a hand over her mouth. Tinkie never said such things. I had no idea she even *knew* such things. "He gets it, Tinkie."

Goode was laughing so hard he started coughing. "You look like a refined lady, but you sure talk like you know your way around a barroom brawl."

"I do both." Tinkie was back in matron form. "I just won't put up with anyone messing with my friends."

He tipped his hat at her. "Everyone should be that lucky to have such a loyal friend. Now are you here to help search or to gather information?"

"A little of both, if you need us," I said. "But what exactly did Clarissa say about Coleman?"

Jerry gave me a look that clearly intimated he was debating whether to tell me the truth or not. He shrugged one shoulder and started talking. "She said he was exactly the kind of man she'd been looking for and that she could make sure the Columbus city council offered him the position of police chief if he wanted to move here."

Tinkie saw the figurative steam coming out of my ears; her blue eyes went wide with alarm before she spoke. "Well, Clarissa Olson can keep wishing for that until the cows come home. Coleman is true blue to Sarah Booth, and besides, he's an elected official in Sunflower County."

Goode chuckled. "I'm sure she's aware that she's playing with dynamite. That's part of the appeal for someone like her. She's bored. It takes more and more danger to keep her interest up. Best thing you can do is just avoid her. Keep Sheriff Peters out of her cross-hairs."

"We're working for her," I reminded him sourly.

"Quit. No law says you have to keep doing her dirty work."

"We aren't doing dirty work," Tinkie said, a little in-dignant. "Our work is just as honorable as yours. We're both looking for justice."

"Not if you're working for Clarissa. Justice isn't even on her agenda. Getting what she wants is the *only* thing she cares about. No matter what she told you she wants, what she wants is pleasure for herself. Just keep that under your hat."

"Thanks for the tip," I said to Goode, and I really meant it. At least Tinkie and I were forewarned. "Maybe we will quit." But until we did pull the plug on the case—which would require some discussion—we were still on the clock. "Jerry, do you think it's possible Kathleen's . . . disappearance is related to the things that have been going on in Columbus? The shocking karaoke, the tum-ble down the stairs, the cemented Caddy."

"Kathleen wasn't part of the swinger clique," Goode said. "She was a nice lady. She was shy and found it difficult to make friends here. Darla Lofton was really the only person who stepped up to befriend her. Those other women . . ."—he shook his head—"they were aw-ful to her. The answer to your question is no. I don't think Kathleen's disappearance is connected to the other things . . . unless she was collateral damage. What we don't know is if someone pushed Kathleen into Clarissa, like using Kathleen as a cue ball."

Now that was an interesting theory, and one I hadn't even considered. "Any reason you'd think of that?" I asked.

"Those women always use someone else to do their dirty work. Like Colton. He's just a guy making a living hauling dirt and delivering cement. He's got no grudges against anyone, minds his own affairs, doesn't gossip. Yet now he's caught up in something that may cost him his business. That's how those women operate. They're like crows pecking at each other's eyeballs but it's always the passerby who gets the blame."

"Did you talk to Colton about the woman who hired him?"

He scoffed. "Colton has his head in the clouds most of the time. He didn't pay attention. He said she was wearing a wig and that's about all he can remember. He honestly thought it was Bricey."

"If we can find who hired him, we'll be a lot closer to figuring out who's behind these dangerous pranks."

"But no closer to finding Kathleen Beesley. Now I have to make sure the searchers are working a grid and being careful." He tipped his hat and headed back to the dock area, where a tent had been set up. Tinkie and I headed that way, taking in the dozens of volunteers who'd come to assist. Several police officers sat at a table with a map and they assigned an area to each volunteer and sent them to search.

"They aren't going to ever find her, are they?" Tinkie asked.

"I don't know. The river looks languid, but I suspect there are treacherous currents. If she's caught in one along the bottom, it could be days before it releases . . . the body."

"Poor Kathleen. Jerry Goode seemed to know her better than anyone else but Darla."

"You know, we really don't know much about her." Kathleen talked about herself less than almost anyone I'd met. I knew far more about Bricey or Clarissa than I did about Kathleen or Darla.

"Are we going to search this morning?"

"Can you bear to forgo shopping?" I teased her.

"I'm kind of done with shopping for right now."

I glanced at my partner. She looked a little down, which wasn't like her. The tragedy wore heavily on her. Tinkie was a society girl, but at the heart of it all, she was tender and kind. "I'm sorry this happened. Sorry for Kathleen and Darla, and sorry for you, Tinkie."

"I just hate tragedy. I wish I could make all tragedy disappear."

"I wish you could, too." I put an arm around her shoulders and gave a good squeeze.

Just then a voice sounded behind us. "You two abandoned the rest of us, but we tracked you down."

I whirled around to find Coleman, Oscar, Jaytee, Cece, Harold, and Millie standing behind us. "We were kind and let you sleep," I corrected. "Tinkie was all for dumping a bucket of ice cubes on you in the bed, but I wouldn't let her."

"Like I would believe that," Coleman said. "Tell me, girls, what's on the agenda for this morning?"

Before anyone could answer, a Lexus SUV pulled to a halt and Clarissa Olson, dressed in a wet suit and dragging scuba tanks out of the back of her car, came down the dock. The suit left little to the imagination, and I had to admit, she had a terrific body. She stopped at our group. "I have another set of tanks and a wet suit that would fit you perfectly," she said to Coleman. "Care to join me in a dive? There's a deep pit just off this dock where the body may be trapped. I thought I'd check it out."

"We have plans," Tinkie said, stepping between the two of them.

"Too bad." Clarissa ignored Tinkie and spoke to Coleman. "No one else around here knows how to dive. You look the type who enjoys an underwater . . . adventure."

Oh, it was clear exactly what she was inviting Coleman to do. My hands curled into fists. I wasn't normally a brawler, but this heifer needed a smack in the snout.

"Not interested, Clarissa. Not interested in any kind of adventure with you. Look elsewhere for your entertainment." Coleman turned on his heel and slipped my hand through his arm, and we all began to stroll away. My heart was doing a little fluttery dance of joy.

"You get an A plus on the boyfriend score sheet," Millie said, taking Coleman's other arm. "Ah, the satisfaction of seeing someone put right in their place. Sarah Booth, you'd better give Coleman an extra special Christmas gift, if you catch my drift."

It felt good to laugh with my friends. The sun broke free of the clouds, and the whole day took on a different color. I couldn't stop tragedy from happening, not even to those I loved so desperately, but I could enjoy each moment I was lucky enough to share with them. I sighed. Duty called, though.

"We should go back and search," I said reluctantly.

"I don't think they need us," Millie said. "Look."

There were at least fifty volunteers already walking

grids and examining every square inch of ground. In my heart of hearts, though, I didn't believe that Kathleen had come up on the bank. "Do you think they'll find her body in the river?"

"Only if they go farther downstream," Harold said. "I regret this. I liked Kathleen. She had a sweet temperament."

Harold had taken a shine to both Kathleen and Darla, and I'd seen potential for a wonderful friendship, if not more. Another regrettable factor in this whole mess.

"We have a little final work to do on our surprise," Coleman said. All the men nodded.

"Will the surprise be ready before we finish our holiday?" Cece asked. There was a glint in her eye.

"Absolutely."

"Is it bigger than a bread box?" Millie asked.

"Considerably," Jaytee said, "but no more questions. You'll get the surprise when it's finished. But we have to go."

Rex pulled up with the limo and I realized this was a coordinated abandonment of us females. "Coleman, you're stacking up a bill that's going to come due."

"Promises, promises," he said, waving cheerily as they loaded into the limo and took off.

"What *are* they up to?" Tinkie asked.

"Cece, why don't you and Millie follow. I can call a great Uber driver. You can get loads of gossip for your Sunday column."

"Perfect," they said.

I called Dallas Sweeney, and within five minutes she was there. Unfortunately, the limo was long gone.

"No worries," Dallas said, "a limo is going to be really easy to track down. I have my sources."

Cece and Millie hopped in and they were gone. Tinkie and I looked at each other.

"How are we going to find out who really hired Colton?" Tinkie asked.

"Let's check to see if anyone nearby has security cameras. You would think Colton would have some with all that expensive equipment around."

"We didn't ask him," Tinkie pointed out, biting her bottom lip. "We should have."

"Yes, we should have," I agreed. "So let's do that."

18

We called another Uber and headed back to the heavy equipment business. Sure enough, there were cameras focused on the front door, the supply shed, and the mechanic shop. It crossed my mind that Colton had deliberately not mentioned the security footage, but I reminded myself that neither Tinkie nor I had thought to ask. It could be innocent.

Colton was out on a job, but the office manager showed us where the camera feed was stored—after I convinced her we were working on Colton's behalf.

"Colton is supposed to review the footage and delete it every day, but he doesn't," she said. "He forgets it until I think of it and remind him. How far back do you need to go?"

I didn't recall a specific date that Colton said he was hired, but it could have been only a day or so before it happened. Otherwise he would surely have come to his senses and thought to check with "Bricey" again to be sure she still wanted to destroy her car. Then the fake phone number—and ultimately the fake ID—would have come into play. "Let's go back a week."

"Colton is a good man, a truly decent guy. He doesn't deserve what's happening." The receptionist sat us down at a computer in a small room. "Knock yourself out. I hope you can prove who hired him. Otherwise we all know he's in a pickle." She was at the door before she turned around. "Would you like some coffee?"

"Best offer we've had this morning," I said. Watching grainy, boring videotape was going to require some caffeine if I wanted to stay awake. "I take mine black and so does Tinkie."

We were already going through the footage when she returned with two steaming cups of freshly brewed coffee. She was about to leave when I stopped her. "Do you remember the woman who hired Colton to fill up the car with cement?"

She shook her head. "She must have come at lunchtime when I wasn't here. I never saw her, and I haven't missed a day of work."

Interesting. "Do you go to lunch at the same time?"

She nodded. "Twelve-fifteen to one-fifteen. I meet my sister."

"Thanks so much." She'd just helped us more than she knew. We could skip a lot of footage and just explore the times she was away from the office at lunch. That would cut our search time by hours, and lucky for us the security footage was time stamped.

"This woman who hired Colton had to know he was here alone at lunchtime," Tinkie said.

"You're right. This was a setup from the get-go."

"It has to be someone who either knows his schedule or was told." Tinkie was biting her lower lip, which was a sign of either concentration or male manipulation. In this instance, the former.

"A friend? You think a friend would set him up like this?"

She tilted her head. "Someone in his circle of business acquaintances or friends."

We kept going through the video, slowing considerably as we reached the hours between eleven and two. We both pointed to the screen at the same time. "There she is."

It was a woman with sunglasses in what looked like an expensive wool coat and muffler. She wore fashion boots. Very little of her face could be seen between the sunglasses, the coat collar, and the longish dark hair that framed her face.

"Who is that?" Tinkie asked as she froze the images so we could study a still. "She looks familiar."

"Let her walk." I wanted to see if I could place her gait. There was something very familiar about her, but I couldn't put my finger on it.

Tinkie turned the video back and the figure walked up to the door and reached to grab the knob.

"Stop!" I didn't want to believe what I saw.

"Do you know who it is?" Tinkie asked. She was staring at the grainy figure as if she could squint and see more clearly.

I didn't want to say it, but I had to. "I think it's Kathleen Beesley."

"What?" Tinkie leaned closer to the screen. "Are you sure?"

"Look at the curve of her jaw, the way she reaches for the door, the tilt of her chin." The more I talked, the more certain I became. "It's Kathleen. Her red hair is covered by a wig, just as Colton thought."

"I see it now. That's her. Petite, a little slump to her shoulders," Tinkie said. She rewound the tape and played it all the way through, then rewound and played it again. "It's her. I see it." She leaned back and sighed. "Why? Why would Kathleen do something like this?"

"Those women were bullies to her. Even Jerry Goode knew they were awful to her. And you saw how Clarissa treated her on the boat, like she was a servant or paid help instead of a guest. They even threatened each other. Maybe she got fed up and decided to make them pay."

"But she trapped Colton Horn and he may lose his business if Bricey really sues him."

I didn't have any answers. Kathleen was literally the last person I would have suspected. "We'll have to talk to Darla about this." I didn't relish that thought. Darla was very protective of Kathleen. "The good news is that if Kathleen is dead, she won't suffer any punishment for this." It was kind of a bleak way to find a silver lining, but nonetheless I tried.

"Well, aren't you a bundle of joy," Tinkie said. "Sheesh, Sarah Booth. Are you going to call the law?"

I didn't know what I wanted to do. Kathleen wasn't there to defend herself. What if we were wrong? I mean really, I was basing my identification on a minuscule amount of flesh. Most of her was totally covered up. And the wig—if it was a wig—hid her real hair. Could I be certain enough to ruin a reputation? A reputation of a woman who was likely dead and couldn't fight back?

"Let's search her place. If we can find the wig, we'll have to tell the police."

"Good idea." Tinkie was ready to move along. "Let's get out of here before Colton comes back and asks questions."

We replaced the video and cleaned up the room, taking our coffee cups back to the receptionist.

"Did you find something to help Colton?" she asked.

"Maybe. We need to do more checking, and please don't mention this. I don't want to get his hopes up if we fall flat."

"Colton's a good man. If you can help him, please do. I don't know why someone would use him that way— for pure devilment and to destroy property." She looked down at her computer keyboard. "He never thinks that people can be cruel."

"We'll do what we can," I promised.

"We'll be in touch," Tinkie said as she led the way to the door.

Kathleen lived in an older home with a wraparound front porch and heritage camellias and azaleas that covered the foundation of the house. It wasn't a fancy house, but it was solid and gracious and lovely. The kind of home I'd have if I lived in town. The front door was locked, but it wasn't much of a challenge for Tinkie and me. My partner, among her many talents, was actually a very good picklock, and I was a good lookout.

The street was quiet as Tinkie worked her magic while I kept an eye out for passing motorists or kids on bicycles. It was that kind of neighborhood—where someone would be looking out for Kathleen's house if they noticed any strange activity.

When we were safely inside with the door closed again, I stopped at the sound of a kitty crying. "She has a pet," I said. "Damn. We have to do something."

"Maybe we can take it to Darla's. Maybe she'll keep the cat until Kathleen is found."

"And after that?" I wasn't going to leave town until I was certain the cat had a home. Darla was the best shot at a permanent residence, but if that didn't pan out, Pluto would have a sibling.

"Kitty, kitty, kitty," I called to the cat, who turned out to be a friendly little calico. She came up and purred as I petted her. I knew she was missing her mom. When I went in the kitchen, I found water and food on the floor. Kathleen must have prepared to be gone for the evening. "At least she isn't hungry." I found the litter box and gave it a cleaning. I'd have to ask Darla before I brought the cat to her. And I didn't want to move the baby until I knew she had a permanent place. Cats were very territorial. She would be happier in her home alone than being carted all over the place.

"Let's look for a wig," I said to Tinkie.

The logical place was Kathleen's bedroom, so we headed that way. The cat followed, rubbing against my legs whenever I stopped walking.

In contrast to the neatness of the front rooms of the house, the bedroom looked like a tornado had struck.

"Someone went through here like a crazy person." Tinkie picked up sweaters that were thrown onto the floor. She folded them and put them on the bed.

I picked up a jewelry box that had been overturned

and the contents scattered around the carpet. "Do you think she was robbed?"

Tinkie stopped. "Maybe we should call Jerry Goode."

"We're trespassing. Remember that. Let's just look around and get out. We can call anonymously when we're safely down the road."

Tinkie stuck her hands in her pockets. "Then we need to leave everything alone just where it is. And wipe your fingerprints off that jewelry box."

I followed her direction and we used the edge of our sleeves to open drawers and look for the wig.

"Got it!" Tinkie said from inside the closet. "This is it." She came out with a blob of dark hair hanging off a pencil she'd found on the floor.

We both stared at each other. There was no doubt Kathleen was the one who ordered the destruction of Bricey's convertible. But what to do with the information? If we called the police, I wasn't certain that Kathleen would get a fair shake in absentia.

"Throw it back in the closet," I said.

"Are you sure?" Tinkie held it up like it was a dead animal.

I nodded. "Look, if the police do the same legwork we did, they can come to this conclusion. But right now we need to give Kathleen a chance. If, that is, she's guilty of destroying Bricey's car—and just remember we have nothing more than Colton's word for that, since there is no contract—then maybe she did try to take Clarissa out by knocking her off the boat."

Tinkie looked glum. "If that's the truth about Kathleen, then I totally misread her."

"Me, too. I thought she was just kind of lonely, you know. She seemed so devoted to Darla and the B and B.

But she did seem to have a crush on Bart Crenshaw. And both Bricey and Clarissa were allegedly former lovers of his."

"That's a point." Tinkie tossed the wig back onto the floor of the closet. "We should leave. What about the cat?"

I bent down to pet the friendly little calico. "I'll ask Darla if Kathleen had a pet. That way maybe she'll bring it up and we can come back to get the cat. If Kathleen doesn't show up soon."

"You think there's still a chance?"

"No." I didn't want to mislead Tinkie. "I'm afraid she drowned, Tink."

"Yeah, me too. Even if she did play Colton Horn for a fool, I still kind of liked her."

"Me too."

"Let's get out of here. This case has put a real shroud over my holiday fun."

"Hey, we have our friends and loved ones. We're lucky, and this evening, we need to celebrate that. We don't have much longer in Columbus before it's time to go home. We can't let this mess up our vacation." I was talking a good game, even though Kathleen's apparent drowning had also depressed me.

I changed the kitty's water, found the dry cat food, and filled the bowl to the brim. We started to leave through the front door, as we'd come, but just as I was about to turn the knob, a car pulled into the driveway.

"Oh, crap. We can't go out this way."

19

"The back door!" Tinkie grabbed my arm.

I was looking through a lace curtain on the side of the door when I recognized the woman heading toward the front door. She was stalking across the yard and had almost reached the front steps.

"It's Tulla Tarbutton!"

"Get away from that door!" Tinkie dragged me into a den and we ducked behind a sofa. The little kitty came to join us, purring and making biscuits on my thighs as we hid.

"What's Tulla doing here?" I asked. "She's no friend of Kathleen's."

"She doesn't have a key," Tinkie said. "She's breaking in, too."

And indeed she was. In a moment the door swung open and Tulla hurried through the house and went directly to Kathleen's bedroom. She was gone less than two minutes, and when she came out, she was carrying the wig. Kitty darted out from behind the sofa and ran up to her. When the cat tried to greet her, she stomped her foot and scared it away. "Stupid cat." She dashed out the front door, slammed it hard, and left.

"She stole the wig." I felt as if I should have stopped her, but since I was trespassing . . .

"Tulla is the same size as Kathleen," Tinkie said. "Could it have been Tulla in the video? Could she have planted that wig to frame Kathleen? I'd never considered how much they look alike in size because their personalities are so different. And Tulla is always frowning."

"It could have been Tulla." The truth was, I couldn't say for certain. I'd never given it a thought, but both women had similar bone structure. Between the wig, the sunglasses, and the high collar of the coat, I honestly couldn't say it was one or the other. My first assumption had gone to Kathleen because I knew there were hard feelings between Bricey and Kathleen. "But why would Tulla want to destroy her friend's car?"

"These women are like a pit of vipers," Tinkie said. "They'd bite their own tail just because they're mean. Maybe they were working together to set Kathleen up. Maybe Tulla hired Colton and then decided she couldn't take the blame."

"Then wouldn't she leave the wig to implicate Kathleen?"

"Not if the purchase of the wig can be traced back to Bricey." Tinkie shuddered. "It's impossible to think like that kind of deviant."

"And yet men find them attractive." That reality bemused me.

"Some men. And keep in mind that crazy in the brain often translates to crazy in bed. Some guys don't look any deeper than that."

"And those are the ones who end up with an ice pick in their spines while having sex." We both laughed at the reference to the Michael Douglas / Sharon Stone classic, *Basic Instinct.*

"Yea, Nick wasn't the brightest lamp on the street. It seems like under certain circumstances, men lose the ability to use common sense and self-preservation."

"Same is true for women." I had to be fair.

"You're right about that. So what are we going to do about Tulla taking that wig? Should we call the police?"

"I don't think so." We weren't in a great position to rat her out. "We know she has it. If we need it, we can let the authorities pick it up."

"Unless she decides to get rid of it. If it were me, I'd destroy the evidence."

Tinkie had a point, but I wanted to work through the implications of what we'd witnessed before I called the law. "Okay, so the assumption is that Tulla wore the wig and then planted it here on Kathleen?"

"But then Kathleen ended up . . . drowned." Tinkie's blue eyes lit up. "Maybe she's going to frame someone else. Someone alive!"

In a cockeyed kind of way, that made sense. If Tulla had set Kathleen up to frame her, and then Kathleen was suddenly out of the picture, perhaps she'd decided to use the frame to her utmost advantage and take out another rival. If Kathleen was even a rival. "We need to see if we can find a notebook or anything where Kathleen might have written things down."

"Like a journal." Tinkie stood up. There was no need to hide behind the sofa any longer. Tulla was long gone and we had work to do. "Maybe a computer. If we could check her emails or text messages, we could learn a lot."

But we couldn't. We didn't have any equipment or authority and Coleman had no jurisdiction to ask for them—if he would even consider doing that. So far Jerry Goode had been helpful, but this would be a bridge too far for him. Even if Kathleen was dead, going into her devices would be akin to an invasion of privacy, and I didn't believe Jerry would go that far for two PIs from Zinnia. But he would if she was a suspect in some crime—hence we found ourselves on the horns of a dilemma.

While I cogitated on possibilities, Tinkie searched through all the drawers in the den furniture and the dining room. I headed to the bedroom. We'd looked there for the wig, but I hadn't been thinking about a thumb drive, disk, or journal. It was a whole new ball game.

It was awkward as hell, searching through things with our hands in the long sleeves of our shirts so we didn't leave fingerprints. Tinkie and I weren't in the habit of carrying evidence gloves or bags with us on vacation. Next time we would. Don't leave home without them.

"Nothing in the den or living room. The dining room is clean, too." Tinkie was exasperated.

"No luck in the bedroom."

"She doesn't even have a desk," Tinkie complained. "No computer. How does anyone live without a computer?"

"With a lot more sanity?" I responded.

"Maybe, but we need to find something and get out of here."

She was right. "Take the bathroom. I'll search the kitchen." Those were the last two places left.

"I can tell from standing outside the bathroom door she has an affinity for coconut shampoo."

Tinkie was really into the girly-girly accoutrements. She could recognize a scent from a hundred paces, especially one she liked. "Just search." I opened the silverware drawer and noted the organization. Again I was struck by the disorder in Kathleen's bedroom when even her silverware drawer was clean with every piece of cutlery in the proper place.

I moved through the cabinets, checking in the cups and bowls to be sure a thumb drive hadn't been stashed there. Then I moved on to the pantry. A terrible image from some horror movie came back to me—a pickled head in the pantry. I was almost afraid to look, but I did, moving things around just enough to make sure there wasn't a little hidey-hole for a book or computer gadget.

"Nada," Tinkie said as she joined me.

"Nothing here that I can find." I was dejected. "Let's get out of here before someone else, like the law, stumbles in."

"Yes, time to go." Tinkie moved back into the kitchen where she looked out the window on a beautiful backyard. The little calico was back, winding around her legs. "This is the sweetest cat," she said. "I want my baby to grow up with pets, to learn to love them and treat them with respect. Maybe if Kathleen doesn't . . . if Darla doesn't want her, I could talk to Oscar about taking her."

"A perfect idea." The kitty would live life in the lap of luxury if she became Tinkie's pet. And Chablis, her little pooch, was cat friendly.

We were exiting the kitchen when the cat jumped on top of the stove, and from there onto a shelf where some knickknacks and cookbooks were stored. "Bad kitty!" I moved the cat to the floor. Had the stovetop been on, the cat could have been hurt. "Stay off the stove." I shooed her into the living room as Tinkie reached up for a cookbook. Kathleen wasn't a tall person, so the shelf was within Tinkie's strike zone.

"Look at this, Sarah Booth. *Antebellum Recipes from Lorilee's Kitchen*. This is a collector's cookbook."

"Put it back. You know you can't cook worth a lick. Don't even pretend. I don't want you to give Oscar food poisoning."

She gave me a sour look and reached up to return the book to the shelf, but holding it in her sleeved hand made her clumsy. Several books came tumbling down. The one that fell on top was a slim leather-bound journal. I picked it up and realized our search had been rewarded—maybe. "It's a book of poems, and it looks as if Kathleen wrote them."

"They could be loaded with clues."

"You're exactly right!"

20

Standing in Kathleen's house was no place to examine our find, so I reluctantly left the kitty alone and we made our way, shrub by shrub, out of the neighborhood. When we were several blocks away from the house, Tinkie called a ride for us. Within twenty minutes we were getting out in front of the B and B.

"We should have stopped for lunch somewhere," Tinkie said. "I'm starving."

She'd eaten at least three biscuits for breakfast. I'd had only one and I wasn't hungry. "That baby must be growing by leaps and bounds. You're going to have to buy some kind of a sling to support your belly if you keep eating." I was only half teasing.

"Maybe I do eat a lot, but I still have the trimmest

ankles in Mississippi." She held up one foot to show how dainty her ankles were.

"I am not even going to think about that." I took her elbow and helped her up the stairs to the front door of the B and B. Before I could reach for the knob, the door flew open. A very startled Darla stopped before she ran both of us down.

"Are you okay?" Tinkie asked her. She had a panicked look on her face, and when she stared at Tinkie, it was as if she didn't recognize her.

"I have to go." She tried to brush past us, but I caught her arm. She didn't look to be in any condition to be running anywhere, especially if she intended to drive.

"Darla!" I jiggled her arm. "Darla!"

At last she registered who I was. "Sarah Booth, let me go. I have to leave."

"Not until you tell us what's going on. Maybe I should drive you."

She shook her head vehemently. "No! No time. Let me go." She tried to pull free, but I kept my grip.

"Hey, hold on just a minute." I didn't really want to stop her, but I was afraid she wasn't thinking clearly—or thinking at all. She seemed in a terrible panic. "Just tell us what's going on."

Tinkie put an arm around her waist and held on. "We're here to help, remember? But you have to clue us in. And Darla, we can't let you leave acting so erratically. You could hurt yourself or someone else."

"I have to go." She made one more minimal effort to pull free, staring at the driveway where her car was parked.

"Where are you trying to go?" I asked.

"Kathleen. She has a kitty. I forgot about Gumbo. I need to make sure she's okay and has food."

I heaved a sigh. "Let's go inside for a moment. Then Tinkie and I will drive you over to pick up the cat, maybe bring her here."

"I should do that, but what if some of my guests are allergic to cats?"

"Confine Gumbo to your quarters for the time being. We'll help you find a more permanent solution if that becomes necessary," Tinkie said. She gave me a nod to let me know she was still willing to take the kitty, should it be necessary.

"I should get her now." She started to pull away, and again I just held on.

"We'll go shortly," I promised her. "You may need help catching the kitty. For right now, come back inside and let me make some coffee." I didn't know exactly what had happened to upset Darla to the point that she was acting a little unhinged, but I knew if we could keep her safe, she'd come around.

Tinkie and I led her back inside and I put on the coffeepot for a quick cup. We sat at the kitchen table and sipped the strong black brew, giving Darla a chance to recover her wits. And it didn't take her long.

"I am so sorry, ladies. I realize I was out of it when I tried to leave. I've just been distraught, and I went back to bed this morning and fell asleep. I had a terrible nightmare. About Kathleen."

"What was it?" Tinkie asked.

"She was down at the bottom of the river, wearing this white gown with lots of material floating out behind her. Her hair was spread out in the water. And she was calling for her cat, Gumbo. She was so forlorn and sad, and she was searching everywhere for her kitty. I woke up from the nightmare and I had this compulsion to go and make sure Gumbo was okay. It was an overwhelming sensation. I couldn't stop myself."

I'd had a few nightmares that had driven me to rash action. And if I wanted to have the pants scared off me, all I had to do was listen to Madame Tomeeka's dreams, which were often prophetic—if I could decipher them. I had great sympathy for the panic Darla must have felt, realizing that her friend's little kitty was alone and confused about where Kathleen must have gone.

"We'll check on the kitty soon," I promised her. "But we have some questions about Kathleen."

"Questions? Can't you wait until they find her?"

I didn't want to say she wouldn't likely be able to answer questions when her body was found, so I ignored it. "Just basic things."

"Like what?"

"Did Tulla Tarbutton have it in for Kathleen?"

"She did, and as it turned out, the eyewitness who saw Kathleen pull Clarissa over the side of the boat— well, that was none other than Tulla Tarbutton. She was on another boat because I wouldn't let her on mine. And she claims she saw the whole thing. I don't know why those women had it in for Kathleen. She never bothered them or ran in their circles. Now they're determined to pretend that Kathleen was trying to knock Clarissa into the river."

"But Kathleen did have a crush on Bart Crenshaw, didn't she?"

"So what? Bart wouldn't give her the time of day. She didn't have enough money to be attractive to him.

And besides that, she was a decent, caring woman who would have wanted a bond, not a one-night fling. Kathleen may have thought Bart handsome, but she'd never have acted on any crush she had. She's smarter than that."

Darla had calmed down considerably, and I was concerned for the cat. My cat, Pluto, had a sixth sense when something was up. I suspected that Kathleen's kitty was also perceptive. "Why don't we go with you to check on Kathleen's cat?"

Darla stood up. "I'll go. There's no need for you to spend your time tracking down a cat. I'm perfectly fine now and I'm not certain the cat will take to strangers. You know how fickle cats can be."

I did, but Kathleen's cat was a sweetheart. I couldn't say that, though. "Don't forget the litter box and litter," I said.

"Good thinking." Darla appeared to be a little rattled still. "Yes, I'll get those things and the food."

"Maybe Kathleen will be found," Tinkie said.

Darla's eyes filled, but she blinked back the tears. "Yes. That's what we're all hoping for. Now let me get Gumbo before any more time passes."

"Darla, do you know anyone who'd deliberately hurt Kathleen?" I asked.

She stopped and thought for a full minute. "Kathleen was kind of a loner, except for our friendship. I don't know why anyone would want to harm her."

"Why did she move to Columbus?" Tinkie asked. "She doesn't have family here."

"I never pressed Kathleen about her past. She was shy, and reluctant to expose herself in anyway. I believe she came here because of a man."

This piqued our interest. "Bart?"

"No, not him. I don't know who it was. She never said a name. But she said something about a poet. Maybe a songwriter. Someone she'd met because those were also interests of hers. Whoever it was, she never introduced him to me. Once she was here, she liked Columbus, and she was here to stay."

"She's such a pretty woman and so sweet-tempered," Tinkie said. "Seems like any guy would be crazy to be with her."

"You would think," Darla said with a bitter laugh. "You would think. But sadly, a kind heart and pretty face aren't the coin a lot of men trade in."

"The right men do," Tinkie said stoutly. "There are good guys out there. I promise you, when we find Kathleen, I'll make it a point to introduce her to some of them."

At last Darla smiled. "I know you will, Tinkie. Thank you. Now I have to go."

After the front door closed, it took Tinkie and me several minutes to pull ourselves out of a funk to get busy with our case. I came to the surface with one question for my partner. "Do you think Darla could be involved in all of this?"

Tinkie bit her bottom lip. "Of course she could. But why would she? She's got a successful business and the goodwill of the town. I'm leaning more toward Sunny Crenshaw."

Tinkie was correct there. Sunny had a lot of motive and so far she'd dodged our calls. I still had her number, so I called from the Bissonette House phone. Eureka! She answered.

All face-to-face meetings were nixed, but she did tell us something very interesting. "Bart's a fool," she said. "But he is a money-making machine. I don't really care what he does as long as he keeps the money coming in." With that, she hung up.

Tinkie looked at me. "We have to keep her on the list, but Sunny Crenshaw, despite the slap she gave Bart at the restaurant, stikes me as someone far too pragmatic to be driven to murder."

Tinkie made perfect sense to me.

Darla's offer to use her computer was coming in handy. Though I was curious about the journal we'd found, we first went to look up Kathleen's tenure in Columbus. There wasn't much to find. Her name was mentioned in a few Columbus social columns, mostly as attending or as cohosting with Darla. I put the other names we had through the same procedure—Tulla, Bricey, Sunny and Bart Crenshaw, Clarissa Olson. The results were the same. Gardening or historical awards, community service notices, hosts of gala events, and serving on planning commissions and various government agencies like the zoning board.

"Both Clarissa and Bart are on the zoning commission," Tinkie said. "Strange."

"It's probably a lot more common than you'd ever imagine." Self-interest seemed to be rampant among "public servants." "The takeaway is that we haven't discovered any new information that helps us."

"I need a drink," Tinkie said, even as she held up a hand. "I know I can't. I'm just vocalizing my needs."

I put a hand on her shoulder. "Soon!"

I wanted a drink, too, but I wasn't going to rub her nose in it. "Let's go down to the river and check in with the searchers."

She nodded. "It's better than sitting and moping."

Before we could get to our feet, my cell phone rang. Cece was calling.

"The men are in some big warehouse on the outskirts of town," she said. "We've tried every which way to sneak a peek inside, but the place is airtight. There's a ten-foot chain-link fence with razor wire all around it, and there's no way to get in. They have cameras everywhere. Something is going on in there, though. Lots of folks are inside."

"What the heck." I was puzzled. Coleman and his he-man contingent weren't likely holed up in a warehouse drinking away the day. They could do that with us. "Come on back to the B and B. Darla has gone to get Kathleen's cat."

"That's hard," Cece said. "We're on the way. Maybe we can cheer her up. What's on the agenda for this evening?"

I relayed the question to Tinkie, who was a little miffed no one had actually read her itinerary. I didn't point out that we didn't have to because she'd lined everything up and all we had to do was get dressed and be there for her to order us about. No decisions to make—no pressure.

"Tonight Darla is supposed to help us come up with some costumes for mumming."

I put the phone on speaker and relayed that to Cece, who responded with "Are you sure she's up for that?"

"If she doesn't feel up to it, we can head out for some shopping and put together our own costumes. The stores will be open later tonight. We can find something appropriate."

Cece was laughing at us. "We'll be home shortly. You be thinking of ways to make these men spill the beans about what they're up to."

"You ran them to ground, but you don't have any idea what they're doing?" I asked. "Did your driver, Dallas Sweeney, have any ideas what was going on?"

"I had a sense she knew something but wasn't talking. We're on our way." The phone went dead.

I was overjoyed at the idea of mumming. My love of acting hadn't died with the disappointment of my thwarted career. Dressing up and pretending was just as much fun as it had always been, but before we got to that, I held up the book of poetry Kathleen had written.

"Let's go through some of this before Darla returns. Chances are this will only upset her if she sees us working on it."

Tinkie nodded. "Good thinking."

Tinkie and I took a seat on the sofa in front of a fire that was burning to embers. I made myself a glass of Jack on the rocks and opened the little journal we'd found at Kathleen's house. We didn't have long before Darla would be back with Gumbo.

We started at the back—the last things written. There were snippets of a scene or complete poems, mostly about loneliness. And some about love. Kathleen had found someone she seemed to care deeply about. Someone who returned that emotion. She wrote sonnets, a difficult form. She was pretty good in some instances. And the best poems, the ones that really worked, made me feel like I was violating her privacy.

There were also things written that I couldn't make any sense of. Tinkie was as puzzled as I was. But it made perfect sense that Kathleen, in writing only for herself, had not felt the need to be linear or logical.

"Do you think she was depressed?" Tinkie asked.

"She was lonely for a bit, but that seemed to have passed." I thought back to the time I'd spent with her. She'd seemed happy enough, and her friendship with Darla seemed like a linchpin in her life.

Tinkie tossed the journal at me. "If there's anything declarative in there, I couldn't find it. It's mostly things about feelings and emotions, being on the outside looking in. Just fragments of things."

Tinkie was right about that. Perhaps someone better trained in literary symbolism could find substance in the journal. That wasn't going to be me or Tinkie. I'd been so hopeful when we pulled it off the shelf that we would have answers to some of our questions.

"What's our next step?" Tinkie asked. Normally she was the person setting out the agenda.

"We can check out some wig shops in town. We can call Dallas for a ride and pick her brain. Or we can join the search for Kathleen." Those were the options, as I saw them.

"What about talking with Clarissa about what really happened last night?"

That was, indeed, another way to go. "I'm in."

"I'm just not buying that she's paying fifteen grand to 'protect the town cheaters.'"

"I'm having a lot of trouble buying that, too."

"It might be best if we aren't here when Darla brings the cat in," Tinkie said. "She can have a good cry or whatever she needs without feeling she has to be the perfect host."

21

I dialed Dallas Sweeney and booked a ride. "The Uber will be here in ten minutes."

We left a note on the kitchen counter for Darla and asked her to tell Cece and Millie we'd be back as quickly as we could. Whether Darla was up to helping us prepare our costumes or not, we still had to find something festive to wear to the mumming. And I had a lot to learn about the ancient tradition.

Grinning widely, Dallas pulled up, and Tinkie and I hopped into her car.

"Where to?" she asked.

"Rook's Nest."

She glanced at us in the rearview mirror. "You want to stop for a Kevlar vest and some weapons?"

We both laughed. "That won't be necessary," Tinkie said. "But tell us about the mumming festivities. What should we expect?"

"Are you going in disguise?" she asked.

"We are. I'm not certain what Darla has in mind, but we're participating," Tinkie said. "I should have asked more questions about this."

"It isn't rocket science," Dallas said. "Darla will pick out a well-known story or fairy tale. You'll dress up as the characters and act it out. Some of the mummers request pay, which is then contributed to a local charity. Do you know what story she's focusing on?"

I didn't, but Tinkie did. "She mentioned Robin Hood."

Dallas nodded. "That's a great one. Back in the day, almost all of the mumming companies were all male, so many of the stories focus on that kind of story. But Robin has Maid Marian. And my personal favorite, the Sheriff of Nottingham. I always like to play the villain."

This did bring up some interesting casting decisions, but Darla—or perhaps Tinkie—was in charge of that, not me. Thank goodness. I would be happy to play one of the Merry Men of Sherwood Forest. It was going to be a fun time.

"Dallas, you hear a lot of things. What's the score on Clarissa?"

"Capable of anything. She can turn a house or property like no one you've ever met. Her listings don't last for more than a week before the SOLD sign goes on them."

"She said Bart Crenshaw handled her real estate." The image of him tumbling down the stairs came back to me.

"He does, but Clarissa gets the listings. She scouts property around her and up toward Oxford. She has a reach into Tennessee and even Alabama. And she has her hooks in a lot of wealthy investors from out of state."

This was interesting to know. "Were there any rumors about her when she moved here from Oxford?"

Dallas pulled to the curb in front of Rook's Nest. "Look, there are plenty of rumors. Gossip was that she'd seduced an elderly man in Oxford and that she was his sole heir."

That was Johnny Bresland. I could fit that puzzle piece in.

Dallas continued. "It's how she got her nest egg to start really high dollar sales. Hence the name Rook's Nest. She bought the house with some of her money and then bought her first property with the rest. She turned it in less than a week and made a handsome profit. She was on her way to wealth."

This was pretty much the same story we knew. "There was never talk she may have killed her elderly benefactor?" I asked.

"He died in a hunting accident," Tinkie added.

"I wouldn't be surprised if she'd pulled the trigger herself. Clarissa is ruthless, from every story about her I've ever heard." Dallas had a call on her cell phone, but she ignored it.

Someone at the front door of Rook's Nest looked out. Tinkie and I had to get moving. "Thanks." I paid the fare and we got out.

"You need me to wait? Or maybe it would be better to call the ambulance before you go in." She was teasing us, but there was concern in the features of her face, like she really thought Clarissa would harm us.

"We're good. I don't know how long we'll be, so it's best you make some money. We'll call when we're done."

Clarissa met us at the door with arched eyebrows. "Shouldn't you be sleuthing or detecting or whatever it is you do to find out who's playing dastardly tricks on the people of Columbus? I've paid you a lot of money and I don't expect to see it used for making the rounds at teatime."

"Not exactly 'the people of Columbus.'" Tinkie used air quotes. "But a few people in town who have earned a lot of hard feelings."

"I don't even like tea" was my snarky contribution. Tinkie frowned at me. I was losing my razor wit.

"What do you want?" Clarissa asked.

"We have some questions." Tinkie brushed past her and entered the house. I started to follow, but Clarissa barred the door. "I'm a little busy here."

"So are we. We're working during our holiday for you." I pushed the door open and stepped past her. The first thing I saw was a pair of shiny black shoes on the floor beside the sofa. Along with two wineglasses, one sporting red lipstick, and a blue shirt. A uniform shirt. Clarissa had bagged a boy in blue.

Tinkie, too, had read the signs, including Clarissa's frowzled hair, smeared makeup, and hastily tied dressing gown. "Sorry to interrupt," I said. "Some coffee would be nice." I hoped it might draw out her lover. I was curious.

The hostess code of the South is pretty rigid, whether for a true Daddy's Girl, one of the older DAR, a DAC, or even a garden clubber. Refreshments must be offered and served. No exceptions. I'd played the coffee card and Clarissa had no choice but to prepare and serve the java, with whatever pastry or morning treat she kept on hand. All society ladies always kept an assortment of tidbits in the pantry for just such a social emergency.

"Have a seat in the parlor," Clarissa said through gritted teeth.

I hadn't expected to have fun with this visit, but I'd been wrong. "I take my coffee black," I sang out. "I don't want to be any trouble."

Tinkie covered her laughter with her hand as we heard Clarissa bustling about in the kitchen. If she'd been a kettle, she would have been singing because stream was coming out of her ears.

Instead of sitting, I walked around the parlor. During the Christmas pilgrimage party, I hadn't really had a chance to look around the house. The decorations, which were fabulous, had captured all my visual interest.

The house had great bones. The parlor was lovely, with a turret with stained-glass windows that cast a rainbow of light across a cozy breakfast nook, complete with a window seat that would be perfect for reading. The peach walls were complemented by fabulous floral draperies that puddled on the hardwood floors. The furniture, covered in floral silk, was both historic and comfortable. Clarissa had built herself something of a wonderful nest in the old house.

Clarissa returned with a silver coffee service that looked freshly polished, which made me wonder where Clarissa's household help might be. Milady didn't strike me as someone who would perform her own polishing. Maybe she'd given the help the day off so she could continue her dalliance undisturbed. She wasn't expecting me or Tinkie.

"What is it you want?" she asked.

"Why do you dislike Kathleen so much?" Tinkie asked the question.

"What does it matter? She's dead." Clarissa poured the coffee with a steady hand.

"Call it curiosity. Why?" Tinkie persisted.

"She showed up in town expecting to be the toast of the city. She was too big for her britches, as the common people would say."

My hold on the fine china coffee cup tightened to the point I thought I might snap the delicate little handle off the cup. I put it down, though tossing the hot liquid on Clarissa was tempting. She was just so damn superior, and if there was anything that got under my skin, it was the attitude that one person was superior to another because of money.

"She's a beautiful woman," I said. "Seems she would have been an asset to your social set."

"She didn't have the . . . spine. She was a milquetoast. She made it clear she thought she was better than we were."

"Because she didn't want to sleep with other people's husbands?" It had to be said.

"Because she judged others. On a superficial basis. She was . . . tedious. And that, Sarah Booth, is the most unforgivable of sins. You're bordering on tedious."

"Heaven forbid." I made an aghast face, and Tinkie laughed out loud.

"Look, Clarissa, Sarah Booth and I don't care what goes on between consenting adults. Have at it. But you've hired us to find the person responsible for dangerous actions. It seems to me that Kathleen's being pushed overboard—or attempting to knock you into the river—might be considered the most dangerous action so far. You were almost drowned and Kathleen is still missing. Now we have to determine if you were the target or Kathleen. I don't exactly see that as a tedious endeavor." Tinkie put her untouched coffee cup on the small table in front of the sofa. "If you don't want to cooperate, we can leave."

Clarissa sighed. "Look, the simple truth is that Kathleen wanted to run with the big dogs, but she couldn't keep up. She was mired in old-school beliefs. She wanted all of us to abide by her views and values."

It was clear to me that Clarissa expected everyone to abide by her rules, while she had no intention of respecting anyone else's rules. She was a perfect example of a narcissist, and a narcissist, as I'd learned the hard way, was capable of almost anything. A person suffering from this personality disorder could convince themselves that whatever they wanted or did was the right thing.

"I think Tulla may be behind all of these attacks." I didn't really believe that, but I wanted to see Clarissa's reaction. Which wasn't what I expected.

"Can you prove it? If so, have her arrested."

"I can't prove it yet," I said. "What I need from you is a reading of Tulla's personality. Why would she take actions like this, even to the point of willingly shocking herself? I mean, that is the perfect explanation of how she was shocked and no one else."

"And how, exactly, do you explain Kathleen's trying to drown me? Tulla had nothing to do with that," Clarissa said. "Were it not for that very handsome sheriff you brought to town, I'd likely be dead."

"Keep it up and you will be," Tinkie said just loud enough for me to hear.

"Did Kathleen truly attack you, or did she lose her balance when the boat lurched?" This was the heart of what I wanted to hear.

"I was leaning on the rail, watching the fireworks. I was staring out into the river. I don't remember Kathleen or anyone else being nearby. When the boat lurched, I stumbled and hit the rail pretty hard. Before I could regain my balance, Kathleen came hurtling out of the darkness. She knocked me over the rail."

"It could have been an accident?" Tinkie asked.

"Out of all the people on the boat, Kathleen grabs me and takes me over the side? Hardly an accident."

"You actually believe Kathleen wanted to drown you? At the risk of drowning herself?" Tinkie asked.

Clarissa hesitated. "I believe she wanted to knock me into the river. I don't know that drowning was her end goal."

"Once you hit the water, what happened?" I asked. "Did she cling on to you? Did she make any efforts to push you under the water?"

Clarissa shook her head. "No. She let go of me before we hit the water."

"And you didn't clutch on to her?" I asked.

She gave me a dark smile. "You think I drowned her?"

"Covering all bases," I said. "That's what you paid me to do."

"Look, Kathleen was a fly in the pudding. You don't

go all nuclear on a fly. She wasn't worth the effort to kill her. That's just a blunt fact."

Perhaps. But I no longer doubted that Clarissa was capable of eliminating whatever stood in the way of what she wanted. What, exactly, did she want? I didn't believe she'd been truthful with me or Tinkie about why she hired us. It was far more likely that her intentions were to put the blame for all of this on someone else— someone whose fall from grace would benefit Clarissa.

"Once Bricey and Bart parted ways, was the path clear for Tulla to go after Bart?"

"Absolutely. Tulla never seemed to mind picking up where Bricey and I finished. Keep in mind that his wife, Sunny, was long done with him."

Oh, the cat was out to play now! "I'm sure the pool of eligible partners demands that the men be recycled. It is a small town, after all."

"Part of the fun is getting there first. We are competitive, as all animals are. And don't look so put out. We are just animals, especially when it comes to sexual conquest. The survival of the fittest. It's how the species improves."

"That is the craziest bull—" Tinkie sputtered before I cut in.

"Suffice it to say, we don't see eye to eye on this. But it's neither here nor there to our case. So do you know if Tulla had made a play for Bart?" I was looking for a reason Kathleen would be interested in knocking Clarissa into the river—and then why Tulla might want to frame Kathleen for the dirty deed of destroying the car.

"I don't know. Ask Tulla."

"I doubt she'll be as open about her . . . sexual proclivities as you are."

"Try her. You might be surprised." Clarissa waved toward the door. "Now, you should leave. I have to finish my morning business."

I wanted to ask who her business was, but I didn't. I had a better idea for that. "We'll speak with Tulla. I hope she'll be truthful. You might encourage her if you really want us to close this case."

"I can do that." She led us to the door and opened it. "No car?" she asked.

"Uber." Tinkie held out her phone. "We'll call one now."

"Good idea." Clarissa couldn't push us out of the house fast enough. She closed the door while Tinkie was still looking up Dallas Sweeney's number.

"Hold off on the Uber," I said as I edged Tinkie across the porch and down the steps. When we hit the sidewalk, I urged her left. The tree-shaded street, so beautiful, was empty of traffic. The sidewalks had all been swept clean. This was a neighborhood of big houses, spacious lawns, established gardens, and a sense of the old South that made me realize how barren of character so many of the new subdivisions were.

"Where are we going?" Tinkie asked when we'd covered half a block.

"To that big shrub."

"For what?"

"To hide in it. I want to see who pulls out of Clarissa's house. Remember, there was someone in there. A cop, I believe."

"Right!" Tinkie was all in.

We ducked into the thickness of a huge Indian hawthorn that provided plenty of cover. It wasn't five minutes before a silver Mustang came out of Clarissa's drive, moving far too fast for that neighborhood. Luck was with us—the driver came in our direction. The man behind the wheel was tall, broad-shouldered, and most of his face was hidden in shadow, but I clearly saw a Columbus city police officer's hat on his head, the old Smokey variety of hat.

"That looks like Jerry Goode!" Tinkie said, as shocked as I was.

Indeed, it did appear to be the lawman who was suing Bricey Presley for the death of his grandmother. How in the world had he fallen into Clarissa's clutches?

22

We needed to talk to Coleman about possible ways to get Goode to talk to us. I didn't see that Tinkie and I had any leverage to make him spill the beans about his relationship with Clarissa. Perhaps Coleman had a solution.

Dallas Sweeney answered the call for an Uber, and before long we were on the outskirts of Columbus headed to the Bissonnette House. "Dallas, what's the story on Jerry Goode. He seems like a good guy. Is he a good police officer?" I asked.

"Never heard anything hinky about him. Lost his grandmother at that Supporting Arms nursing home. There was something not right about that situation, but if I heard the details, I don't remember."

"We checked the place out," Tinkie said. "It looked well run. There was an issue with a private nurse."

"Right!" Dallas snapped her fingers and gave us a grin in the rearview mirror. "I remember. Sounded to me like he had a case against Bricey Presley."

"Is Jerry known to be a player in town?" I asked.

"He's dated above his station, as the elite class would say." She was mocking them big-time.

"Why would anyone in law enforcement get involved with a group of cheaters?" Tinkie asked. "I don't much care what people do in the bedroom, as long as all parties involved know the score. But isn't adultery illegal in Mississippi?"

"It's a crime." I knew that from listening to my parents talk. My dad, a lawyer and judge, enjoyed discussing the law with my mother at the dinner table. I learned a lot just by listening. "And it's also a cause for calculating alimony for the injured spouse."

"Now wait a minute," Dallas said. "Sleeping with another consenting adult is a crime in this state?"

"Sleeping with a married consenting adult." I clarified the point of the law. "If you aren't married, you're just easy." I gave her my smartass grin. "If you are married, then you're breaking the law if you sleep with someone other than your spouse."

"Are you sure that's still the law?" Dallas asked.

I had to smile. I wondered if she was worried about her conduct. "It's the law, Dallas. Just steer clear of married men and you'll be fine."

"Sometimes you don't know they're married," Dallas pointed out.

"In that case, I believe ignorance would be taken into

consideration." I didn't know for absolute sure, but she looked way too worried.

"That sounds a little better. It's just too easy for someone to get tricked."

There was definitely a story behind that statement. Too bad we were pulling up in front of the B and B.

"Will we see you during the mumming?" I asked Dallas.

"Not me. I'm working. I like the idea of acting out an old familiar story, but it's a matter of economics."

"Thanks, Dallas." We hopped out and hurried inside.

When we opened the front door I stopped so suddenly that Tinkie bumped into my back.

"Move it along, Sarah Booth," Tinkie grumped. She looked around me and froze.

The entire parlor was strewn with colorful costumes. There was a monk's robe, a chain mail outfit, a green jersey and tights with a bow and quiver, a gorgeous dress cut for a lady of the court, and plenty of foot soldiers and supporting cast characters.

"Take your pick," Darla said. She'd returned from her errands, and judging from the claw mark on her arm, I gathered she'd managed to get Gumbo the kitty into a carrier.

"Any trouble with the cat?" I asked.

"She was afraid of traveling, but I managed to get her here. Just until Kathleen returns." She lifted her chin as if challenging me to say different.

"Are you sure you're up to this mumming thing?" I asked. "I know you're upset."

"It's better for me to keep busy." She turned away and went to the beautiful gown. "This is for our Maid

Marian. Care to help me cast the show? Since everyone really knows the story of Robin Hood and the Merry Men of Sherwood Forest, there can be a lot of ad libbing. The central part of the tableau is the fight between the Sheriff of Nottingham"—she gestured at the chain mail costume—"and our fair Robin."

I had no desire to cast the production, but Tinkie stepped right up. She was at heart a director. "Coleman should be Robin. Oscar can be the Sheriff. Jaytee can be Little John. Harold can be Sir Guy of Gisborne. I'll be Maid Marian and Sarah Booth, Millie, and Cece can be Mortianna, Aria, milady's observant handmaid, and Friar Tuck, respectively."

I actually loved the idea of Mortianna, and I found her costume on the far end of the sofa, complete with a straggly wig and pasty makeup. This was going to be some party. "I get a solo scene where I predict the return of Robin Hood." I was already highlighting my stage time. "How do you think Cece will react to being cast as a fat friar?"

"Cece doesn't care. Maybe we can work in a scene where Little John plays the harmonica and Friar Tuck sings." Tinkie, in her mind, had made the casting decisions and was moving on to scene development. "How many houses do we mum at?" Tinkie asked Darla.

"As many as you'd like. It's only the big houses with lawns that participate, but there are plenty. I'll give you a list and you can pick where you'd like to go. If you collect any money, it has to go to charity."

"Certainly," Tinkie said. "This is for fun, not profit."

The front door opened and Cece and Millie joined us. The men were only ten steps behind. They entered in a huddle that reeked of conspiracy. I really wanted a word with Coleman about another law enforcement official—Jerry Goode. I certainly had not foreseen Goode's entanglement with Spider-Woman Clarissa.

Before I could take action to get Coleman alone, Darla herded us all to the parlor. "Tinkie has cast the story for tonight." She gave a little drumroll, and I had to admire her ability to push her grief over Kathleen down deep inside in order to entertain her guests. "Tinkie, reveal your casting."

Tinkie assigned everyone their roles, and when she pointed to me and said Mortianna, everyone laughed.

"I see we're going with the Hollywood version. *Robin Hood: Prince of Thieves.*"

"Of course," Tinkie said. "No one will ever top Alan Rickman as the Sheriff of Nottingham, unless it's Oscar."

Cece found the fat pads she'd wear under her monk's robe and held them up. "These will be very warm."

"And protect you if someone throws rotten eggs at you," Jaytee said.

We sat down and worked out the simple story of Robin robbing a rich noble, to be played by Cece in a double role. The scenario would open with Mortianna speaking of Robin, describing how he made the sheriff and his followers furious by interfering with their robbery of local citizens to fatten the rulers' purses. Robin would give a little talk about his love for Marian and his joy in his Merry Men. The rich noble would arrive on scene, and Robin would cleverly rob him, with some slapstick antics involved in distracting the noble. The sheriff would arrive and try to capture Robin. The Merry Men would suddenly appear to help Robin. Marian and her clever handmaid Aria would arrive to distract the evil sheriff.

A sword fight would ensue; Robin would escape with his Merry Men. Mortianna would close out the scenario with another sinister prediction of future encounters between the bandit and the evil sheriff.

"We can do this." Tinkie was deeply invested.

"Is anyone going to write lines?" Cece asked.

"Ad-lib," Tinkie said. "Improvise. But there is one thing we need to do. Set up a scene where Jaytee plays the harmonica and you sing the blues."

"There's a pretty cool song called 'Robin Hood Blues,'" Jaytee said. He hummed a few bars.

"They could perform that for the finale, and we could all do a court dance," Millie said, getting into the mood.

"Do you know a court dance?" I asked. This was turning into a real production.

"In fact I do." Millie almost smirked. "I went to a Renaissance faire not so long ago and learned several. Very easy steps. Forward, back, walk around with your partner in a half circle, hands up—very simple." She demonstrated as she talked.

It *was* simple, and it would be fun.

"We need to keep the play within about fifteen minutes," Darla said. "And we'll try to hit about six or seven houses. What are you going to do with the money you collect?"

"How about the local animal shelter?" Cece suggested. "We can have a good time and help the local animals."

"Perfect," Darla said. "And speaking of animals, I have Kathleen's cat, Gumbo, in my apartment here. She's very sweet. Is anyone allergic?"

"No one in this group," Jaytee said. "We're cat lovers, in fact."

"She's only here until Kathleen—" She broke off and turned away.

"You don't have to keep her shut away," Tinkie said gently. "We'd love to have her roaming about the B and B. We'll be careful not to let her get outside."

"Thank you." Darla had composed herself. "That's good to know. Now, while you rehearse, I need to finish baking some goodies I promised my neighbors."

"Darla, has there been any word from the searchers?" Coleman asked.

"Nothing. No sign of her, alive or dead." She turned away from us to hide her raw emotions. "One of the police officers said we should know something later today."

I didn't know how anyone could predict when a body would rise from the depths of a river—if the body was even still in this vicinity and hadn't been swept downstream—but if it gave Darla some comfort, who was I to open my yap otherwise? "Which officer said that?" I asked.

"Officer Goode," Darla said absently.

I exchanged a glance with Tinkie. Our local police officer was Johnny-on-the-spot wherever we went. It was time to speak with Coleman about using his badge to check into Jerry Goode.

23

We took our costumes to our rooms and agreed to meet in the parlor to run through the story of Robin Hood that we were presenting. We had a little time to perfect it, and then we'd set out to the list of houses Darla provided. These were wealthy people we could count on for a significant donation toward our worthy goal. I hadn't anticipated doing a fundraiser, but now that I was involved, I was eager to get after it. Animal shelters were always in need of food, veterinary care, money for spay/neuter surgeries, and a million other things that made living in a cage while waiting to be picked tolerable.

After one run-through of my part in the play, I was comfortable enough to abandon the merry crew and step outside on the terrace for a moment of reflection. The image of Jerry Goode driving away from Clarissa's house nagged at me in an unpleasant way. Goode's role in this whole mess concerned me—a lot more than I'd let on to Tinkie. He was a key figure in so many aspects of what was happening in Columbus. He was investigating the woman who'd hired Colton Horn—without any success, I might add. He was investigating the dumping of the cement into the car and Bart Crenshaw's tumble down the stairs—also without any arrests. It was almost as if he were stalling the investigations rather than looking for the guilty parties. Now he was also in charge of discovering what had happened to Kathleen. If she had been knocked off the boat, this was a murder investigation that he might be deliberately obstructing.

There was a rustle in the lower branches of some thick shrubs surrounding the patio. I froze. The plants formed what was almost a solid wall around the outdoor area, which included a pool, a tiki hut and bar, and a pool house. The rustling came again, as if some creature crept along the ground. It could be a possum, a raccoon, or a dog, or it could be something more dangerous.

I edged closer to the shrubs and tried looking into them, but they were so thick and lush I couldn't really see past them. I held very still and waited. Farther to my right, the rustling came again.

The creepy sensation that someone was spying on me crept down my back. I hadn't brought a light or even my cell phone, and dusk had fallen. Night was quickly coming down. The B and B was on a bluff with a stair-like walkway that clung to the side of the cliff and zigged and zagged down to the river, where the *Tenn-Tom Queen* was tied at the dock.

By rights, no one should be anywhere near Darla's backyard, which probably meant it was a wild animal I was hearing. Still, the creepy sensation persisted, until I realized it was also possible Jitty had returned to have more fun messing with me. "Jitty?" I waited. "Jitty, if you're trying to scare me, I'm going to do something awful." As I looked toward the river, there was only darkness except for the beautiful stars beginning to blink awake.

The sound came again. I moved along the hedge, hoping to catch a glimpse of whatever was rummaging in the leaves. In the night, though, I couldn't see anything. All the creepy stories about hauntings and ghosts that I loved to read about came back to me, and I thought of Kathleen, returning one last time to visit her friend Darla. Except the place Kathleen had fallen into the river was several miles south of here.

I was so deep in thought that when a Texas twang came right behind me, I almost jumped out of my skin.

"Sin doesn't just happen."

I whipped around to confront a very young Sissy Spacek, all wide-eyed and cautious. As a fan of horror movies, I recognized her from *Carrie*. That movie had scared ten years off my life and became a classic trope-setter for future horror movies.

"I don't want to talk about sin with you." Even though I knew this was Jitty pretending to be Sissy pretending to be Carrie, I didn't want any part of this conversation. When dealing with someone with telekinesis, one didn't take any chances. As if to prove my point, the cocktail I'd been sipping—a very tasty old-fashioned that Harold had made—flew across the patio table and into Sissy's outstretched hand.

"Good idea. Have a drink," I said.

"Are you a fanatic about sin?" she asked, her face so pale her freckles seemed electric.

"Nope, not me. I have no quarrel with sin." The plot of the movie came back to me clearly. Carrie had been abused by her crazy Bible-thumping mother. Then she was abused by the popular girls in high school. Then she lost her mind and burned the school gym down, stabbed her mother in a reimagined crucifixion, and finally burned her own house to the ground, with herself and her mother inside. She was dead, dead, dead. Until that one hand came out of the grave to grab her high school friend, the only survivor of the fire.

Whew! Just remembering all of that had my heart pumping and my feet itching to make a run for it.

"My mama says we're born in sin."

Uh-oh. She had that crazy look in her eye. "Sip that nice cocktail," I said.

"I'm only sixteen. I'm too young to drink. That would be a sin."

Oh, legions of the devil, that was the wrong thing to say. "Sure." I reached up for the drink. "I'm old enough to drink." I knocked it back.

"I'm going to the prom."

I realized then she was in a pastel prom dress. "Maybe you should rethink that choice."

"Tommy is taking me. I'm his date."

"Eh, maybe go to dinner instead of the prom."

She shook her head. "I have a date. No one is going to stop me. Not my mother, and certainly not you." Sparks flicked in her eyes and I saw dancing flames.

"Right. I have no desire to stop you. Just giving some alternatives. Dances are so . . . last year." I had little experience talking with teenage girls. Especially not fictional teenagers from a bloodbath horror movie.

Carrie held out her hand and a little flame jumped up from her palm. That was my signal to head inside and alert the others to run for their lives.

"Ha-ha, hold up, Sarah Booth." The voice that called out to me was rich, lazy with an old Mississippi Delta drawl. "I really had you going, didn't I?"

When I turned around, Jitty stood there with buckets of blood dripping off her. I gave a little shriek and nearly tripped over a wicker chair.

"Hold up there, missy," Jitty said, wiping the blood out of her eyes. "I never realized scaring you could be such fun!"

"If you weren't dead, I'd kill you." I had been within twenty feet of rushing in the door of the B and B and making a total fool of myself.

"Now, now. I was just spoofin' you."

"I think you just aged my ovaries another two years." That would get her goat. "Stress isn't good for the reproductive system. What if you killed off my last viable egg? And what are you doing pretending to be the victim in a horror movie from the 1970s?"

"Makin' a point about sin."

Her very direct answer stopped me in my tracks. "What point?"

"What was the biggest sin in that movie?"

It was so Jitty to answer a question with a question. "Why don't you just tell me to be sure I get it straight?"

She grinned, and slowly the blood disappeared and my favorite haint, wearing some really bad 1970s fashion, took a seat on the arm of a sofa. "You can figure it out if you give it some effort. And you'd better figure it out."

"Jitty!"

She was starting to fade just as a choir began singing an old classic hymn. "Are you washed in the blood, in the soul-cleansing blood of the Lamb? Are your garments spotless? Are they white as snow?"

"Jitty, you are going to burn in hell for co-opting a real hymn in your foolishness," I whispered fiercely after her. Just as the back door opened I heard a little yip of laughter and she was gone. Cece stepped outside.

"Are you out here rehearsing by yourself?" she asked.

"Exactly." It was better to own up to being an insecure actor than a crazy woman who talked to dead people and fictional characters.

"Come back inside. It's cold out here."

And indeed it was. I simply had been so scared that I hadn't noticed. "Good plan." I picked up my empty glass and hurried inside behind Cece before Jitty decided to pop out and scare another ten years off my life.

At last I had a moment alone with Coleman and I was able to share with him Jerry Goode's actions. I tugged him toward the terrace to talk. He slipped on his heavy coat and followed me.

"You sure you saw his shoes and shirt?" Coleman was having difficulty buying into the story that Goode was bumping uglies with Clarissa Olson.

"The uniform shirt and those spit-shined black shoes were in her parlor."

"There's more than one police officer in town," Coleman pointed out.

"I know what I saw. And then Tinkie and I both saw him driving away."

"In a patrol car?"

"No, it was a silver sports car."

"Did you get the plates?"

"No. But we saw him. He was wearing his uniform hat."

"That's what I'm having trouble with."

I leaned my head against Coleman's shoulder. "Why?"

"Most officers don't wear their hats when they're driving. They take them off, then grab them as they get out of the vehicle, and put them on."

It was an action I'd seen Coleman perform at least a million times. He was right. Driving in a hat wasn't all that comfortable. "So what are you thinking?" I asked him.

"Not certain. Yet. Waiting for a hunch to kick in."

Coleman certainly had hunches, but he didn't base his law enforcement decision on his "gut." "I'm serious, Coleman, what do you think?"

"I think I'm going to have a conversation with Goode. Until then, I withhold an opinion. Now . . ."—he checked his watch—"I'm going to find the good law officer. Make my excuses to Darla and the others. I'll be back in an hour, in plenty of time to get into my costume and be ready for the mumming."

"What about something to eat?"

"I'm stuffed full of Darla's party snacks. She sure knows how to bake. And I think Harold was offering her some solace about her friend."

"Good." Harold was tenderhearted to a fault.

"Darla writes poetry. Harold says she's pretty good."

That would be another shared interest between her and Kathleen. "Is it really good poetry?" Meaning, could I understand it?

"Haven't sampled the wares yet, but when Harold mentioned it, while you were outside, he said she'd been published."

"She and Kathleen had a lot in common. Darla is really going to miss her friend."

"And there's nothing you can do about it." He sighed. "The big Christmas parade is tomorrow, and then we head home."

He said the last with some longing. I understood. I, too, was missing Zinnia and Dahlia House. Mostly I was missing my critters. "I hope we can wrap up this case."

"Any indication of who's behind all of this?"

I thought about it. "I have a list of suspects, but no solid evidence. When you talk to Goode about Clarissa, get the latest on the search for Kathleen, please. That's a murder, though not one Clarissa wants us to investigate. She's interested only in herself."

"I'll see what I can find out." Coleman took off toward the driveway.

"You want me to call a ride for you?"

"Not necessary" were his final words as he disappeared behind some hedges.

"What are you up to, Coleman Peters?" I asked the Bissonnette House's empty patio. I was just glad he was working with me instead of against me.

24

I didn't have time to fret about Coleman's disappearance. When I went back inside, Tinkie was in Darla's office on the computer. Cece, Millie, Harold, Oscar, and Jaytee were in the parlor playing a raucous game of poker. I was glad to see that Darla had allowed Gumbo to join them. The little black, orange, and white kitty was perched on the arm of a sofa watching the humans with what could only be described as superior tolerance.

Watching Gumbo, I felt a pang for Pluto and a wave of homesickness. I'd be back in Sunflower County in no time at all, and until then, I needed to find out who was playing deadly games in Columbus.

I played five-card draw for a few minutes—until I realized I was outclassed by everyone at the table. Amidst good-natured teasing, I left the card table. I made a call to Coleman and got his voicemail.

I went to Darla's office to catch up with Tinkie. "Hey, Tinkie," I called out.

"Hey, Sarah Booth," she said back, laughing at me. "What?"

"Coleman should have some updates about Kathleen, but he isn't answering." I paused. "I'm going to call Jerry Goode."

"We shouldn't tip our hand and let him know we're onto his affair with Clarissa."

Tinkie was right about that—if we were on the nose about the affair. Coleman had made me question that assumption. I dialed Goode's number, and he answered on the third ring, sounding as if he were coming out of a deep sleep.

"Hi, Officer Goode. I'm looking for Coleman Peters."

"Why are you calling me?"

Coleman had had plenty of time to get to the officer. "He went to talk to you."

"Never made it here."

"Are you messing with me?"

"I am not." Goode was suddenly wide-awake sounding. "Where was he going to look for me? I've been home, dead asleep."

If he'd been with Clarissa, he probably needed to sleep a lot to allow his blood supply to recharge, blood-sucking vampire that she was.

"He may have been on his way to the river." I didn't know where else he might have gone.

"Meet you there." Goode hung up.

"I need to go to the river to look for Coleman," I told Tinkie.

"I'm right behind you." She slipped into her coat while I called for a ride. Dallas didn't answer, so we chose another Uber, and by the time we walked outside, our ride was there. We were about to step into the car when my phone rang.

Coleman was calling, but there was only the sound of heavy breathing. "Coleman? Coleman? Are you there?" The line went dead.

Tinkie was watching me as she ordered the driver to the site on the river where the search had been organized.

As the car took off, I dialed Officer Goode again. The phone rang and rang. No one answered and it never went to voicemail.

"What's going on?" Tinkie asked.

"I don't know."

"Can you drive faster?" Tinkie asked the driver as I tried again to call Coleman and Goode. Neither man answered.

The driver's response was to press the gas pedal and the car sped into the night.

We arrived at the river to find that the search was basically shut down. The tent on the dock was still in place, but no one manned it. The tables and chairs where volunteers had organized grid searches were abandoned. And there was no sign of Coleman.

Just to be sure, Tinkie and I split up and searched the area. She took the dock and I edged around the bank of the river. I didn't go far enough to find alligators—there was no reason for Coleman to be wading around in marsh grass. Since we'd put flashlights in our purses, we also had the benefit of good light and I could keep track of where Tinkie was. After ten minutes, it was clear Coleman had never made it here.

"Where could he be?"

Our ride was still waiting for us, so we jumped in and headed back to the Bissonnette House. As we were pulling up, a man staggering along the edge of the road was highlighted by the car's headlights. "Stop!" I yelled. I was halfway out of the car before it came to a complete stop.

I recognized the man stumbling toward the B and B. It was Coleman. In the lights from the car, I saw that blood was trickling down the side of his face from a blow to the head.

"Are you okay?" I grabbed his arm to steady him. Tinkie arrived to shore up his other side.

"I think so," Coleman said, wobbling a little.

"What happened?"

"Someone came out of the darkness and hit me while I was waiting for a ride. I tried to call you, but I was too fuzzy to say anything."

"Let's go to the hospital," Tinkie said. The Uber was still waiting. "Come on, just get in the front seat." She was leading us both toward the waiting car.

"No." Coleman stopped, and he was rooted like an old oak. "I'm okay."

"What would it hurt to get it checked out?" Tinkie insisted. "Don't be a hardhead."

"I'm really okay. I was caught by surprise."

I waved the Uber on because I knew Coleman well enough to know he wasn't going to cooperate with Tinkie's plan. With me on one side and Tinkie on the other, we made the forty-yard walk up the sidewalk to the front door. Before we went in, Coleman stopped us.

"Don't say anything to anyone."

"Why not?" Tinkie asked.

"Whoever attacked me came out of the backyard."

"I thought I heard someone earlier," I said, "but then I thought maybe I was just imagining things. I looked, but the hedge was so thick, I didn't see anyone or anything suspicious." Except for Jitty. And if someone saw that exchange, they'd believe I was completely nuts.

"Why not tell the others?" Tinkie persisted. "They may need to be on the alert."

"I don't want Darla worried that I was injured on her property," Coleman said. "She has enough on her with Kathleen's disappearance. I'm really not hurt." He rubbed the side of his head. "I was just stunned."

"And knocked unconscious." I didn't buy his self-diagnosis at all, but I wasn't going to argue with Coleman in front of Tinkie. "What are you going to tell Darla about the mumming?" I checked my watch. It was time to put on the costumes if we were going to participate.

"Nothing. I'm ready to play Robin Hood." He used the sleeve of his jacket to wipe at the blood on his face.

Tinkie rolled her eyes at me as she opened the front door of the inn. "If you two ever had a baby together, it would have a skull as hard as a granite slab."

"Hurry, hurry," Darla said as she pulled us into the house. "Get into your costumes. It's time to perform."

Coleman grabbed my hand and dragged me up the stairs. "Get into your costume," he said. "It's important if we want to resolve this matter."

"I'd feel better if you got into a hospital gown and had your head checked out."

"Dream on." Coleman pulled me into our bedroom and closed the door. It was time to suit up for the evening's festivities. I supposed we could all ignore that a serial attacker was on the loose, a woman was still missing from a boating incident, and Coleman had been attacked outside the B and B.

25

By the time we started toward Rook's Nest, we'd already hit a bunch of homes with our Robin Hood act. We'd perfected our drama and gathered over five thousand dollars in donations for the Columbus animal shelter. Darla had not been kidding. People in Columbus had money and were willing to donate it to a good cause. With each successful performance, we grew bolder and bolder in our presentation. And the feather in our cap—the "Robin Hood Blues" duet with Cece and Jaytee—brought the house down as far as raking in donations. Rook's Nest was our last stop, and Darla had insisted we go there. She said Clarissa had a small gathering of friends over and they were expecting to see us. Clarissa had promised a substantial donation and Darla pleaded with us to go there on behalf of the shelter animals. Though I was loath to go to Clarissa's, the needs of the shelter animals won out over my reluctance.

"We have just one more night in Columbus after tonight," Tinkie said to me as we clanked along the sidewalk toward Clarissa's house. The Sheriff of Nottingham, with his armor and sword, was rather noisy. Coleman, Cece, and Jaytee were in front of us, and Tinkie let out a wolf whistle. "Nice legs, Robin! And Friar Tuck, those fat pads are very becoming."

Despite her protestations that she wasn't an actress, Cece had perfected the waddle. And Coleman did have great-looking legs. They were shown to advantage in the green leggings and tunic. Even better, he seemed to have completely recovered from being hit in the head.

"I wouldn't kid too much. Coleman and Cece will get even, you know." I thought it wise to warn my teasing cohorts.

"I'm counting on it," Tinkie said. "Coleman's been too quiet, and Cece is plotting something. She's not going to leave Columbus without some kind of final flare-up!"

She was right about that. "It's been an . . . activity-filled trip, Tinkie. Thank you. What a great idea. Maybe if we can figure out how to avoid mayhem, we can make it an annual tradition to travel to a Mississippi town to celebrate the holidays."

"I'm going to ignore the snark and just say that can be arranged."

"Excellent."

"Has Coleman said anything about who attacked him?"

It was a curious thing that Coleman had avoided all conversation about how he'd been set upon outside the

B and B. He'd hushed me whenever I tried to bring it up, saying Darla had enough woe and worry without knowing her guest had been whacked upside the head by a derelict lurking about the property. I knew there was more to his reluctance than he let on. I just didn't know why he was so reticent to tell us what had happened.

"Coleman hasn't said a peep. He says Darla is too stressed. That I should just let it go. He knows more than he's letting on."

"Maybe his brain is rattled."

I pushed Tinkie on the arm. "That's not very nice."

"I meant from being struck. Coleman isn't making a lot of sense in his conduct, protecting someone who attacked him." She grinned wickedly. "On the other hand, he sure fills out those tights and he's doing great as Robin Hood."

"And you're the perfect Maid Marian." Tinkie's costume was beautiful, and it suited her. Even the long chestnut wig.

"You're pretty convincing as Mortianna. The way you're shuffling around, dragging a foot and acting like some kind of wicked witch, predicting all kinds of dire things. You scared those children at the last house. Maybe you should take off the wig and get rid of those awful contact lenses."

"Nah, I love to scare children. Just wait until yours is born. I'm going to teach that baby to love scary movies and stories."

"You're probably going to be a terrible influence. I've already accepted that." She gave me a quick hug. "And it's perfectly fine. Just watch the Mortianna act. If you come out of those bushes and scare someone like you did at the last house, they may shoot you."

"Me?" I pretended outrage. "When Friar Tuck burst out of the shrubs just as the sheriff grabbed Maid Marian, I almost wet my pants."

Tinkie was laughing. "Cece's comic timing is great, isn't it?"

In front of us, Oscar stumbled in his armor, and Tinkie doubled-timed it to get to him. He had a hard time seeing through the visor, and if the sidewalk was uneven, he was prone to trip. "Let me help my husband," she called over her shoulder.

I dropped back to talk to Harold. "How is Darla doing?" He'd spent more time talking to her than any of the rest of us.

"She's having a very hard time. She was going to come mumming with us, but at the last minute she just couldn't bring herself to do it. She's holding it together because we're still her guests, but she canceled all the reservations she'd made for the rest of this year. After we leave Sunday, she'll be alone. She said she just needs to grieve, but it worries me. I'm afraid she'll slip into a serious depression."

"She's given up on Kathleen?"

He nodded. "She has. She won't say that, but she feels there's no way she could still be alive."

"Is that a good thing? I mean, is accepting reality better than clinging to false hope?"

Harold sighed softly. "It's never a good thing to believe a friend is dead." He lowered his voice. "*I* believe Kathleen is gone. If she didn't drown, the hypothermia got her. It's possible she hit her head going over. And she had on so many clothes. She was really bundled up."

"It was cold on the water, and she knew it, so she was dressed appropriately. Her jacket was thick. And

she had on gloves, boots, and even a thick cotton hat."
I remembered what Officer Goode had said about how
if her clothes became waterlogged they would take her
straight to the bottom. Unless she could shed those
clothes.

"Without a body, there's no way to tell what really
happened. Clarissa was absolutely no help, Coleman
said. I just feel Darla needs to get angry before she ac-
cepts this. Stages of grief and all. If she simply gives up
all hope, it could be very hard for her."

"Did Darla ever find out what happened to the boat?"

"She had it looked at. The propeller was terribly
damaged, but the mechanic didn't offer any definitive
answers about what happened. As I understand it, it
could have been an accident or it could have been sab-
otage. I believe the insurance company is looking into
the circumstances. Right now Darla doesn't care about the
boat. It's her friend that she's focused on."

It was hard. One moment Kathleen had been on the
boat, partying and drinking. The next she was over
the side and gone, swept along in the dark currents of
the river.

Tinkie rejoined me and Harold. "Look, we're at Rook's
Nest. Let's put on the show, get it over with, and then go
back to Darla's. I'm so tired my collarbones ache."

"Tinkie, if you're too tired, we can stop right now.
As you are wont to remind us, you are pregnant." I gave
her a hug. My partner was a real trouper, so I had to
look out for her.

Tinkie squared her shoulders and lifted her chin. "I'm
perfectly fine. The show must go on."

Under Tinkie's direction, we found our places for

the first scene. I hid in the bushes while Millie rang the doorbell and then rushed across the porch to get into place. Clarissa opened the door to what appeared to be an empty yard. She stepped out onto the porch, followed by a cluster of houseguests. "Oh, mummers! We're here to watch you perform," she called out.

She was indeed expecting us. I came out of the bushes with my slanting crab walk, frazzled white hair, and completely white eyeballs, compliments of costume contacts. I heard the sharp intake of breath from Clarissa and her friends. I was a bit more than they'd expected, and I was convincing!

I scuttled up to the porch where I could look up at Clarissa and mimed cracking an egg. I pretended to roll the egg around in the bowl and cast the shells down. "Look, milady, the twin yolk of the pigeon egg predicts foul trouble will befall all who hamper the green men of the forest. See the blood in the yolk! Beware the arrows that fly!"

"You are one scary piece of work," she said. "I don't know who you are, but you are ugly. In fact, you're so ugly, I'll bet your mother had to tie a pork chop around your neck to make the dogs play with you."

For a moment her venom knocked me out of character. She was really a very mean person. But I recovered. Waving a hand over my pretend bowl of cracked egg, I gave a high-pitched cackle. "I see the future for you, my lovely. I hope that STD is something antibiotics can cure. Some are antibiotic resistant."

"How dare you!"

I saw Tinkie as Maid Marian laughing in the wings, but it was Harold who stepped out to confront me. "Oh far-seeing Mortianna, the Sheriff of Nottingham needs your counsel." He grabbed my arm and began to move me away from the porch.

"Robin! Oh, Robin! Beware the traps being set for you. Great evil lurks within the walls of yon castle." I was having a hard time holding back the laughter myself. Judging from Clarissa's expression, she was sizzling with anger at my remark.

Millie burst into laughter, and Jaytee turned away to hide his amusement.

"I recognize the voice of my hired help," Clarissa said, putting her hands on her hips. "Sarah Booth Delaney! You look like something that crawled out of a nightmare. And you aren't nearly as clever as you think you are."

I was outed, and I didn't really care. "My name is Mortianna, my pretty." I sounded like a blend between a dying hyena and the Wicked Witch of the West. Coleman and Oscar were behind a shrub laughing. Cece, Tinkie, and Millie were ready to come to my defense, if needed. I escaped Harold's grip and sidled closer to Clarissa. "Would you like me to tell your fortune?"

"Oh, yes," she said. "I can't wait."

"Give me your hand." I reached up to grasp her hand, aware of the perfectly manicured nails and the two very expensive rings. I really couldn't see very well with the opaque contacts in, but I didn't need to. I had no skills at reading palms; I was just going to wing it as I went along. I pinched the area at the base of her thumb. "Ah, a fat and juicy Mount of Venus. You are a girl who loves her pleasures. Beware that you don't run to fat in your middle years, which aren't that far away."

Behind Clarissa, a few twitters arose from her guests. Tulla and Bricey brayed with laughter, and for a split second hatred crossed Clarissa's features.

"She got you, Clarissa," Tulla said. "You absolutely look marvelous for your age, but you are getting on up there. Better up the time you spend with your personal trainer."

Clarissa threw a withering look over her shoulder and tried to snatch her hand away, but I held on.

"Your life line and your head line intersect," I said in my falsetto cackle. "You've managed to blend what you love and what you do." I was really racking my brain trying to remember anything Madame Tomeeka, Zinnia's resident psychic and medium, had ever said about reading palms. "And here, that mark on the mount at the base of your forefinger—the Mount of Jupiter—a message is coming for you. An important message. There is news you don't want to share. The resolution of a puzzle is on the way, and it is not what you anticipated."

"It had better be coming soon, since you've been paid handsomely to find those answers." She finally freed her hand. "I thought you came to perform. Get on with it. It's cold standing out here on the porch."

And with that, Harold whipped out a bugle and blew it—off-key. "The story of Robin Hood begins," he said, motioning me forward.

I spun around with a cackle. "The Prince of Thieves is a tale oft told about a man who robbed from the rich to give to the poor. Robin"—Coleman bowed—"will do battle with the Sheriff of Nottingham." Oscar took a bow. "And win the hand of Maid Marian." Tinkie curtsied. I introduced the rest of the players and set up the story.

Clarissa's guests were on her front porch, but a crowd had also gathered on the front lawn of Rook's Nest, and they applauded in anticipation. The lawn was large and filled with beautiful landscaping. A lover's bench was tucked among some trees, and a fountain tinkled behind some other shrubs. Tulla, Bricey, and Bart and Sunny Crenshaw, among other guests I didn't know, were leaning on the balustrade around the porch. They held drinks and were in high good spirits.

I continued. "But there is evil afoot in the land of King John. Persecution of the poor is rampant, and Robin will defend those without protection until King Richard is placed upon the throne. I predict a bad ending for the minions of King John, especially the Sheriff of Nottingham, a blackhearted villain. The play begins!" I bowed and slipped away to find a place to hide until it was my turn to burst out of the shrubs. We were all about dramatic entrances.

The highlight of the story was the sword fight between Oscar and Coleman and they'd become pretty good at acting it out, even following the blocking I'd done for them. The finale involved Robin shooting an arrow that strikes the sheriff so that Robin can swoop in and save Maid Marian. We had a rubber-tipped arrow and a child's toy bow.

The crowd laughed and applauded, and I had to admire the fervor that my friends put into the play. The sword fight went off without a hitch and impressed the audience. We were almost at the finish, and Coleman drew back the bow to let his arrow fly.

Friar Tuck, or Cece, as she was better known, had been off her mark the entire play. She was supposed to hide in the shrubs and come out during the sword battle to act as Robin's second. Instead, she'd been walking back and forth in front of the porch and at the last minute had run into the thick shrubs at the side of the house. I wondered what bee had gotten up her bonnet. She was supposed to be stage left in preparation for the duet with Jaytee, but she was stage right. I'd round her up when it was time for her song.

Coleman made a big production of drawing back the little plastic bow. When he loosed the rubber-tipped arrow, it stuck Oscar in the shoulder, and he fell back, pretending to be gravely wounded.

The crowd was whooping and clapping as Robin raced across the lawn and swept Marian into his arms. "My maiden is safe!" he cried out.

From somewhere in the landscaped yard, there was the twang of a powerful bowstring, and a real arrow shot across the area and struck the front porch post only inches from Clarissa's head. The arrowhead dug deep into the wood.

Clarissa screamed, which made Tulla and Bricey scream, too. Pandemonium broke out on the porch as everyone pushed and shoved to try to get in the front door.

Another twang cut through the noise and a second arrow whistled toward the front porch. This one grazed Clarissa's head, slamming into the front wall of the house.

"I've been hit!" Clarissa screamed. She placed a hand on the side of her head, and blood seeped through her fingers. It looked like the arrow had taken part of Clarissa's ear with it.

The porch audience screamed louder. Individuals dropped to the floor as the spectators on the lawn, realizing this was not part of the play, scattered and ran for their lives. Coleman discarded his bow and Maid

Marian and ran toward the area the arrow had come from. I grabbed Tinkie and Millie and nudged my friends to the ground. "Stay down," I said. Cece was nowhere to be seen.

Jaytee, Oscar, and Harold were hot on Coleman's heels. They paid no heed to my admonitions to be safe.

"Someone is trying to kill you, Clarissa," Tulla said. She grabbed Bricey and made for the door, pushing Clarissa and the Crenshaws out of the way. Clarissa grabbed Tulla's ankle and brought her down with a whump.

"Damn you," Tulla said.

Clarissa punched her and crawled on top of her, using Tulla as a doormat as she made for the door.

"Halt!" Friar Tuck came out of the shrubs with a crossbow and hunting arrows. "In the name of justice, take this!" And he shot another arrow right at Clarissa. Luck was with her and the arrow narrowly missed.

"Cece!" I ran toward my friend, who'd obviously lost her mind, intending to knock her down before she got another shot off. Where had Cece even gotten a real crossbow?

To my astonishment, another Friar Tuck—a second plump man of the cloth—came stumbling out of the bushes. He tumbled forward, tripped over his robe, and rolled into the Tuck with the bow. They both went down in a heap. In the dark they rolled around, one on top of the other, slugging away. They would flip, and the Tuck who'd been on the bottom would be on top, punching the one on the ground. They were grunting and cursing.

"What the hell?" Tinkie asked. "This has gone way too far now."

"Indeed it has." I rushed forward and hurled myself at the Tuck on top. I had enough speed to knock him off-balance. He hit the ground with an *ooffph* and rolled over me, crushing the wind from my lungs. I felt like I'd been run over by a linebacker.

Before I could do anything except heave for air, Tuck got up and ran in the opposite direction from the one Coleman had taken. The remaining Tuck got off the ground and waddled over to me, offering a hand. Her fat pads had shifted so that she looked like Quasimodo, and with her makeup all smeared and blurred, she could have been anyone. I was more than a little suspicious.

"Sarah Booth. Snap out of it. It's me, Cece." She jammed the hand almost in my face. "Take it. I'll pull you up."

I did as she suggested. The yard was finally quiet. The spectators had scattered to the winds. Tinkie ran up to join us. "What the hell happened?"

"There was a second Friar Tuck." It was like a bad hallucination. Where had the other Tuck come from? And where had he gone?

"I saw that," Tinkie said. "Who was it?"

I looked at Cece, who shrugged. "Sorry, he didn't leave a calling card," she said.

"We need to be on his tail. Was he the person who shot Clarissa with an arrow? He could have killed her."

"I think he meant to," Cece said. She was busy untying her friar's robes. In a moment she had shucked out of the costume and was unstrapping the fat pads. Beneath it all she wore jeans and a sweatshirt.

Coleman and the men returned. "We lost him," Coleman said. "He took off down the street and disappeared."

"We need to see how badly Clarissa is hurt." It had looked like a mere brush with death, but we needed to be sure.

"That arrow almost took her ear off," Harold said, and he wasn't being clever. He was worried. "Whatever is going on in this town, it's dangerously out of hand."

"Any idea—other than Cece—who was in the friar's costume?" Coleman asked.

We all shook our heads. "I don't think it was a man. Beneath the fat pads, the body seemed lean but compact. I had some close personal contact when he, or she, rolled over me."

"Tulla, Bricey, and Clarissa were all on the porch. Sunny and Bart Crenshaw were there, too," Tinkie pointed out. "That means the archer wasn't part of Clarissa's inner circle of wild things."

"Jerry Goode is unaccounted for, but he's too big to be the second Friar Tuck," I said. Tinkie and I looked at each other. "Who else could it be?"

"We have to consider that there are multiple bad actors here," Tinkie said. "Each incident may have a unique villain."

She had a point, and she was aggravated. She started to stomp toward the porch.

"Where are you going?" I asked.

"To get our donation. We aren't leaving without it. We were promised a donation for the animal shelter and I can't help it that Clarissa's ear got skinned a little. We need that money."

I knew there was no dissuading her, and I watched her knock boldly on the front door. In a few minutes she returned with a check. "Clarissa is fine. She didn't want to cough up the money, but I told her I'd take out an ad in the newspaper to say she'd reneged on her donation."

"Was she hurt?" I asked.

"The arrow nicked her earlobe, but no serious damage. It isn't even bleeding. Much." She waved the check. "And we have a nice contribution to the animal shelter." She tucked it in her pocket. "Now we're going to resolve this so we can go home day after tomorrow without having to think about Clarissa Olson. I have a plan."

26

Coleman joined us wearing latex gloves and holding what looked like a very expensive crossbow. "I found it in the ditch. Whoever shot this could have killed Clarissa," he said. "This isn't just practical jokes, this is attempted murder. I'll call the police."

"I don't trust Jerry Goode," I told Coleman.

"We have to report this."

"Shouldn't Clarissa report it? It was her ear that almost got snicked off by an arrow."

"She should, but we're witnesses. I have to uphold the law," Coleman said. "Even when you don't like it." He rumpled the frizzy white hair that was my wig. "I'll tell you what. You guys go on back to the B and B and I'll wait here for the law to come."

It was an offer I wasn't about to turn down. After my exchange with Clarissa, I wasn't eager to end up inside her house, listening to her berate everyone. We helped Cece pick up the parts of her costume she'd scattered about the yard. I wanted to pull the arrows out of the front porch post and the wall, but I knew Coleman would never hear of it. He would leave that for the Columbus police.

I sidled up to Cece. "Do you know who your doppelgänger was?"

She hesitated. "Not really."

"A guess?"

She shook her head. "Let me think about all of this."

Before I could offer to call a ride, Rex appeared with the limo to get us all back to the inn. Either he was psychic or Tinkie had already called him. Tinkie and I piled up in the far back seat. She sighed. I could almost guess what she was thinking.

"Whoever shot at Clarissa had to know we were going to do the Robin Hood story," Tinkie said. "They came dressed exactly like Friar Tuck. They had the crossbow. They knew where we were and the time we'd be there."

"You're right, Tinkie." I'd already come to that conclusion. There was only one person who knew all of that. And she had a very personal reason to hate Clarissa Olson. "Darla?"

She nodded. "Yes. I don't know that she's involved in the earlier shenanigans, but this one, I'm willing to bet she's in it up to her ears."

"I know."

"Her best friend is dead, and Clarissa was awful to Kathleen. I think this has driven Darla to madness. She's been too calm. Too accepting of Kathleen's death."

"I know." Everything Tinkie said made perfect sense, even though it hurt me to admit it. "I think that's why Coleman didn't want to tell Darla he was attacked outside the Bissonnette House. He was already suspicious. The evening Coleman was attacked, when I was outside, I felt like someone was watching me. Do you think Darla has someone helping her do these things?"

"Let's not jump to conclusions. Maybe Darla is at home and has plenty of alibis. She really seemed to have a headache. Wouldn't that be great?" Tinkie brightened at the possibility.

"It would." I smiled, too, but it was a false smile that only hid my deep concern.

We arrived at the B and B just as Darla pulled up in her car. She greeted us with a warm smile. "How about a nightcap? How did the holiday mumming go?"

She was a better actress than I'd ever assumed. "Fine. Where have you been?"

"I ran to get some cranberry juice and champagne." She clicked her key fob and the trunk of her Lexus opened. Sure enough, grocery bags cluttered the back of the car. It looked like a member of the Donner Party had finally made it to a grocery store. There were at least thirty bags of groceries. We each grabbed a couple as we headed in through the back door. When we finished unloading the trunk, the counters were completely covered by sacks of food. It had to have taken Darla at least two hours to buy all of those groceries. Tinkie and I nodded at each other. Perhaps Darla did have an alibi.

"Where's Coleman?" Darla asked once we had everything from the car in the kitchen.

"He stayed behind to talk to Clarissa."

Darla's eyebrows arched. "You left your man alone with that she-devil?"

Even though I trusted Coleman with my life, my gut took a little twist at her words. Clarissa knew no boundaries. She'd move on anyone's territory no matter how many no-trespassing signs were posted. "Coleman can handle her. Besides, someone almost killed her tonight."

"What?" Darla looked genuinely surprised. "Who?"

"Someone in a Friar Tuck outfit," Harold threw in.

"I didn't realize any of the other mummers were dressing as Robin Hood and the Sherwood Forest crew," Darla said. "I picked that because I thought it was original."

"Who else would know that was the theme you'd chosen?" Tinkie asked the question gently, but there was still bite in it.

"Anyone in town," Darla said. "The costume shop is a din of gossip. Those theater types love to shuffle scandal around town. And of course I knew. And Kathleen. But anyone who wanted to know could have found out just by asking."

"Between eight and ten o'clock, you were grocery shopping?" I asked.

She nodded. "Call Kroger. They know me in the store." Her voice registered hurt. "A dozen employees saw me shopping, and then I stopped at the pet food store to pick up some more food for Gumbo."

The cat appeared as if she'd been summoned—very un-catlike behavior.

"Ask the cat," Darla said, moving the conversation to a more lighthearted plane. "If Gumbo could talk, she'd tell you."

Even without the cat, Darla had a solid alibi. And I

was relieved, but I had other questions. "Darla, what's really going on in this town?"

"Clarissa and that crew have hurt a lot of people. Folks who were just trying to lead their lives, provide for their families. When you deliberately interject yourself in a relationship and blow it up, there can be all kinds of fallout." She sighed. "I agree with Clarissa on the point that most humans can't deny their animal nature. Put sex in front of them and they are going to go for it. But decent people try hard to follow a code of conduct."

"Did they ever take a romantic interest away from you?" Tinkie asked her.

She stopped with a can of tomatoes in her hand. The cabinet door was open and the shelves were already packed with food. "No. But it could have been me easily enough. Clarissa, Tulla, Bricey—they've run roughshod over polite society. Someone has just had enough."

Darla tried to close the cabinet door, but it was jammed too full. For someone who had canceled all of her future guests, she'd really forked out some bucks for food. "Who is going to eat all of this?" I asked.

"I'm going to prepare some food for the Angel's Wings Shelter for the Homeless. Christmas will be here, and without Kath—" Her voice broke and she turned away.

I nodded, feeling only slightly like a heel for asking the question.

"Darla, you're welcome to come to Zinnia," Millie said. "You can stay with me. I hate to think of you here alone."

"That's very kind." Darla dashed her tears away with the back of her hand and stood taller. "I'll be fine. This is the hard part of really having a friend of the heart.

To care for someone so much leaves you wide open for terrible heartache." She inhaled and forced a smile. "Enough doom and gloom. Tell me more about what happened. I should have gone with y'all instead of letting my depression get the better of me and going to the grocery store. I would have given a lot to see Clarissa's face when that arrow almost got her."

"She was frazzled," Harold said. "As were all of her guests."

"How close did the arrow come?" Darla asked.

"The second one nicked her ear," Jaytee said. He'd taken a seat at the breakfast nook and was busy unsacking the groceries and organizing them. When Darla opened another set of cabinets, I saw that she, too, was obsessive about organization. The canned goods were put away in alphabetical order, by vegetable *and* can size. She even took the time to move the older cans to the front as she put the new ones in back. I, on the other hand, just jammed things onto shelves, which sometimes resulted in cans of tomatoes on the verge of explosion. The way I looked at it, it just kept life interesting.

Darla opened a bag of cat food and poured some kibble into a bowl for Gumbo. The little kitty daintily crunched a nugget or two, and then turned to the kitchen window that looked out on the pool and patio area. The kitty jumped up above the sink and batted at the window, obviously asking to go out.

"Did Kathleen let her kitty go outside?" I asked.

Darla shook her head. "No, she has to be inside. I promised Kathleen that if anything ever happened, I'd keep Gumbo safe." Tears brimmed, but she blinked them away. "I couldn't bear it if something happened to her cat."

"I understand," Tinkie said gently. She rubbed Darla's back lightly. "Gumbo will adjust to being indoors here. This is a wonderful home for her."

"I'm going to check the trunk to be sure we got everything," Jaytee said.

"Thanks." Darla gave him a wan smile.

The minute Jaytee opened the back door, Gumbo leaped from the window, hitting the floor halfway across the kitchen. She was out the door before Jaytee even knew to be on guard.

"Gumbo!" We all cried the cat's name as Darla and I darted after her. I saw the tip of her tail disappearing around a neatly trimmed bottlebrush plant. My legs were longer than Darla's, and I scurried after Gumbo, with Darla following behind me.

"Kitty, kitty, kitty!" I called. "Kitty, kitty."

Darla, too, called for the feline, but Gumbo paid no attention to either of us. She streaked across the patio and through the dense hedge. She was gone before I had half a chance to convince her to come to me.

"I'll go around the hedge," I told Darla. "I need a flashlight."

She hurried inside and returned with a small flashlight. Once we left the patio, the yard sloped gently to the bluff overlooking the river. While it was a large, well-maintained lawn, it was also inky dark. Away from the patio illumination, I couldn't see what was in front of my face. I could run into a shrub or step in a hole and break my neck. The flashlight helped, but overhanging limbs caught in my hair and brushed my face. The big benefit of the flashlight was that I might be able to pick up the cat's golden eyes.

Tinkie, Cece, Jaytee, Harold, and Millie came out on the patio, braving the brisk wind that blew up off the river, to keep an eye out for the little cat. Darla was beside herself. Her agitation would send the cat running in the opposite direction. Cats were like that. They didn't like any drama unless they created it. "Darla, maybe you could get some food to rattle for her." I needed to get her away from the cat's hiding place if I ever intended to get my hands on the kitty.

"Of course," she said, hurrying inside.

I made it around the dense hedge that marked the parameters of the patio and walked toward the river. The drop-off on the bluff was very steep, and I didn't believe the cat would attempt the zigzagging stairs that seemed to cling to the clay bank of the river in a very precarious way.

I swung the beam of the flashlight from left to right, hoping to see the cat's eyes. The skin along my arms prickled. I had the sense I was being watched. It was the same sensation I'd experienced before.

Out on the street in front of the B and B, I heard yelling. I couldn't be certain but it sounded like Coleman . . . and another man. An argument. I decided to give Gumbo one last try before I had to rush back to see what was going on with Coleman. I knelt down and aimed the flashlight into the thickest part of the hedge. Gumbo looked back at me.

She was curled up in a piece of cloth tucked in the compost at the base of the hedge. I reached into the bush and grabbed the kitty. She was purring and didn't offer any resistance. When I drew her out, she dragged what looked like a stocking cap with her.

I tucked the kitty inside my costume and coat, calmed by the loud purr Gumbo made. She truly didn't object to being captured, thank goodness. When I turned the flashlight on the hat, I couldn't help gasping. It was a red hat with a snowman on it. Exactly like the hat Kathleen had been wearing on board the *Tenn-Tom Queen*. When she went over the side, she'd had that hat on.

So how had it gotten under the hedge in Darla's B and B lawn?

With the cat tucked inside my clothes, I started back to the inn. Whatever hullabaloo that had started in the front had stopped. Now all was quiet. Darla was watching from the kitchen window. Relief touched her face when I brought Gumbo from inside my jacket. "Kitty safely returned."

"Thank you!" She hugged the cat to her. "I'll be a lot more careful when I open any doors."

I held the cap back. I wanted to talk to Coleman first. My mind was going a thousand miles a minute and I couldn't settle on an answer that explained how the hat had come to be where I'd found it. By all rights, it should be in the bottom of the river, along with Kathleen's body. Yet it was here. In the hedge—exactly where I'd heard someone earlier. In the same vicinity where Coleman had been attacked.

Either someone had stolen Kathleen's hat and planted it there. Or . . . Kathleen was alive.

27

Tinkie followed me through the house, aware that I was keeping something from everyone.

"Coleman and Jerry Goode got into it out on the street," she said. "Goode must have given Coleman a ride over here from Clarissa's house. Anyway, Goode was angry that we left the scene of the arrow shooting. He tried to take it out on Coleman, but he got an earful. So what are you hiding in the coat?"

I'd done my best not to give away the fact I had something. "I'll tell you outside. I need to talk to Coleman."

"He left with Goode."

"Voluntarily?"

Tinkie laughed. "Yes, I guess so. I went out to talk to

him and he was gone." She grabbed my arm and moved me out to the porch. "Show me what you've got."

When the front door was closed behind us and I knew we had some privacy, I pulled the hat out and watched her expression go from confused to amazed to wary. "It's Kathleen's hat she was wearing when she went overboard. Where did you find it?"

"In the shrubs."

"And no clue how it got there?"

"None." I shook my head for emphasis. "Last night I had a sense there was someone hiding out in those hedges, watching us. But I never saw anything concrete."

"So whoever was hiding in the hedges with Kathleen's hat was likely the person who attacked Coleman last night?"

"That's what I'm thinking. That and a lot more. How did the hat get in Darla's shrubs?"

"And who knew to dress as Friar Tuck to get in the middle of our mumming?" Tinkie was both excited and a little angry. "Someone on the inside is involved in our case, someone who had a lot of access to this B and B. And I believe they're the same person. Either Kathleen is very much alive or someone is working really hard to make us believe she is."

Tinkie pulled her phone from her pocket. "Dallas, we need a ride. We're at the Bissonnette House." She looked at me. "You've got five minutes to get out of that costume before someone thinks you're celebrating the wrong holiday, like Halloween."

"Where are we going?" I asked.

"To find Jerry Goode. And Coleman. We're going to get some answers. Let me grab my Taser. Early Christmas present from Oscar."

Dang it. Tinkie was one step ahead of me in being properly armed. "You're going to tase Coleman?"

She laughed, a tinkling bell-like sound. "Not Coleman."

Which could mean that her focus was Jerry Goode or just about anyone else in town. It was going to be a long night.

We sent a text to Cece and Millie to let them know we were safe and sound and working on our case. They both responded back with whines and complaints that we'd left them behind. Now was the time, though, for action. Tinkie and I needed to carefully prepare for what lay in front of us.

If Kathleen was alive, how had she managed to survive the fall into the river, especially with all the clothes she'd been wearing? The weight of the water, the temperature of it, which would throw her into hypothermia within minutes—how had she avoided all of that? Coleman had saved Clarissa only moments after she'd gone into the water, and the gossip among the EMTs was that another ten minutes and she might have been dead.

Sitting in the back of Dallas's vehicle, we discussed all of this.

"Pardon me for butting in," Dallas said, "but what if she had a wet suit on under all those clothes?"

"You think Kathleen wore a wet suit because she intended to go overboard?"

"Actually, I was thinking about Clarissa. What if she wanted to take Kathleen out and she came prepared? Clarissa is always writing opinion columns for the local newspaper about her scuba diving experiences. I hate to admit it, but she's shared some pretty great photos."

A wet suit was an idea that hadn't occurred to me. "Is there a place to rent wet suits?"

"Yes, and I know the owner." She made a sharp U-turn and headed in the opposite direction from where we'd been going. "I'll give him a call." Which she promptly did. In a moment, she'd convinced the scuba shop owner to meet us at his place of business. Fifteen minutes later, we were in the parking lot as he was pulling up. In a small town, people could get to their destination with great speed.

Tinkie took one look around as we got out of the car, and I realized she was thinking exactly what I was thinking. This was kind of a seedy part of town. There was a booger light in the parking lot, but the bulb was broken. Only the moon, slipping between clouds, shed light on us, causing strange lunar shadows. I could hear the sound of traffic in the distance, but at the Snorkel and Fin, the parking lot and surrounding area was almost empty.

The man who got out of the car was tall and slender, and he motioned us to follow him. He opened the front door of the shop with his key and we all marched inside, including Dallas. "Thanks for opening for us, hon," Dallas said to him. "These ladies need to know if someone rented a wet suit?"

The man was about sixty, and he arched one eyebrow, inviting us to speak.

"Did this woman rent any diving equipment from you?" I showed him a photo of Kathleen on my phone.

He shook his head. "Nope."

"Are you sure?" Tinkie asked.

"Absolutely. It's winter. Not a lot of diving going on

except for the search party looking for that drowned woman."

He was right about that. "Is there anywhere else someone might rent a diving suit?"

Frowning, he considered my question. "Well, there are people with personal gear. Sometimes they get new equipment and dump off the old at Goodwill or a charity. Unless that's what happened, they'd have to go to a bigger city." He shook his head. "Or they could order online."

In other words, what had looked like a great lead was kaput.

"Thanks for looking," I said, about to put my phone away. I stopped. "Did *any* of these women buy diving equipment?" While I was there it just made sense to ask about the whole cheaters club.

He flipped through the photos on my phone until he grinned and tapped the screen. "This one, she's an avid diver. Goes down to Florida regularly and about twice a year dives off an island in the Caribbean."

I took the phone, expecting to see that he'd picked out Clarissa Olson, who'd already said she was a diver and had shown up at the search in her formfitting wet suit. To my surprise, the woman he'd pointed out was Tulla Tarbutton. I showed Tinkie, whose face lit up.

"Where do folks around here dive?" I asked.

He shook his head. "Rivers are muddy. Only reason to dive there is to look for something lost. The pleasure divers go south to the Gulf waters."

We thanked the shop owner and headed back to Darla's vehicle. "Clarissa and Tulla both dive." I spoke softly to Tinkie.

"Do you think Clarissa or Tulla may have found Kathleen's cap and planted it back at the B and B?"

"I don't know what to think. Clarissa was scuba diving in the river during the search. She could have found the hat, brought it out, and left it in the hedge, maybe to lead people to believe Kathleen is still alive." I clenched my fists in frustration. "I thought we were onto a solid lead, but now I'm not sure."

"Let's ask Tulla about it." Tinkie tapped Dallas on the shoulder as she was about to slide behind the wheel. "Do you know where Tulla Tarbutton lives?"

"It happens that I do."

"Take us there," Tinkie said.

28

To my surprise, Tulla lived in an apartment complex on the beltway off the bypass. I'd imagined she'd have a small house in one of the older residential areas, but she'd gone for sleek, modern, impersonal, and no lawn maintenance.

Tinkie knocked on the door and then knocked again. She was antsy, and I wasn't going to get between her and the door. She knocked a third time.

"Calm down! I'm coming." Tulla's voice held annoyance. Good, now we were all aggravated. And it was only going to get worse for her when she opened the door.

She stood in the doorway, feet apart. "You! What are you doing here?"

"We came to talk about scuba diving," I said as I pushed past her.

"You two have done nothing but make my life a misery. I don't know why Clarissa hired you, but—"

"She thinks one of her friends is trying to kill her," Tinkie cut in. "So we're either your best friend or the posse on your tail. It all depends on your answers to my questions." She sidestepped past Tulla and joined me in a living room completely devoid of any personality except for a sad ficus tree that was surrounded by a mountain of dead leaves. One fell as I was looking at it.

"I'm calling security." Tulla went to pick up her phone, but Tinkie struck first and swiped it.

"Give me that." Tulla's cheeks flared with red spots of anger.

"When we're done." Tulla didn't know Tinkie, but had she known her, she would have been wary about that glint of blue steel in Tinkie's wide eyes.

"You can't—"

"I suggest you sit down and listen to our questions." I pointed to an ugly armchair and she dropped into it. "Now, tell us about scuba diving. Have you been in the river since Kathleen went overboard?"

Her mouth opened and her eyes blinked. "How did you know I liked to dive?"

"We know a lot more than anyone suspects. When was the last time you went diving?" I asked.

"It's been almost five months. I didn't make my Thanksgiving trip to the Caymans this year."

"Do you ever dive with Clarissa?"

She looked away for a split second, just long enough

for me to see the hurt rush over her face. "We used to dive together. Not anymore. Our schedules conflict."

"Did you hire Mr. Horn to dump cement in Bricey's car?" A swift change of subject was sometimes a good tactic to throw a suspect off her stride.

"I—I," she sputtered.

"We know you were wearing a wig that you also tried to plant on Kathleen."

She bit her bottom lip and tears welled in her eyes. "Okay, yes. Bricey just rubbed my nose in that car all the time. I slept with Bart Crenshaw, too, and all I got for my trouble was diamond earrings and a UTI."

"Oh, brother." Tinkie flopped in the chair across from Tulla. "You destroyed a beautiful car because you felt you hadn't gotten your due?"

"I thought Bricey had it insured. I just wanted to hear her scream." She looked at us both. "What fool would get a new Caddy like that and fail to take out an insurance policy? I only meant to inconvenience her."

"And defraud the insurance company," I pointed out. "Not to mention putting Mr. Horn in a very precarious position."

"Oh, fiddle-dee-dee." She tried to emulate Scarlett O'Hara and failed dismally. "Bricey won't ever pursue this. Horn is too good-looking."

"Wrong. Horn is being sued. Did you know that?"

Tulla rallied at last, trying to get out of the chair until I pointed a finger at her and she sat back down on the edge. "Bricey won't sue that man," she insisted. "She'll get Bart to buy her another car and this will all blow over. Bricey and I are Bart's past. He'll do what's necessary to quiet this down and then he'll be on to a new woman. Or maybe he'll take up with Clarissa again. I think she's still got the itch. You should be working on something more serious, like how Sunny rigged the top step in Clarissa's house. I don't know if she was trying to kill Bart or Clarissa."

This was all news to me. "Who let Sunny into Clarissa's house to tamper with the stairs?"

"No one had to let Sunny do anything. She does exactly what she wants. Bart has a key to almost every house in our set. He's sold everyone their homes. Sunny takes the keys and goes in houses any time she feels like it. Sometimes she just leaves something out of her cat's litter box. Sometimes it's a dead reptile. She put a dead snake in my mailbox. She thinks she's so clever, but everyone knows it's her."

"And people put up with it?" Tinkie asked, clearly finding it hard to believe.

"It's kind of amusing, don't you think?"

"No." Tinkie put her hands on her hips and leaned forward. "Did Clarissa know Sunny was in and out of her home?"

Tulla shrugged. "Maybe. Maybe not."

"And Sunny Crenshaw? Did she care that her husband was sleeping with others?" I asked.

"Sunny's got everything she wants. A handsome man who put a ring on it. He's always there to squire her to social events. He serves his purpose. No one is complaining about any of it."

"You are pathetically jaded," Tinkie said. "Haven't you ever really cared about anyone in your whole life?"

"Yeah, once. And it got me exactly nowhere except in a lot of pain."

Tinkie wanted to pursue this, but I shook my head. We had to stay on focus unless we wanted to spend another week in Columbus. But Tinkie ignored me. "Who did you love, Tulla?"

She turned away and brushed at her cheeks. "Stay out of my business."

"Too late for that. We are all *in* your business. Someone tried to kill Clarissa tonight. If the archer had been a better shot, Clarissa would be dead. Next time it could be you."

The expression that crossed Tulla's face told me a lot more than her words did. "You know who the archer is, don't you?" I asked.

She stood up. "I don't have to talk to you."

"Tinkie, search her bedroom for that wig." I watched closely for her reaction, and I got more than I'd ever hoped for.

Panic streaked across her face before she regained her composure. "You can't search my place. You don't have a warrant."

"We aren't the police," I said. "We don't need a warrant."

Tinkie took off toward a hallway that obviously led to the bed/bath area of the apartment.

"You can't do this."

"Watch us," I said, standing so close to her that she couldn't get out of the chair. I hoped Tinkie would hurry. If Tulla really objected and tried to evade me, I wasn't going to slug her—no matter how much I wanted to.

"Even if you find a wig, you can't prove anything." She glared at me.

"Except that we were in Kathleen's place *filming* everything you did when you paid your little visit. We saw you take the wig. You were stealing from a dead woman."

"Show me the video." She tried to stand up, but I could see in her eyes this was a last-ditch attempt to save herself.

"Coleman has it. He's taking it to the police," I bluffed. I gave it three beats. "Unless you're willing to cooperate with me." Blackmail was an ugly thing, but it was one of the very best tools in my PI kit. And I didn't have a lot of time to squeeze Tulla.

"Here it is!" Tinkie came out of the bedroom holding the wig on a coat hanger. "I found it in the back of the closet."

Just for show I made a photo of Tinkie holding it. "You marked the spot you found it?"

"Of course," Tinkie said. "The crime lab guys will need to know the exact location. To gather evidence."

Tinkie was really rubbing it in. To add to the heat, I pulled out my phone and started punching in a number.

"Who are you calling?" Tulla asked.

"Coleman. He needs to get that video to the Columbus police. If he waits any longer, they may think he was trying to protect you."

"Stop!" She reached up for the phone, but I stepped back, then slowly put it in my pocket. "Are you ready to talk?

"I did steal the wig, but I didn't plant it on Kathleen. I lent it to her. I was helping her."

"Helping her what?"

"Get even with Bricey."

"I don't believe that for an instant," Tinkie said. "Call Coleman." She started back to the bedroom.

"It's the truth. I swear it." Tulla squirmed in her chair.

"Kathleen hated all of you—Bricey, Clarissa, all of you," Tinkie said. "Why in the world would she work with any of you?"

"We had a common enemy," Tulla said. "We both wanted to put Bricey in her place. She was so full of herself over the car and how much more Bart Crenshaw gave her than the rest of us. She rubbed our faces in it. We decided we'd had enough and to get even."

"You knew the car wasn't insured?"

Tulla lifted her chin. "I was the one who told Bricey to wait until after the first of the year to insure the car. I told her the insurance rates would drop."

"That's not even true about the rates dropping after the first of the year," I said, awed by her evil genius.

"Of course it isn't true. Bricey is a moron. She believed me, and that's all that matters."

"So you went to Colton Horn and hired the cement truck."

Tulla shook her head. "No, that was really Kathleen. It's just that when she went overboard and didn't resurface, I knew I had to get that wig out of her house before someone found it. It was my wig and it would trace back to me."

Tinkie had returned the wig to the closet and came to stand beside me, hands on her hips. "I don't believe a word that comes out of your mouth."

"Oh, boo-hoo, don't make me cry," Tulla said. "Like I care if you believe me. I'm telling the truth. That's what you asked me to do."

"Kathleen wouldn't work with you," Tinkie said. "She wouldn't. She despised all of you."

"The enemy of my enemy is my friend." Tulla spouted the aphorism as if she'd coined it herself.

"Can you prove any of this?" I asked.

Tulla actually paused long enough to think for a bit. "I don't have any physical proof, but I can tell you that Kathleen had it bad for Bart Crenshaw. It drove her crazy to know that Bricey, Clarissa, and I had sampled a piece of that tempting pie. She didn't know how to go about snaring him for herself. She was so . . . pathetic. She'd moon over him at parties and call him about ridiculous real estate listings that she didn't have the finances to afford. But he would show her houses and property. He wasn't into her, so he never acted on her flagrant invitations."

"Why not?" I asked. "Kathleen was beautiful. And nice. He's slept with everyone else in town."

"You are as big a fool as she was," Tulla said. "It was the nice part that kept him away. Kathleen wanted more than just a roll in the sack or some firecracker-hot sex. She was nice. That meant she had expectations for a relationship or some such foolishness. That's like a stake in the heart of a vampire to a real swinger. She'd be gum on his shoe he could never get rid of."

I didn't want to admit it, but her rationale made sense. No swinger would deliberately bed a romantic. The only thing that could come out of that would be hard, hard feelings. Bart would feel trapped and Kathleen would get her heart broken.

"Tulla, you slept with Bart," Tinkie pointed out. "Why would Kathleen join up with you?"

"I was no longer a threat," Tulla said.

"But Bart had broken up with Bricey," I said. "He gave her that car as a parting gift."

Tulla shook her head. "No, he hadn't. That was all a farce. He wouldn't give a $70,000 car to a woman he was cutting loose. Bart's wife, Sunny, was on his ass all day long. She said he was embarrassing her in town. So Bart agreed to break up with Bricey—*pretend* break up. It took the heat off them for a while."

She had a point. One I should have considered before now. "So you and Kathleen called the cement truck. What about the shock at karaoke?"

"It was a setup. I knew about it and made it happen."

"You could have killed yourself," Tinkie said, her voice rising in frustration. "How stupid can you be?"

"I knew it wouldn't kill me. I'd rigged the circuit. I had to make it look good."

"For what purpose? Not just to keep you off the suspect list for a ruined car." Suddenly the bigger picture snapped into focus. "You had something else planned, didn't you? Something where someone was really going to be hurt? Surely you weren't going to kill Bricey? Or maybe you tampered with the stairs at Clarissa's house. You have plenty of access there."

"Of course not!" Tulla finally stood up and began pacing the room. "We weren't intending to kill anyone."

"We?" Tinkie said. "Who is this we?"

"Me and Kathleen."

I was still finding it hard to believe that Tulla had joined forces with Kathleen, a woman she clearly viewed as her social inferior.

"When pigs fly," Tinkie muttered under her breath. She rounded on Tulla. "You would never really be friends with Kathleen. You were just setting her up. I know it. We all know it. So why did you steal the wig back? You could have framed her, and a dead woman has no defenses."

Tulla didn't bother denying her lack of good faith with Kathleen. "Like I said, I was afraid the wig would track back to me. I'm the one who bought it. It was my idea that Kathleen dress up and hire Horn. Kathleen was so eager to be part of my world that she did it."

I didn't believe that, either. Whatever else Kathleen had been, she wasn't a blind follower.

"Who set up Bart Crenshaw to take a tumble?" I asked.

"Not me. It could have been Bricey or Sunny."

"Not Clarissa?" I asked.

She shook her head. "Clarissa still has it bad for Bart. She denies it all over the place, but she yearns for his touch." She laughed. "That's the truth. It wasn't me or Clarissa. If Bart refused to give Bricey a new car, I wouldn't put it past her pushing him."

"And why wouldn't he just say so and have her arrested?" Tinkie asked.

"That's just not done. We deal with things ourselves." She looked toward the door, clearly eager to be away from us.

"That's an ominous statement," I said. "You're like a secret nation unto yourselves. You have your own laws, your own punishments."

She glared at me. "I'm done."

"Not yet." Tinkie stepped to block her from moving. "Did you deliberately push Kathleen into the river and drown her?"

"No. That's the truth. I would never be friends with her, you're right about that, but I wouldn't kill her."

"I'm not so sure I believe you," Tinkie said, echoing my own thoughts.

"I don't give a rat's patoot what you believe," Tulla said. She was finding her backbone and about to bolt.

"Who shot the arrow at Clarissa?"

"It clearly wasn't one of us. As much as I'd like to pin it on Bricey, we were all on the porch. You saw us."

"Like I believe you five are the only swingers in town," I said. "It's likely someone in your group who has decided to settle a score. Put your thinking cap on and tell us before someone is killed. Is Officer Goode one of your swinging group?"

"Him? Heavens no. He's too straitlaced. He'd never play by our rules, and we're the only ones that matter," Tulla said with some of her old arrogance returning.

"Who else is involved?" She exhausted me, but it was time to wrap this mess up.

"None of your business."

"What about Colton Horn?" I asked. If he were in this up to his ears, it would throw a completely different light on the whole car episode.

"He's a stick-in-the-mud. Handsome man. He could have been fun, but too uptight."

"You legitimately hired him to fill Bricey's car with cement?"

"I didn't hire anyone to do anything. I've told you already, Kathleen hired him." Tulla all but dusted her hands to show her lack of involvement. I didn't buy it for a second.

"It was all Kathleen. That's what you're saying?" I asked.

"Looks that way to me," Tulla said. She had begun to

enjoy herself. She intended to push the blame for everything onto a dead woman.

Tulla waved a hand. "Look, you need to leave. I haven't done anything illegal. None of us have." She went to the front door and opened it wide. "Make your exit now, please."

29

Exhausted, I trudged up the stairs at the B and B to find that Coleman had the sheets deliciously warmed. He'd been listening to some Christmas music on an app on his phone, and he snuggled me to him as Mariah Carey sang, "All I Want for Christmas Is You."

"That's really all I do want," Coleman whispered in my ear, sending chills over me. He had the magic touch when it came to me. "I only want you."

"Okay, I'll send those presents back to Santa." I couldn't be all soft and gooey—I had a reputation to uphold.

He chuckled. "Not a chance of that. And I have a really big surprise for you tomorrow."

"Tomorrow isn't Christmas," I said.

"But you're getting a present anyway—if I can lure you away from your case long enough for a little fun."

"What kind of fun?" He'd really gotten my curiosity bone to itching.

"Oh, something you may never have experienced."

Now he was definitely working on me. "I've never bungee jumped."

"Not that."

"Vacationed in Denmark."

He laughed. "For someone who didn't want a present, you have some big dreams."

I kissed him. "I'm just playing along. You want me to guess, and I know even if I guess correctly, you won't tell me."

"You're right about that." He smothered my protests with another kiss, which quickly turned into something that canceled all thoughts of trying to trick him into telling me his secrets.

When we were both spent, we snuggled close, and I fell asleep to the mellow sounds of Bing Crosby singing "White Christmas."

The next morning, I was tapping on Tinkie's door before sunrise. We'd finally reached the time of year when the days would get longer—by about a minute a day. I was ready for the longer days. Outside the windows of the B and B, night still held sway.

When Tinkie didn't answer the door, I tapped again. And again. Oh, I had some payback in store for her. At last the door cracked open.

"What? It's not even six A.M. It's still dark outside."

"I know that. Get dressed. We have work to do."

"Don't forget the Christmas parade is today," Tinkie

said. "Oscar has made me promise that we'll be there. No excuses. Not even for a case."

I liked parades. I looked forward to the Columbus Christmas parade. "Fine by me. So let's work this morning. The parade isn't until tonight."

"Meet me downstairs. Give me fifteen minutes."

I didn't hear Darla rattling around in the kitchen yet, so I poked up the glowing embers of the fire in the parlor and threw on two more logs. Gumbo came to join me as I waited for my partner. The little kitty was so dainty and feline, gently kneading my thighs. At last I put her aside and began to explore the room. It was spacious and lovely, with built-in bookshelves on either side of the fireplace.

Anxious to get busy but stuck waiting for Tinkie, I examined a bust of William Faulkner. Judging from the books on the shelves, Darla was quite a reader. She had bestsellers, classics, childhood favorites, and a dozen slim volumes of poetry. I could spend a week going through her books.

I saw a volume with a brown leather cover and picked it up. It was a journal. When I opened it, I discovered it was handwritten, like a diary. I wondered if I'd stumbled on the musings and thoughts of one of Darla's ancestors. Perhaps someone connected with the Bissonnette House, which had once been a private home.

I turned on a reading light beside the fire and dropped into a chair to read until Tinkie came down. The first page of the journal involved the B and B and the beauty of the structure. There were no dates or signatures—no way to know who wrote the journal or when it was created.

The journal detailed holiday celebrations, complete

with menus and comments about guests—who were named only with initials. Darla was obviously the author, and the journal was a neat look inside Darla's time as a hostess. She obviously enjoyed her role and her work.

I heard footsteps and closed the booklet to greet Tinkie, but it was Darla. I stood up and the journal slipped from my hand and dropped to the floor. A piece of paper fell out. Darla swooped down to get it, but I picked it up first. Written in blue ink was a simple message: "I'm sorry, Darla. Meet me at three where the moon and tide hold sway, where Artemis and the feminine rule. I shall sing an ode to the huntress."

Darla flushed as I handed over the journal and note. It was clear this was an assignation of some type that I'd stumbled onto. "I'm so sorry. I wasn't trying to pry."

"It's embarrassing, this communicating by written notes in such poetic language. It's so . . . old-world."

"And rather lovely," I said. "So genteel."

Darla rolled her eyes. "You can take the gal out of romance, but you can't take the romance out of the gal, I suppose. Please don't mention this to anyone. It's just that since Kathleen . . . I'm so very lonely. I lost my best friend, perhaps my only friend in Columbus. It's probably jumping out of the frying pan and into the fire, but I renewed an old relationship." She flushed and looked away.

I was happy she had someone else in her life, but she'd opened the door, mentioning Kathleen. And I had to walk through it, even if I knew it would upset her.

"Darla, is there anyone who would want to hurt you by leaving something of Kathleen's on your property?"

"Something like what?"

"An article of her clothing."

"What?" She put a hand to her throat and I could almost see the pulse jumping there. I'd really caught her unprepared. "Why would you even say anything like that?"

"When I was hunting for Gumbo, I found something under the hedge. A cap."

"Kathleen's cap?" Her eyes were wild and her voice was rising. She sank onto the sofa.

"Please calm down. Yes, I believe it was Kathleen's snowman stocking cap. She was wearing it on the boat the night she . . . fell overboard."

"That bitch Clarissa!" She was off the sofa like a cork flying from a champagne bottle. "She was scuba diving, pretending to be so concerned she was searching for Kathleen. She found the cap, brought it up, and left it in the hedge for me to find so I would get upset."

"Why would she do that?" I asked.

"Because she's a terrible person. She loves to inflict pain on people she doesn't like. Even on people she does like. There's something very wrong with her. Surely you've seen it."

My opinion of Clarissa wasn't far off from Darla's, but my opinion wasn't the point. The cap was physical evidence. It was true Clarissa had been diving in the river, saying she was helping with the search. It was possible she could have found the cap, brought it up, dried it, and put it under the hedge. But I wouldn't have found it unless Gumbo had gone there. And how would Clarissa think that Kathleen's cat would escape and find the hat? Still, maybe Clarissa was spying on the inn and accidentally dropped it.

"Can you think of any reason Kathleen would pretend to be dead?" I asked her.

She scoffed. "Not one single reason. She wouldn't do that. She'd never have people searching for her just to play a prank. You don't understand. Kathleen and I were close. Like sisters. She'd never do any of this."

"And would she throw in with Tulla Tarbutton to get even with some of the swingers in town?"

Darla shook her head vehemently. "If someone is saying that, they're lying. Who said that?"

I was spared from coming up with a response when Tinkie came down. "Darla," she said. "You don't have to get up and cook for us. We can fend for ourselves. You've been the perfect hostess, but just take a rest."

"I love cooking for my guests. And tonight is the final Christmas event, the big parade downtown. You'll want to get there early to find a spot on the street if you want to catch the treats that Santa and his elves will be throwing. I'll get you started off with a hearty breakfast. How about a grits soufflé? Filled with cheese and eggs and other yummy stuff."

Darla found solace in her cooking. I wasn't about to take that away from her. "Sounds delicious."

"I know you and your partner are always rushing out the door, so I'll get busy in the kitchen." She turned away, the journal forgotten in her hand. Tinkie jerked her head toward the door.

I followed her out the front into the still-dark morning. Dawn was just peeking over the eastern horizon. "Darla doesn't believe Kathleen was involved with Tulla," Tinkie said.

"I know," I said. "She also doesn't believe there's a chance Kathleen is alive. She was adamant that Kathleen would never pretend to be drowned."

"So where does that leave us?" Tinkie asked.

"Tracking down Jerry Goode."

"Coleman isn't going to like this."

That was an understatement. "We need to return before Darla makes breakfast. Let's just make it quick." I called Dallas. She sounded like she'd been up for hours. And she knew where Jerry Goode lived. "Remind me next case we work to hire an Uber driver who knows everything," I told Tinkie as we walked to the curb to wait for our ride.

30

Dallas did know where Goode lived, but she wasn't magic. She couldn't make him be at home when we knocked on his door.

"His car isn't here," Tinkie said.

"You know his car?"

"When he was leaving Clarissa's, if that was him, he was driving a silver sportscar. There's no vehicle here at all."

"Good, let's break in."

Tinkie grabbed my arm. "Bullying Tulla is one thing. Goode is a member of law enforcement. He could really put us in jail."

"Only if he catches us." The first pink glow of dawn was moving up the horizon. Soon it would be daylight.

It was now or never if we intended to break into the small brick house. Soon the neighbors would be up and poking around.

"What are we even looking for?" Tinkie asked.

"Goode has investigated every single incident. If he's part of the cheaters club or somehow beholden to one of them, maybe he's protecting someone."

"And we're going to find that out how?" Tinkie asked. "It's not like he's going to leave a written confession on the kitchen table."

"If we don't look now, we may never have another chance." I walked back to Dallas, who was waiting at the curb, and asked her to drive around the block and park. "Leave the motor running," I said. "We shouldn't be long."

"If I see him coming back, I'll drive by and blow the horn three times."

"Good plan." I waved her off and rejoined Tinkie.

"We don't have to do this," Tinkie said. "Let's just give the money back. Really, Sarah Booth. It's almost Christmas. We could end up in jail, or worse. I don't like our client enough to ruin the holidays."

Her words gave me pause. She was right—I knew that. But we were so close. "Let's do this. If we don't find anything, we'll talk about dropping the case."

"If we do this, we might as well hang on until we flush out the culprit," she said, almost under her breath. "You're going to deal with Oscar if we get caught."

Saying no wasn't an option. I checked the door—unlocked. "See, it's not even breaking. It's just entering." I tried to put the best face on it.

"Shut up and let's get inside." Tinkie all but shoved me in the door and closed it.

Goode's house was eerily neat—almost as if no one actually lived there. There was a sense of emptiness about the place. Except for the sound of something moving around in the back of the house.

"We should announce ourselves," Tinkie said.

"Like what: 'Private investigators, please don't shoot?'" I tried to curb my sarcasm.

"We could say we're the police."

"Follow me." Tinkie and I both had guns, but they were back in Zinnia, locked safely away. We didn't travel with firepower—except for Tinkie's brand-new Taser.

I crept down the hallway toward the sound of shuffling.

"What is that?" Tinkie whispered.

"I don't know. Maybe a dog."

"Don't open the door!" She tried to step in front of me, but I blocked her.

"Stay back. Oscar will kill me if you get hurt. The good thing about Coleman is that he'll only blame me if I get hurt."

"Because he knows how hardheaded you are."

I gave her an eye roll and put my hand on the doorknob to a back room. The sound was definitely coming from inside. I couldn't tell if it was a dog trying to escape or something more sinister.

Tinkie put a hand on my shoulder. "What if it's something we shouldn't let out?"

"What if it's someone in trouble and we're too cowardly to look?"

"Go ahead." She released my shoulder.

I turned the knob slowly, praying that I wouldn't feel resistance on the other side. The door opened easily and I peeked through the crack. The room was dark. Nothing. I pushed the crack wider, searching carefully before I stepped into the room. Before I could do anything, something hit the door with great force—so much force that the wooden door flew back toward me and smacked me in the forehead. The pain was instant.

"Damn!" Tinkie ran to the kitchen and grabbed wet paper towels. She held them to my forehead and wrapped my hand around them before she shoved the door, hard. There was a muffled moan. "What the hell?"

Before I could stop her, she forced her way into the room and flipped on the light switch. "Holy Christmas," she said. "It's Goode. He's been hog-tied on the floor."

Even though I was in pain, I knew I wasn't seriously hurt. My head was as hard as it was reputed to be. I pushed into the room. Behold! The lawman was on the floor on his stomach, his feet tied together and pulled up to his butt and then tied to his hands. He was also gagged with duct tape.

"I'll get a knife," Tinkie said. "Looks like the drawstring from the curtains." She looked around, and sure enough, the curtains were torn down and thrown on the floor. But how in the heck had anyone gotten the better of Goode? He was about six-three and looked to be very fit.

"Crime of opportunity," I said.

"Murrahahahah!" Goode said, thrashing about on the floor.

"Okay." Tinkie leaned over and snatched the duct tape from his mouth. I could almost hear the hair follicles ripping out of his skin.

"Owwww!" Goode yelled. "Cut me loose this minute."

Tinkie shrugged. She'd had enough of being ordered

about. "I'm good with leaving him tied. How about you?"

That set up another howl, and I took the knife from Tinkie and sliced the cord that bound him. At first he couldn't use his arms or legs—he'd apparently been tied in that position for a good while. At last he sat up. "How did you know I was here?"

"We heard what sounded like a struggle." We had to have a reason for breaking and entering or we'd be in legal trouble. We were the rescue squad—the good guys—but we'd still broken the law.

"How did you hear me?" He looked at both of us.

"Tinkie has bat hearing. She heard something and I walked around the house to look."

Goode struggled to his feet and searched his pockets. "Cell phone?"

I handed him mine and he called the police. He gave me back the phone. "Units are on the way. You should put ice on your forehead. You've got a knot."

"Who did this to you?" Tinkie asked.

Goode thought a minute before he answered. "I'm not certain. When I was leaving the B and B, I saw someone on the property. I didn't get a clear look, but whoever it was knew I saw them. They took off and I pursued on foot, but I lost them. There are too many places to hide on those big properties. Anyway, I stopped by the PD to file a report and then went home. Someone was waiting on me."

"You were struck from behind?" I asked.

"I came in the front door, put the keys on the little table in the entrance, and headed to the kitchen. I heard something in the back, so I went to check. I opened the door. I remember . . . someone on a chair. Behind the door. They struck me on the head." His hand went up to rub at a bump on his head.

His story made complete sense. He'd been struck on the back and side of his head, so likely he'd fallen forward. He'd landed in the perfect position to be hog-tied. "You think your attacker was on a chair?"

He nodded. "That has to be right."

There'd been no chair in the back bedroom when we'd arrived, but that didn't mean the attacker hadn't moved it. "Did you see who struck you?"

"No, but it was a short person."

"Because of the chair?"

"A tall man wouldn't need a chair. He'd have the reach."

"Was it the same person you saw at the Bissonnette House?" I asked.

He nodded slowly. "I think it must have been. They might have thought I could identify them. So they ambushed me and put me out of commission."

"Maybe Tulla got mad at you," I said.

"Tulla Tarbutton?" He looked genuinely confused.

"She said you were part of their swingers group." That was actually a lie, but I wanted to hear his response. "We saw you leaving Clarissa's place yesterday morning."

"Have you lost your ever-loving mind? I wouldn't touch that Medusa with a ten-foot pole."

"Tulla said you got into the kinky stuff." Another lie, but I was getting to him.

"She's crazier than you two. I have a steady girl. And for that matter, an alibi."

"We're listening."

Goode's mouth was a thin line. "I'll hold my piece, I

think. But if you're believing anything Clarissa or Tulla tells you, you're not as smart as I thought you were."

"Why would Tulla lie?" Tinkie asked.

"Because she's breathing? Because her lips are moving? Because she's completely amoral? To throw you off the trail? Shall I go on?"

I had an unresolved question from an earlier incident. "Officer Goode, did you ever figure out what made those marks in the riverbank? You said it might be some kind of boat. Any idea whose?" I needed to know who else had been on the river.

"I talked to some search-and-rescue guys, who said it was a small skiff, flat-bottomed, likely aluminum. They'd been on the river the day before and saw it pushed up on the bank."

"A fisherman's boat." I knew exactly the type of vessel he was talking about.

"Correct."

"So someone left it there and then paddled off in it. Maybe even picked up Kathleen."

"It's the theory I was working on, but everyone in town was looking for Kathleen. If a fisherman had taken her to any of the docks, we would know. She would have been rushed to the hospital."

He had a point. But it was still a clue that needed to be pursued further.

We didn't have any time for more questions because the police and paramedics arrived. Tinkie and I were pushed out of the house and told to wait. We were going to be questioned like we were part of the problem, not the solution. And in fact, we did have a little breaking-and-entering charge to avoid. We glanced at each other, and after a quick stop for a washcloth and some ice, we took off into the rising dawn. Dallas was waiting around the corner.

"What happened to your head?" Dallas asked, and there was real worry on her face.

"We ran into a little trouble." I didn't want to go into details. "Let's hurry back to Darla's place."

Dallas turned around in the seat to look at me. "Is Jerry okay?"

Something about her tone told me everything I needed to know. "He's okay, except for a bump on the head and being hog-tied for a while. Jerry said he was dating someone. It's you. That's why you know so much about everyone in town."

Dallas pinched her lips together. "I should have told you. But I really did want to help. That's why I know he's not involved in these dangerous games. He's been with me almost every minute he's not on duty and I'm not working. I keep that man plenty busy."

Tinkie sighed and sank into the seat. She was tired. "We should have asked Dallas more questions," she said. She sighed again. "And Dallas, you should have been more forthcoming."

"I swear, I really wanted to help."

And she had been a big help. And maybe more.

31

Breakfast was ready when we returned and no one was any the wiser we'd been out on the case. I came up with a clever lie about my forehead, saying I'd run into a low-hanging branch. We ate the delicious food Darla prepared, and the men took off on their "secret mission." I had a quick word with Coleman about my case. "There has to be more at stake than cheating." This was the thing that niggled at me.

"What's your gut tell you?" he asked.

"Money or revenge."

"Pick one. I'll wager the other."

"What's the wager?"

"A whole day of total pampering." He grinned and the very devil was in his eyes.

"You're on. The motivation is revenge." I'd come to that conclusion about the case from the very first.

"You were always a bloody gal," he said. "Okay, I'm betting on the fact that money is at the root of this." He kissed me in a way that was a promise. "Now I have to finish my mission. Tonight, after the parade, I'm all yours to do with as you will."

"Great. Just great." I couldn't really begrudge Coleman his fun. It was our last night in Columbus. It gave me pleasure to see them having so much fun. I was dying to know what they were up to, but at this point, I could wait until tonight for them to spring the surprise. I'd gone all week without spying on them, and even though Millie and Cece had tried, they weren't successful at finding anything out.

As Darla was picking up dishes from the table, she cleared her throat. "I won't be here to fix lunch, but we'll have a lovely celebration tonight after the parade."

"Darla, go have some fun," Tinkie said. "We'll find a nice place after the parade and just have some drinks and eat in town. We'll have time in the morning before we leave to tell you goodbye and thank you for the wonderful week."

"Have you resolved your case, then?" she asked. "Do you know who's after Clarissa?"

"Not yet. Not all of it," Tinkie said. She was more troubled by this than I was.

"We have a lot of leads but no real suspect." I wasn't totally truthful. "Darla, if the basis for all of the mean things that have happened is revenge, do you know who might be seeking revenge against Clarissa. And for what?"

Our hostess shrugged her shoulders. "I don't have a

clue. I don't run with that crowd, but I'd be willing to bet they've left a slew of people perfectly willing to tack their hides to the wall."

She was likely right about that—and the truth was no help in solving the case.

We waved the men off, and Cece and Millie took off with Rex and the limo to tour Friendship Cemetery. Cece was going to do a feature on the cemetery for the newspaper, and Millie wanted to see it. Tinkie and I had a scant six hours to finish up with finding the culprit involved in shooting arrows at Clarissa.

Tinkie and I had one excellent clue to run down, which came from the night of the mumming. We walked into town and headed straight for a store that sold hunting supplies, including crossbows. The one we'd found at Clarissa's house—sans fingerprints—had cost someone a pretty penny. The owner of the hunting goods shop was the first positive lead we'd had.

"Sure, I remember selling that exact bow," he said when I showed him a photo. "Bart Crenshaw bought it. Said he was going to take up crossbow hunting." His lips curled into something of a sneer. "I didn't think the pretty boy had it in him."

"Did you sell him hunting arrows, too?" I asked.

"Sure did." He led us to an aisle where he showed us several different arrows. "He bought these. Fletched with these feathers."

Identical to the arrows lodged in Clarissa's front door.

"I told all of this to that policeman name Goode," the owner said. "It seemed to mean something to him."

Goode had done the preliminary investigating. Coleman's instincts were good. "Thanks."

We left the shop and Tinkie blew out her breath. "It

all circles back to the swingers. Every single lead. But Bart Crenshaw was standing on that front porch when the arrows were fired. He couldn't have done it. Nor his wife. Nor Tulla, Bricey, or Clarissa. How did the archer get Bart's bow and arrows?"

"He could have given them to someone. But who? All of the swinger participants we know were in plain sight when the archery session occurred."

"There's someone we're missing." Tinkie had reached the same conclusion I'd come to earlier. "Someone in this group that so far hasn't shown his or her face."

"How do we find this person?" I asked. That was the issue to resolve.

"Clarissa."

We had to do it. We could dislike her, but it was time to quit dithering. Either solve the case or give her the money back. Since I'd ordered Coleman's saddle and paid special delivery to have it at Zinnia for Christmas morning, I didn't have the luxury of a choice.

The day was sunny and warm, and we'd done nothing but eat for an entire week, so Tinkie and I opted to walk to Clarissa's. The old historic neighborhood where Rook's Nest was located wasn't that far from downtown. I could easily visualize a time when the downtown, also situated near the river, had been the center of a booming residential area that included the W.

Clarissa was surprised to see us, and at first she tried to stall us at the door. When we got inside, we realized why. A carpenter was at work on the top step. "A repair?" I asked pointedly.

"Yes, it seems the riser wasn't firmly tacked into place.

I guess when Bart tumbled, the step tilted and he lost his balance. He wasn't pushed. He said that all along."

"If he had been injured, he or Sunny could have sued the pants off you," Tinkie said. She knew a lot more about liability than I did.

"But he wasn't hurt. And he isn't going to sue. And neither is Sunny."

The way she said the last made me wonder. Everyone had said Sunny was on the porch when Clarissa was nearly killed, but I didn't remember seeing her. She could have been. Or she could not have been. If anyone had a reason for revenge, it was Sunny. She was almost too obvious, and also very evasive. We still hadn't run her to ground and today was our last chance.

"Do you think Sunny would want you dead?" I asked. Her husband had bought the crossbow. It was a perfect opportunity.

"Why? Over Bart?" She laughed that Southern belle laugh. "Sunny wouldn't care if Bart was hit by a septic tank truck. In fact, it would simplify life for her. She could find another man like that." She snapped her fingers. "One not so inclined to share his charms."

"Has Sunny ever been alone in your house?"

Clarissa realized I was serious. "She has, but so has every person involved in our group. Sometimes I leave the key under the doormat for lovers to meet if I'm going to be out of town. We all do that."

So everyone in the group had access to the staircase. Any one of them could have loosened the step. And that also answered our question about how the archer could have gotten his or her hands on Bart's crossbow and arrows. "Did you ever consider that perhaps *you* were intended to take the fall? Not Bart."

At last I truly had her attention. "No one would dare try to kill me."

"Remember the arrow that nicked your ear." Tinkie pointed to the ear Clarissa had covered with her longer hair. "You've sincerely pissed someone off."

"Who?" Clarissa asked. "That's what I paid you to find out. So far you've been about as useless as teats on a boar hog."

"We're working on it."

"Well, I hope you find something before I'm a dead woman, since you've convinced me I'm a target. Maybe I shouldn't lead the parade this year."

"You're Santa Claus?" Tinkie asked.

"Of course not. I'm the hot elf that stands on the back of the lead convertible and sets the parade in motion. Kind of the drum majorette elf."

I had no doubt. "Clarissa, did you find Kathleen's stocking cap when you were diving in the bottom of the river?"

It was almost as if I'd punched her in the gut. "Absolutely not!"

"You did, and you left it at the Bissonnette House for Darla to find."

She had the grace to look down, but her shame was short-lived. "I didn't. But what if I did? Darla came to town all better than us. We did invite her to join us, but she didn't want to. She said she was a romantic and believed in true love and that we were the antithesis of everything she believed."

That pretty much summed it up, to my way of thinking. "So you thought you'd just leave something from her dead friend. A little memento that might indicate Kathleen was alive?"

"That's really cruel," Tinkie threw in.

"Oh, grow up. I didn't do it, but I see the humor in it."

"I don't. That isn't funny at all, and it had to be you. You were diving. The only one diving other than the police department volunteers." I shook my head. "I'll find out who's after you, and then Tinkie and I are done with you and your group of friends. I don't want to be standing by you when karma finally decides to roll up in your front yard."

"Piddle posh. There's no such thing as karma. That belief, like all other religious superstitions, is a sop to make the poor feel better about their pathetic lives."

I decided to try another tactic. "Who was the police officer whose clothes were scattered around your place?"

"Have you never heard of role playing?" Her mouth opened. "Oh, you saw the uniform and thought it was . . ." She laughed. "You're too easily fooled to be detectives. I was just having a little law-and-order fun before you so rudely interrupted, but it certainly wasn't with a real police officer."

One mystery solved. It was time to move on. "Clarissa, I'd forget riding exposed in the parade tonight."

"I've given that some thought. Nope, I'm doing it. It's my night to shine. No one is going to cheat me out of it."

"Fine." Tinkie and I gathered our coats. "See you tonight. We hope to have an answer for you."

Before we went back to the B and B, we stopped by Sunny Crenshaw's house. It was in the same neighborhood as Rook's Nest. The Italianate design was beautiful, but out of place in the older antebellum neighborhood. Sunny was home and invited us in, but we didn't make it past the foyer before she blocked us. She took her stand in the doorway before I could even ask a question.

"You're wasting your time here. I'm not involved with Clarissa and her games. I don't care what Bart does as long as he doesn't publicly embarrass me—hence the slap you saw me give Bart when I caught him with Tulla. He's on a short leash now. If he steps out on me in public again, I'll divorce him. Believe me, that will hurt him a lot more than it will hurt me."

If Sunny was pretending, she was very practiced at not giving a damn about what her husband did.

"Bart could have been killed in that fall."

"And?" She arched her eyebrows and waited.

"You really don't care," Tinkie said. "You really don't. Why not divorce him?"

For a moment she looked away and I could see that she was tired. "Bart's a habit. And sometimes he's really funny and good company. I've thought of divorcing him, but before I file the papers, I always relent. It's just too much work to find another partner, and I admit I'm a woman who needs a man."

"Do you need him enough to try to kill the competition?" Tinkie asked.

She laughed. "Not that much. I'd rather find a new husband than do a stretch in prison."

I could imagine that under different circumstances, I might actually like Sunny Crenshaw. "Who do you think is behind all of the mayhem? You know it was your husband's crossbow used to shoot at Clarissa."

"I told Bart not to buy that thing. He's never even shot it. He was going hunting with some local men, but Bart doesn't care for the woods or hiding in the bushes.

When it came time for the big hunting trip, he found a convenient excuse not to go. Frankly, anyone could have taken the bow from the garage. Or any number of useless things he's purchased in pursuit of a recreational activity. I honestly don't know what happened to it. I wasn't even aware it was missing. Neither was Bart. He was shocked when the police came to question him about it. Look, Bart has his . . . hobbies, but he isn't a cruel man. And he's not desperate enough to harm anyone. Neither am I. Whatever is going on can be traced squarely back to Clarissa. I don't know what she's done, but someone means to make her pay."

I had the strongest feeling that Sunny was telling the truth. She was a beautiful woman, accomplished, and loaded. Why she would tolerate a husband who had such different values was not a question I could answer. But I didn't believe she was trying to kill the female swingers to protect her marriage.

"I have an appointment in town," she said. "I have to go." She reached over to a table and picked up a business card. "This is my private number. If you call, I'll answer. Right now, though, I have to go."

Tinkie took the card and we found ourselves on the sidewalk. We still had a lot of ground to cover.

We arrived back at the Bissonnette House at two-thirty to find Darla wasn't at home. I remembered the note in the journal. Darla had an assignation at three with a mystery man. Whoever it was didn't impact our case, and Tinkie and I had only a couple of hours before the parade was due to take off. Coleman and the men had asked us to meet at the tourism center, where the parade was to begin. The house was Tennessee Williams's birthplace. If I had time in the morning before we left Columbus, I wanted to take a quick look around.

"Where's Darla?" Tinkie asked when she realized the house was empty.

I explained about the note I'd found in her journal.

"Intriguing. I wonder where the location of the rendezvous might be."

"We can't solve our own case. We don't have time to spy on Darla."

"I'd kind of hoped she and Harold would hit it off," Tinkie said. "What did the note say?"

"Just something about the pull of the moon and the flow of the tides, and something about Artemis."

"Sounds like the beach," Tinkie said.

There was a knock on the front door and I went to open it, feeling only a bit awkward. The young couple standing on the porch—with five pieces of luggage—looked a little shell-shocked. "We need to register."

I knew that the Zinnia gang had taken every single room in the inn. And we had one more night before we were due to check out. Clearly this young couple had made a mistake, but Darla was going to have to sort that.

"Come in. You can put your bags in the parlor," I said. "Tinkie, stir up the fire, please. Darla has guests."

Tinkie peeked around the corner. "To stay here?"

"Uh-huh," I said. I walked over to her. "Darla will have to handle this. We need to find her."

"Pronto. These guys will need to find another accommodation tonight, and that may not be easy to do with Christmas and so many people traveling. The sooner we find Darla, the better."

Tinkie and I scampered out before any more questions were thrown at us. "Where do you think Darla is?"

I pulled out my phone. "Simple enough." But when I called Darla, I got a message that her mailbox was full and to call back later. "That's really strange."

"Maybe we can find her. She couldn't be far."

"She was meeting someone at three." My watch showed three o'clock on the dot. "And since there's no beach here, maybe at the river?"

"Good idea. Her car is still in the garage." Tinkie pointed. "She must have gone on foot."

The obvious place to look was at the edge of the Bissonnette House property, where the zigzagging staircase that clung to the river's bluff led down to the river. When we got to the edge of the lawn, I looked down, feeling only a little of the vertigo that came along with fear of heights. Tinkie grasped the handrail and started down. When I didn't follow, she looked back at me. "Are you coming?"

"Maybe." The whole wooden structure looked pretty rickety to me. When we'd boarded the boat for the flotilla, we'd driven down to the dock. My gut clenched with apprehension at the idea of descending those steps.

"Come on, Sarah Booth. There's someone down on the shore."

Indeed, someone was on the dock where the *Tenn-Tom Queen* was tied up, waiting for someone to repair her propellers. A solitary person paced, as if anxious. I couldn't tell if it was Darla because the person wore a parka with a hoodie obscuring the face, but I was relatively certain it was a woman. Likely Darla. "If I make it down these stairs, I'm never going back up them."

Tinkie only laughed. "You need therapy to get over this fear of heights."

I had a snappy retort about fear of cooking, but I didn't deliver it because I was grasping the handrail in a death grip and forcing my feet to move one at a time onto the stairs. It took all of my concentration to inch forward step by step, slowly going down toward the shore.

When we were nearly to the bottom, I realized that the woman had disappeared from the dock. She'd either entered the boat or taken the road that wound past several other houses with river docks.

"Did you see where she went?" I asked Tinkie when my feet were on solid ground.

"No, she was right there and then she was gone."

"Let's check the boat." I started on deck. "Darla! Darla!" She had to be nearby.

Tinkie started around the wheelhouse to the front of the boat and I was close on her heels. Before I could even say a word, someone barreled around the wheelhouse and straight into Tinkie, knocking my partner into the railing.

"Hey!" I shouted as the person pushed past me, almost knocking me on top of Tinkie. The assailant rushed off the boat and ran down the dock.

"Who the hell was that?" Tinkie asked.

"I don't know. It wasn't Darla."

"Do you think it was someone tampering with the boat?" Tinkie asked. She'd recovered her cool a lot quicker than I would have.

"I think it was someone up to no good. Let's check the boat to be sure Darla isn't injured inside."

We moved forward with caution, and for good reason. When we got into the cabin, it was clear someone had been living on the boat. The bed was rumpled and dirty dishes were stacked on the floor beside the bed. I found a receipt from the Marine Repair Center with an estimate to replace the propellers. It was clear the boat had hit something.

Tinkie came out of the bathroom holding a brush. "Look at this."

The brush was tangled with long red hairs. We looked at each other. For a long time neither of us spoke. "Kathleen has hair that color," Tinkie said.

Suddenly the fishing skiff tucked up on the bank of the river took on new meaning. If Kathleen was indeed alive, she could have swum to the bank and used the boat to make it to a safe dock. But all I had was a suspicion, no evidence.

32

Tinkie and I were both quiet as we left the river behind us. "Kathleen could have been on the boat prior to the Christmas flotilla," I said. "Maybe she was staying on the boat part-time. That would explain the hair in the brush." Which would have to be tested for DNA to be real evidence.

"Gumbo," said Twinkie.

I glanced over at my partner as we walked up the road that would eventually take us up the bank of the river—on a gentler slope—and back to the B and B. We still hadn't found Darla.

"What's gumbo got to do with it?"

"Gumbo, the cat. Kathleen wouldn't spend nights on the boat and leave Gumbo alone, would she?"

Tinkie had a point. I often had to leave Sweetie Pie, Pluto, and the horses because I was working on a case or vacationing with a friend. But I hired someone to live in the house with the pets to keep them company. Gumbo had been left alone until Darla retrieved her. If Kathleen had a choice and had left her animal all alone, then she was not the person I thought she was. Of course, if she was alive—letting everyone believe she'd drowned—she wasn't that person anyway.

"Why would Kathleen pretend to be dead?"

Tinkie's face went completely still. "She's going to kill Clarissa." Tinkie said it with such authority that I knew she was correct. "Her death is the alibi. She came here and started over. She's built a new life so she could pull this off. Once she's done, she'll move somewhere else. She had to be the one who attacked Officer Goode, too. She must have been afraid he had seen her and was going to tell others. She had to silence him, but she didn't want to kill him."

Tinkie was making perfect sense—but we needed a motive. "Why would Kathleen try to kill Clarissa?"

"I don't know, but Kathleen isn't dead, and there's no other reason for her to pretend to be."

"I agree. She isn't dead." There was too much evidence to prove she was alive. Tinkie and I both had suffered some kind of mental block in this regard. We'd been too willing to believe Kathleen would never *pretend* to be dead. Would never put her friends through such a cruel charade. Good people didn't do such things. "There has to be a reason for this game she's playing."

"We really don't know her background."

"We've been sadly neglectful in that regard. We never considered her a viable suspect."

"Darla will let us use her computer. We have to do what we can."

"And we have to know what Darla's role in all of this is," I said. "Kathleen has been on the *Tenn-Tom Queen*, maybe since the flotilla. We don't know if Darla knows she's alive."

"Maybe not," Tinkie said. "Darla could have met someone else today. I mean, who was that stranger that almost knocked me down? We're assuming that note you saw told her to meet at the river. The moon, tidal pull, and Artemis were the clues. For all we know it could be a seafood place. Maybe Darla hasn't even been back to the boat since the flotilla. We don't know that she knows anything." Tinkie's eyes widened. "And if she was going to meet Kathleen, who's to say Kathleen hasn't harmed her or taken her prisoner. In all the time we've been here, have you known Darla to leave the B and B for longer than two hours?"

She was right. "So let's find out."

It was a longer walk around the bluff to get back to the B and B, but we still had several hours before it was time to meet the men at the parade. Huffing a little from the incline, we made it. Cece and Millie were still hitting the local high points, and the young couple who'd come to stay at the inn had left their bags in the parlor and gone out. We had the entire place to ourselves.

Tinkie went to the computer and I began searching the bookcase. I needed to reread the note I'd found. I should have photographed it, but I'd never considered it was evidence of anything except a romantic tryst.

"I'm going to make some coffee," I told Tinkie.

"Great idea."

The first thing I saw in the kitchen was the journal that had been on the parlor shelf. A ragged piece of paper was sticking out of it. I opened the flap. This was a different note, but the message was clear and explicit: "Stop chasing me or Darla will die. Go home to Zinnia."

I wordlessly took the note, using salad tongs, to Tinkie. She looked up at me, fear in her eyes. "Do you think Kathleen wrote this and that she would really hurt Darla?"

"I don't know, but I'm calling the police. We have to now."

"Wait!" Tinkie grabbed my arm. "You might get Darla killed. If it is Kathleen and she doesn't want you and me investigating, she sure isn't going to want the police."

"Damn." I was caught on the horns of a dilemma. Even if I just consulted Coleman, he would feel obligated to call the police—and that could very well be the smart call. I just didn't know what the best thing to do was. At last I came to a decision. "You're right. We can't call the law. What can we do?"

"If we assume that this person, whether it is Kathleen or someone pretending to be her, has Darla, where might she be?"

"What did you find on Kathleen's background?"

"I don't think anything she told us was true. There doesn't seem to be any record of Kathleen Beesley until the last three years, when she bought a house in Columbus."

"No records of school or anything?"

"None."

"Driver's license?"

"She was issued one here three years ago. She passed

the test, which means she took it without transferring a license from somewhere else. I can't run the background checks we can at home, because Darla doesn't have the software."

"And we can't ask Coleman to do it for us." I arched one eyebrow. "Can we?"

"No, we can't," Tinkie said. "Unless we pretend Darla asked us to find the information so she can write Kathleen's obituary."

Oh, Tinkie was bad! The best kind of bad.

"In fact," Tinkie said, "we can call DeWayne or Budgie to do this for us without involving Coleman."

"*You* can do that." I wasn't about to cross that line with Coleman. He was easygoing, but that was a bridge too far.

"Okay." Tinkie pulled out her cell phone and placed the call to Zinnia. DeWayne answered, and she put in our request, asking if there were any police records for Kathleen Beesley.

"How are the critters?" I asked in the background, trying to sound normal, to act as I would act if I weren't deceiving Coleman.

"Everyone is good. Pluto is really, really miffed at you. Sweetie Pie likes fried chicken tenders. Miss Scrapiron let me ride her without any quibbles. All is good."

"That warms my heart. If you make my dog fat, I'm going to come after you."

"Sweetie Pie will always be svelte, and she will be glad to see you tomorrow. I'll get after this info as soon as I finish up the paperwork on an armed robbery at the vape shop. Tell Coleman no one was hurt and I'll be following a lead as soon as I hang up. Budgie's got my back."

"I'll tell him." I was disappointed DeWayne couldn't drop everything and look up the information I needed, but stopping local crime had to come before helping out a couple of private dicks.

I hung up. "I wonder who would know more about Kathleen's history?"

"No one who is going to help us," Tinkie wisely said. "Did you give Darla Kathleen's journal?"

"No." I still had it. I'd leafed through it, but it was poetry, scribblings of emotions and thoughts, even a couple of grocery lists. Nothing in it seemed useful.

"Maybe there's a clue in there."

I hated trying to decipher cryptic clues, but Tinkie was rather good at it. "We've got an hour before we have to be downtown for the parade. Let's give it a try."

I got the journal that I'd taken from Kathleen's house and we began going through it. I'd started, originally, at the back, thinking the more recent entries might give us more information. This time we started at the front, wondering if we could find a clue to Kathleen's past.

"Look at this reference to what has to be suicide. Like she intended to go overboard into the water," Tinkie said. "'The river pulls the flow of goods from the north down to New Orleans, a city born in a crescent of river. We are water born. The river is my mother. Now that I am orphaned, I return to her sweet embrace.'"

"You think she meant to drown herself?" I flipped through a few pages. "That was three years ago."

Tinkie shrugged. "It could mean anything. It could be part of a poem that was never finished." She flipped through a few more pages.

"This one is dated January three years ago. 'The

lioness, betrayed and beaten, has been killed, yet no one takes notice. A mother is gone without even a whimper of justice. Before she is through, C. will kill the lion. It is her nature. I wonder how she'll accomplish it.'"

One page over. "'Soon the cycle of life—and death—will continue. The huntress will arise from the stars. All sins finally come home to roost.'"

It struck me then. "Aurora Bresland was killed in January. Her husband died the next month while hunting deer. That's the lioness and the lion. And Artemis is the goddess of the hunt. I just can't figure out what any of this means."

Tinkie tapped the page with her finger. "It fits, yes, and we considered the idea that Clarissa had killed both Breslands to inherit. But what is this to Kathleen? As far as we know she doesn't have any connection to Oxford or the Breslands."

I pointed out the use of the word *mother* in the earlier passage. "Could that be the connection? Are Kathleen and Darla somehow related, maybe to the Breslands?"

"That's just it. We don't know. But we don't really know anything about Kathleen Beesley. According to what we can find out, she didn't exist up until a few years ago."

"About the same time that Aurora and Johnny Bresland died so unexpectedly."

I still had the number of Deputy Len Ford of Tippah County in my phone. I made the call, even though it was the Saturday before Christmas. He answered with a warm hello. "I'm on my way over to Columbus," he said. "Please tell Millie I'll see her at the parade."

Well, okay then—now that we had Millie's personal business out of the way. "Deputy, when you were investigating Johnny Bresland's shooting death, did he have any relatives? Any at all?"

"He had none."

I admired that he didn't ask why. "Did Aurora have any relatives?"

"Aurora Bresland had been married previously. When she was very young. I believe there was a child that was put up for adoption."

"Did you look for her?"

"Remember, I didn't investigate Aurora's death, but I did talk to the deputy who did. The woman who inherited, Clarissa Olson, said that the Breslands had severed all ties with the child. There was nothing for her in Aurora's will, no way to find her or contact her. No information about the adoption agency—that's what the Lafayette County sheriff's office told me. I did interview Clarissa Olson, and she said it was a past better left buried," he said. "To be honest, it always kind of nagged at me, but a lot of people who put children up for adoption never want to look back."

He was correct about that. "Did anyone ever say the name of the child?"

"I don't know if they knew it. Ms. Olson said it was a part of Mrs. Bresland's past that was never mentioned. It brought great distress to her."

"Did you happen to know Aurora's first husband's name?"

"I'm sorry. If it was ever mentioned, it didn't stick with me."

"Deputy Ford, I need a big favor. I need you to call Deeter Odom, the chancery clerk in Oxford, Mississippi.

I need the marriage license information for Mr. and Mrs. Bresland. I need Aurora's legal name on the license. And I need it today."

"I'll make the call, but I can't guarantee Odom will cooperate. It's the Saturday before Christmas."

"It can't wait until Monday. Seriously, someone may die here today." I wasn't laying it on thick. Death was an imminent possibility, especially if Clarissa Olson intended to lead the parade standing on the back of a convertible and prancing around like a drum majorette. She would be a standing duck.

"I'll see if I can rouse Mr. Odom," Deputy Ford said. "Just tell Millie she's going to owe me a free lunch when I make it over to Zinnia."

"The lunch is on Delaney Detective Agency," I said. "Thank you."

Tinkie had a question for me when I hung up the phone. "Are you going to call Clarissa and warn her about the danger?"

"No," I said. "I'm not." I gave it a beat. "You can do that since you thought of it. But she won't take your call, I'll bet. I'll call Officer Goode and let him know Darla has disappeared. I don't want to involve law officers, but now we have to."

There was the sound of a door closing. "Someone should have told me I disappeared." Darla stepped into her small office.

"Thank goodness you're okay." Tinkie rushed to hug her. "We've been worried, Darla."

"I had to meet a friend at the River Moon Café. Is something wrong?"

"You had some guests show up." I told her about the honeymooning couple.

"Oh, dear, they weren't supposed to arrive until tomorrow, *after* you left to return home. They were my last booking for a few weeks."

"Darla have you been down to your boat lately?"

"No, why? The repair guys from upriver were supposed to come down and tow the *Tenn-Tom Queen* back to their business. They need to dry-dock her to see to the propeller repairs and make sure there's no damage to the hull."

"Did they determine what happened to the boat?" I asked.

She shrugged. "I hit something submerged in the river. It was an accident." She frowned. "Why are you so interested in the boat?"

"Someone has been living on the *Tenn-Tom Queen*."

"No." Her fists clenched at her sides. "No. That's not right."

"I'm sorry, but Tinkie and I were down at the dock and someone ran into us as they were departing the boat. They'd obviously been living there. Dirty dishes, bed used." I tried to limit the details yet paint the proper picture.

"Who's been living there?" Darla went into the kitchen, and I could hear her running water, but we could still carry on a conversation. Tinkie looked at me and mimed *Show her the note?* I shook my head.

"We didn't get a good look," Tinkie said. "They were desperate not to be caught." She hesitated. "We thought it might be—"

"Probably a young person," I said. "Someone who found shelter and just took advantage." I truly didn't want to bring up Kathleen's name. Now that Darla was safely home—and hadn't been colluding with Kathleen—maybe it was best to let that sleeping dog lie. At least for the moment. Until we found out more about Kathleen.

"Are you going to the parade tonight?" Tinkie asked Darla.

"I had planned to, but I guess I'll find a place for those two new guests. I honestly don't know how the date got mixed up, but since they're here, the details don't really matter, do they?"

"Darla, how did you meet Kathleen?"

Darla came out of the kitchen with a tray of coffee for us. "I met her at the farmer's market maybe three years ago. She'd just moved to town, and we started talking over some homegrown tomatoes. I'd just bought the Bissonnette House and renovations were under way. Kathleen had some experience as a caterer, and I hired her on the spot to help me when I opened. From there, we became friends. She didn't want to work for me, but she liked helping me."

"How did she make a living?" I asked.

"She'd retired as a hedge fund manager. She did pretty well, meaning she had income and never seemed to lack for anything she wanted. Bought her house and a new Lexus. She seemed so happy."

"Except for being a little lonely," Tinkie said softly.

"I didn't see that. Those awful swingers seemed to think she had a crush on Bart Crenshaw, but I don't think so. Kathleen just wanted to be seen. To be truly seen. To be valued. That is the one thing Clarissa and her brood can't give. They can't acknowledge someone who is just kind. It terrifies them."

"Just be careful tonight," Tinkie said. "After the arrow incident on mumming night, use extra caution. Any idea who would have a reason to kill Clarissa?"

"I honestly don't."

"If the arrow was meant for someone else, any suggestion who that might be?"

"I'd guess Tulla Tarbutton, but it could have been Bricey or even Sunny. Maybe Bart. Who knows? It doesn't take much these days for someone to foster a grudge. Any leads?" Darla asked.

"I don't know," I said. "If I find out anything, I'll let you know."

"If you find out who it is, I'll pay for their archery lessons." She forced a smile. "Now you two better get your coats and head down to the tourism center. Dress warmly."

"Will do." We grabbed coats, mufflers, gloves, and hats. It wasn't bitter, but it was plenty cold. We'd meet the men at the tourism center and then find a good place along the parade route to watch. This was the last event of our Christmas vacation. We'd be back in Zinnia shortly after lunch the next day. And I would be glad.

33

Night had fallen as the parade began to line up. The tourism center was closed, so there was no touring the birthplace of Tennessee Williams. But some wiseacre down the street was bellowing "Stella! Stella!" as an homage to Williams's brilliant *Streetcar Named Desire*.

"Where are our men?" Cece asked. She and Millie had found us with ease. The four of us were huddled in a clump at the head of the parade. It would take another thirty minutes for the line of floats, pickup trucks, marching bands, and the fire truck holding Santa and Mrs. Claus to organize into a line. At the very front was a convertible with Clarissa Olson, dressed as a sexy elf, standing in the back seat. She was ordering people around, per usual.

"Clarissa, you should rethink this," I said. "Someone is out to kill you."

"Piddle posh. Let them try."

She was either stubborn or stupid or both, and I was tired. "Okay. We've been paid and you've been warned. Now it's on you."

"Sarah Booth!" Coleman was coming straight at me, along with Oscar, Jaytee, and Harold. Each man was holding a black cloth in his hand. "Come with us."

Coleman didn't give me a chance to refuse. He tied the black bandanna around my eyes and hustled me down the street. Behind me I could hear Tinkie, Millie, and Cece complaining about not being able to see.

We stopped, and Coleman removed the blindfold. I couldn't believe what was in front of me. It was a float, a grand float covered in blinking lights, poinsettias, a big decorated Christmas tree, and four rocking chairs around a fake fireplace. It was the perfect Christmas scene with a big sign: THE ZINNIA QUEEN BEES DO CHRISTMAS RIGHT. Beside each chair was a huge box of beads, Christmas decorations, trinkets, and candy for us to toss.

"All aboard," Oscar said as he handed Tinkie up onto the float. "Ladies, Merry Christmas!"

"This is what you've been doing all this week? Building a float?" Cece gave Jaytee a huge kiss right in front of everyone. People in the crowd applauded.

"There's even a microphone for Cece to sing," Jaytee said when he could talk. "I'll be up there to play the harmonica for her."

"Don't let Sarah Booth near that microphone," Coleman said as he swung me up onto the platform.

"Very funny." I had no intention of singing anyway.

I was already calculating that the float was the perfect vantage point to watch the crowd for any would-be archers. Clarissa in her convertible was only one marching band ahead of our float. I looked around the float at all the great decorating and hard work the men had done. It was phenomenal. I leaned down to whisper in Coleman's ear. "Thank you. This is the best Christmas present ever."

"Better than Ireland?"

"Different better. You do have a knack for giving great gifts."

"Do I get a present tonight?" he asked wickedly.

"Santa will just have to see about that." I kissed his cheek.

"Line up, line up. We're starting to move." The man organizing the parade came by with a bullhorn trying to get the unruly participants into shape.

Luckily the four Zinnia Queens were seated in the rockers when the float lurched forward, and then we were off. The men had gone to find a good location on the street to watch the parade. Their work was done! Now it was up to us to fling the trinkets and candy and celebrate the Christmas season.

We'd made it a half-dozen blocks when the band in front of us began to play "Rocking Around the Christmas Tree" and Clarissa stepped onto the back of the car to dance. She had exceptional balance. I had to give her that. And she was also dumber than a rock. She was a perfect target if anyone cared to shoot an arrow, or something more deadly, at her. With a shotgun, the assailant didn't even need great aim.

Tinkie, Millie, and Cece were having a blast hurling prizes at the crowd, who seemed to really love our float.

And when Jaytee stepped forward and began to blow the harmonica and Cece picked up the song, the crowd was riveted. A group of young people who knew the song followed behind, singing the chorus. It was wonderful and crazy and thrilling. I looked at my friends, and they were glowing with happiness. In each one, I could see the child that had always believed in Christmas miracles. This float and the parade and just the sheer insanity of the surprise our men had sprung on us made this a Christmas to remember.

Up ahead, the band switched to "Frosty the Snowman" and Clarissa was going to town shaking her booty. I tossed a handful of red and green necklaces to the crowd as I watched her gyrate. She did have a body to be proud of.

I saw her stumble at the same time I heard a scream in the crowd. Clarissa staggered on top of the car as the crowd hushed for a split second before it roared back to life and several people ran forward to catch Clarissa before she hit the pavement.

I couldn't see what had happened and I hadn't heard a shot. The parade ground to a halt, and Coleman and Officer Goode rushed to the car where Clarissa had been dancing. Coleman turned back to face me as sirens began to wail and the throng of Christmas celebrants dispersed in all directions.

"What happened?" I asked Coleman when he was close enough to hear me.

"Clarissa was shot."

"Gunshot?"

He shook his head. "Arrow. Exactly like the one the other night. Not fatal, but she was hit in her gut."

Up at the lead car, Tulla Tarbutton had rushed to

help Clarissa. Too late I saw movement across from the car. A woman stepped out from behind a tree and aimed a crossbow.

"Tulla!" I screamed. She stood frozen like a deer as the arrow buried itself in her shoulder. People everywhere began to scatter. I stood, mouth agape. I knew who the shooter was. Kathleen Beesley. I'd seen her clearly before she'd faded back into the crowd.

"Sarah Booth!"

Someone was calling my name from the opposite side of the road. Cece had jumped off the float and was photographing the mayhem. Millie and Tinkie were huddled together in fierce conversation.

"Sarah Booth!"

I scanned the other side of the road and saw her—but it couldn't be. Kathleen Beesley was waving at me from the back of the line that crowded the road. That was impossible. I'd seen her on the other side of the road with a crossbow. Now she held only an umbrella.

"Kathleen!" I yelled her name but she didn't look at me. Tinkie and Millie looked over and saw her.

"Kathleen! Kathleen!" They began yelling at her.

She looked at us, turned, and faded into the darkness on the fringe of the crowd.

"She isn't dead!" Tinkie said to me. "We were right."

"There are two of her," I said. "I saw her on the other side of the road with a crossbow. She's the one who shot Clarissa and probably Tulla."

"That's not possible." Tinkie was just blunt. "Not unless she has a twin."

"I know." It didn't make any sense. Kathleen had disappeared, presumed dead. Now she was back in duplicate.

"Let's go!" Tinkie grabbed my hand as she jumped off the float and into the street, pulling me with her. "Tell Coleman we're on the trail of a ghost," Tinkie said to Millie before she dragged me into the crowd of people.

34

If Kathleen was trying to hide from us, she did a terrible job of it. Ten minutes after we jumped her trail, we found her in a dark corner of a dive bar drinking tequila shooters. I wondered if she'd somehow hit her head and lost her memory, or perhaps suffered from a case of dissociative identity disorder, where an alternate personality had emerged. This tequila-chugging mama in tight leggings and a body-hugging sweater and boots was not the woman I'd met in Darla's kitchen.

"We've been hunting everywhere for you," Tinkie said to her. "You should have let us know you were alive."

She threw back another shot of tequila and ignored Tinkie. That was the wrong thing to do after the week we'd had. My fingers curled in her abundant hair and I twisted until I had her attention. "Where the hell have you been? We've been worried and Darla is sick with all the nightmares she's been having thinking that you drowned."

"Don't mind me, I'm just the diversion," she said.

"You're going to jail," I said. "You can't jerk law officers around and have volunteers spend hours looking for you when all along you were safe."

"I don't think I've broken any laws. Not yet, anyway."

"Not broken any laws? You shot Clarissa and Tulla with arrows." I was furious.

"Did I?"

"You hid a boat in the marsh along the river, and when you knocked Clarissa off the *Tenn-Tom Queen*, you swam to the boat and let everyone think you'd drowned."

"That's not illegal, unless you can prove I deliberately hit Clarissa, and you can't prove that." Kathleen knocked back another shot.

"Why? Why did you do it?" Tinkie demanded.

"I didn't do anything."

"Right," Tinkie said. "Tell that to the law when they get here." She dialed 911.

My phone rang, and I answered, expecting Coleman. "Ms. Delaney, it's Deputy Ford. I have that information you wanted."

"Aurora Bresland's maiden name?"

"Yes, it was Lofton."

"What?" I didn't believe what I'd heard.

"Lofton. I hope that helps."

"Are you with Coleman?"

"He's assisting the EMTs. Clarissa Olson has a severe stomach wound, but the other one, Tarbutton, she's going to be fine."

"Is Officer Goode with you?"

"Yes, why?"

"May I speak with him?"

"Sure."

A few seconds later Goode answered.

"The shooter is Darla Lofton. She's wearing a red wig and is made up to resemble Kathleen Beesley. You have to find Darla and arrest her. And we have Kathleen Beesley here at Dirty Harry's bar."

"Are you sure about this?" Goode asked.

"Positive."

"We'll pick Lofton up."

I turned my attention back to Kathleen. She shrugged. "Clarissa poisoned Darla's mother and then had her father shot. So she could inherit everything."

I'd figured that out. "You couldn't have turned this over to the law?"

She shook her head. "Some scores you have to settle on your own. All of them. All the cheaters had to pay."

"But you were in cahoots with Tulla Tarbutton. You hired that contractor to fill up Bricey's car with cement. We have it on video."

"Yes." She didn't deny it. "I used Tulla's money to make Bricey pay. They all had to pay, and pay hard. It was quite the game to come up with revenge plots and make them pay for their own punishment."

"And Bart Crenshaw? You could have broken his neck."

"Bart was collateral damage. He wasn't supposed to take a fall."

"You sabotaged the step thinking Clarissa would tumble down the stairs." It was so clear now that I had the pieces in place. "Why, Kathleen?"

"I love Darla. You don't go through what we've been through without learning what's important in life. We've been friends since the orphanage. More than friends. We're sisters. We honor that bond of sisterhood above all else. I'd do anything for Darla." She sat up. "Clarissa had it coming, and so did the rest of them. I don't regret a single thing. Darla and I hunted them together, because it was justice."

"Artemis," I said. It was the clue I hadn't fully understood. Artemis was the goddess of the hunt, the protector of children and women, the deity that honored the scared bond of sisterhood. I finally understood.

While Cece, Millie, Oscar, and Jaytee manned the float as the parade continued, Tinkie and I waited until Jerry Goode arrived to take Kathleen into custody. Darla had also been apprehended. Clarissa and Tulla were in the hospital, and initial reports were that they'd recover. Coleman was helping the Columbus PD with their paperwork and filling in the gaps. We'd resolved the case, and no one in Columbus was dead. It wasn't the cleanest outcome we'd ever had, but it was plenty good enough for me and Tinkie. At least it was over.

The next morning Rex had the limo ready for us by ten o'clock. We'd gone back to the Bissonnette House for our final night. Without Darla there, the place was a shell of what it had been. Tinkie had managed to place the newlywed couple in another inn and we had the place to ourselves.

I was still wrapping my head around the relationship between Darla and Kathleen, the close bond that had formed between the women at the orphanage where Darla had lived for most of her childhood. She'd found out about the murder of her biological mother only in the last few years. Before Darla could find the courage to meet her mother, Aurora had been murdered. With all chance of knowing her birth parents taken from her, Darla had set about to seek revenge.

"Ready to go home?" Coleman asked as he hefted our bags into the trunk.

"I am. More than ready." I looked back at the inn, wondering what would become of it. "It's been a fabulous vacation. With a few drawbacks."

"Our time together was fabulous."

"It was." I stood on tiptoe to give him a gentle kiss.

He and the men loaded our bags as I made one final phone call to check on Clarissa at the hospital. She'd made it through surgery and was expected to recover. Tulla had gone home with her arm in a sling. No one died, at least not in Columbus.

Coleman put his arm around my shoulders. "Sorry it ended this way. I really liked Darla and Kathleen."

"As did I." It had given me a lot to think about, how old wounds festered and infected the entire body. "I don't blame Darla for wanting revenge. I don't. If Clarissa truly killed Darla's mother and her father, I can't fault Darla for wanting to kill her."

"Deputy Ford says he's reopening Johnny Bresland's shooting death. He believes Clarissa paid another hunter to do it."

"Do you think he can find the evidence?"

"I do." Coleman rumpled my hair.

"And what about Aurora?"

"The deputy over in Lafayette County said they were reopening that case. It will mean disinterment, but if there was poison, they should be able to find it."

"I can't help but wonder why Darla didn't speak up sooner," I said.

"The cases in both deaths were closed quickly. I'm not faulting the investigators. There was no reason to believe it was other than suicide and accident," he said. "An older woman whose husband is cheating on her in one case. Suicide isn't that far-fetched. Then with Johnny Bresland, a hunting accident. It happens more than people know. It adds up."

"Except for the inheritance. It was right there when we finally went looking. Clarissa was smart to kill the Breslands in two different jurisdictions."

"You're right about that."

"Will Clarissa be charged?"

"Goode has assured me that if the evidence points to her guilt, she'll be turned over to the proper authorities and prosecuted."

"And Kathleen?" The last time I'd seen her, she was being led away in handcuffs.

"Same for her. And Tulla Tarbutton also. She was involved in duping an innocent man into committing a felony."

The others came out of the house. Tinkie locked the front door of the Bissonnette House and put the key under the mat for one of Goode's fellow officers to retrieve. She picked up the kitty carrier. Oscar hadn't stood a chance trying to halt her adoption of Gumbo. Soon the Richmond household would be brimming with pets and a child.

"Our work here is done," Tinkie said, putting the kitty carrier in the limo. "Next year, no matter where we travel or what's going on, we are *not* taking a case."

"Amen to that," Coleman and Oscar said together. They were acting way too much like Tinkie and me.

Millie picked up her bag before Coleman could load it. "Len is going to take me home," she said. She looked at the deputy and her smile held only happiness.

"We'll want details when we get back to Zinnia," Cece said in a whisper loud enough for everyone to hear and for the Tippah County deputy, who took the bag from Millie's hand, to blush to the roots of his hair.

"Then we're off. We still have to get home in time to cook Christmas dinner," Harold said. "The party is at my house."

"But first a little Christmas Eve fun," Coleman said as he patted my butt. "I can't wait."

35

Coleman was sound asleep when I got up Christmas morning. I lit a fire in the parlor and turned the stove on to heat. I wouldn't attempt scratch biscuits, but I'd bought some heat-and-serve biscuits from a little bakery in Columbus.

As I prepared a special Christmas morning breakfast for my lover, my thoughts were on the treacheries of revenge. I'd won my bet with Coleman, and last night he'd gone a long way toward paying off his debt. In a way, though, the whole mess that Darla had set in motion was also about money. She felt cheated out of her due. Part of that rested with Aurora, though, not just Clarissa. And whatever sympathy I'd had for Darla, I lost when I thought of Kathleen. She was a decent person who'd become a criminal because of her love for Darla. It was all just so depressing.

I'd left my cell phone plugged in to the charger on the kitchen counter, and just as I reached for it, "Unfaithful" began to play. My phone was possessed by Rihanna. This was the Christmas that just kept on giving.

I backed away from the phone and it stopped. "Great." I picked it up and examined it. Nothing unusual there. Not until the Eagles took it over. "Lyin' Eyes" started up.

"Nope, nada, stop!" I turned it off. It came back on, still in the Eagles mode.

Suddenly the kitchen fell away from me and I was standing on a street in New York City. The wind was literally howling, and debris was everywhere, blowing in mini-cyclones. I saw a beautiful woman with an armload of packages struggling against the wind. Suddenly she stumbled and fell. When she stood up, her knee was bleeding.

I knew instantly what movie I'd fallen into, *Unfaithful*. And I knew who the actress, Diane Lane, really was. Jitty was welcoming me back home with her usual torment. The movie scene faded away and I was back in the kitchen with Jitty.

"You never know when temptation is going to strike," Diane/Jitty said.

"It isn't the sex that does the damage, it's the lying," I responded.

"No, cheating on someone who loves you does its own kind of damage."

Jitty was right. "Cheating is a bad thing," I agreed.

"And sometimes irresistible."

"What has you in such a charitable mood?" Jitty was seldom forgiving of the foibles of humanity—living humanity at least. And she was pretty intolerant of the shenanigans of some of the residents in the Great Beyond. Jitty believed in doing your duty and shouldering your responsibilities.

"It's Christmas," Jitty said. As beautiful as Diane Lane was, when Jitty took over and Diane faded away, she was even more lovely. And she was wearing my favorite ugly Christmas sweater and some awful plaid sweatpants that I'd been hunting for two weeks.

"You're filled with the Christmas spirit?" I asked.

"I'd rather be filled with some good vittles." She waved a hand at my cell phone and Dean Martin began to croon "Winter Wonderland."

"People make so much trouble for themselves," I said as I took a dozen eggs from the refrigerator. If I hurried, I might be able to serve Coleman breakfast in bed. We had plenty of time before we had to be at Harold's.

"You hit that nail on the head," Jitty agreed.

I glanced at her to see if she was okay. She normally never agreed with me. It was a matter of principle with her. I cracked the eggs, whipped them with a dollop of milk, and put them in a hot skillet. In two shakes of a lamb's tail I had breakfast done and on a tray for Coleman, complete with a red carnation and a candy cane.

"What will you do for lunch?" I asked Jitty. I had a sudden pang of sorrow for her.

"I got my own dinner to go to. Lots of people there, you know."

"My parents?" I smiled at the thought of that Christmas dinner. Aunt Loulane, my great-great-grandma Alice, the various uncles, aunts, and crazy cousins who'd gone before me.

"Your mama said to tell you she loves you."

I felt the tears behind my eyelids. "I know."

"And your daddy says to make that Coleman give you a Taser."

"I'm hoping there's one under the tree." It was just like my daddy to think about the practical aspects of safety.

"Go feed that man," Jitty said as she began slowly to fade. "I'll be here when you get back."

That was a promise I intended to hold her to. Just as I picked up the tray, Sweetie Pie came through the doggie door, with Pluto on her heels. They followed me up to the bedroom, where they knew Coleman would share the bounty of his breakfast. And I would bask in the holiday glow of true love.

Acknowledgments

Books take a lot of work, from the original idea and writing to the editing, art, and distribution. Thanks to my wonderful team at St. Martin's Press, my agent Marina Young, the booksellers who shelve my books, and the readers who have allowed me to write about Sarah Booth and the Zinnia gang for more than two decades. Another thanks to the residents of Columbus, a truly lovely Mississippi city.

Turn the page for a sneak peek at

Independent Bones

the next Sarah Booth Delaney mystery
by Carolyn Haines, available now in hardcover
from Minotaur Books!

1

The first scattering of sycamore leaves tumble across the grass in front of me as I walk with my PI partner and friend, Tinkie Richmond. We cross the newly christened "Erkwell Park" in the heart of Zinnia, Mississippi. Tinkie and I are at the grand opening of the park, a space donated and supported by our good friend, Harold Erkwell. A playground and entertainment center are much needed in our county, and Harold took it on as a personal mission. While parks have not been a high priority in a poor state, Harold donated all the funding to create this little bit of heaven on the outskirts of our bustling Delta town.

"Harold worked on this all summer," Tinkie says as we admire the landscaping of native trees and a host of flowering shrubs that will be Nirvana for butterflies and bees next spring and summer. She points as she talks. "Swing sets, slides, a splash pad, tennis courts, that adorable putt-putt course with boll weevils." She sighs. "My baby is going to love coming here."

I hold my peace. Tinkie, who is pregnant, and as big around as she is tall, looks like she might pop out a two-year-old ready to lift weights and pole-vault.

"I know you're thinking it, so you might as well say it," she says.

"That baby is going to be born with teeth." I grin to take the sting out. This baby is the thing Tinkie wants most in life and all of her friends are anxiously awaiting the birth of the next generation's Queen Bee of the Delta. Even Tinkie's parents, who have been touring Europe for what seems like an eternity, are coming home for the big event, which should happen in two weeks. Tinkie is going to produce a little Scorpio—watch out, world!

The sunny breeze is soft and teases Tinkie's sun-glitzed curls as we watch children and adults play in this wonderful green space. Some forty yards away is a dais with a speaker system. A striking woman with abundant black curls, dark eyes, and red lipstick takes the stage. I didn't realize Harold had planned speeches.

"Who is that?" I ask Tinkie. She knows every woman in the Delta, their pedigree, their political persuasion, and their moral character.

"I've never seen her," Tinkie admits. "But I can take a guess. She must be that professor of Greek literature who's writing a book. She rented the old Compton house not far from Cece. Her name is Alala Diakos."

"She's intriguing." With her perfect posture and toned body, she projects power.

"I've read some of her articles. She's a force to be reckoned with, but I'm not sure Zinnia will be receptive to her . . . philosophy."

"Which is what?" I've never heard of the woman.

"Men who abuse women should be exterminated with the utmost efficiency. Hopefully, by a mob of angry women."

I glance at my friend. "And you disagree with that?"

She laughs. "Nope. But, I just wouldn't say it out loud. She's been giving speeches around the Delta and she's stirred up some hot protest from the Neanderthal contingency." Tinkie glances around the park, where folks have begun to gather at the dais. "Looks like she could start some trouble here."

"In Zinnia? You think there are people who support men who abuse women?"

Tinkie stops and frowns. "Of course there are. We just aren't friends with them. Look under any rock, though, and you'll find a man who thinks males should be able to control women. You know Mississippi didn't vote to ratify the Nineteenth Amendment until 1984."

That tidbit stops me in my tracks. "Are you serious?"

"Deadly serious. Harold and Oscar were approving home loans for women back in the 1990s when other banks wouldn't. If a woman didn't have a husband or a daddy to cosign, a lot of banks wouldn't loan her money. Financially, even today, women are second-class citizens."

I didn't have to respond. The Greek professor with the flashing eyes begins to talk. She introduces herself and explains her presence in Zinnia. She's rented a house where she can write in peace and draft her nonfiction book, *The Moon Rises*, the story of the fight for women's equality.

Dr. Diakos says, "Until we have equal pay and equal say, we are not equal citizens." The statement draws applause from the crowd gathered around the dais to hear her talk, mostly younger women and a few men. Dr. Diakos obviously has a local following.

The professor continues. "Basic fact: retired women are twice as likely to live in poverty as retired men."

"Because they aren't smart enough to manage money!" a man in camo shouts. He stands defiantly at the back of the crowd. "Women need a man to manage their business. That's the fact *you* need to grasp."

I didn't have to ask Tinkie who the man was. We both recognized Curtis Miller, a well-known domestic abuser who Coleman had arrested at least five times. Unfortunately, Miller's wife, Tansy, had refused repeatedly to take legal action. Even now she shifted to take a protective stance in front of her husband, who outweighed her by at least sixty pounds.

"That Tansy doesn't have sense enough to pour piss out of a boot," Tinkie said. "Look at her. Like she's going to go all Rambo on anyone who comes at Curtis."

I shook my head in disbelief and disgust. Curtis had broken her arms at least twice, fractured her eye socket, bitten off part of her ear, and broken her fingers. In a town like Zinnia, everyone knew the dirty details of their marriage and the pattern of violence. But not even Coleman could persuade Tansy Miller to press charges or leave Curtis.

Dr. Diakos ignored the heckling. "Women still shoulder most of the household chores, even if the woman also holds a job."

"That's because cooking and cleaning are women's work," Miller yelled out. "Get over it and get in the kitchen where you belong. If you had a man to keep you satisfied, you wouldn't be yowling in the public park like a cat in heat."

I quietly dialed Coleman. When he answered, I just said, "Better get over to the park. It's going to get bloody. Bring the deputies."

"On the way."

I set my phone to video so I could document what was likely to be a physical encounter as the female supporters of Dr. Diakos began to move toward Miller.

"Y'all better leave my husband alone." Tansy stepped out in front of her husband. "Go on, shoo!"

I thought of a mouse defending a lion. And she was sporting a black eye to boot. Some unfortunate women had no concept of how a real relationship worked, where partners were equal. Too often women caught in the web of men who were bullies had grown up in families where the pattern played out again and again. No matter how smart or talented, they'd find themselves trapped. Tansy's situation was tragic.

As the crowd quickly began to turn into a mob, I saw a flash of wiry gray and white hair on four legs. Oh, how well I knew that devious little fiend. As if things weren't hectic enough, Roscoe Erkwell, Harold's no good, troublemaking, bruise-mashing canine was right in the middle of everything. And Harold was nowhere to be seen. The dog ran to a parked truck with giant mud tires. Someone had left the door open and he hopped up in the seat. When he jumped out, he had a lacy red thong in his mouth flapping in the breeze.

"Roscoe!" Tinkie and I called simultaneously. "Come here!"

Per usual, Roscoe completely ignored us. He ran up

to Tansy Miller and dropped the panties at her feet. Her eyes went big and round and her mouth followed. She picked up the thong with fingertips and held it up, then turned to look at her husband. "Those are Moody Moody's panties. I recognize her getup from the Silver Stallion men's club. How did they get in your truck, Curtis?"

His response was a backhand.

And that's when the fight started. Whether he was bright enough to realize it or not, Curtis Miller had stepped into a fire ant mound. The women, as if reacting to a command, advanced on him all at once, kicking, spitting, and screaming. All hell broke loose. I glanced up at the dais, where the good professor stood with a satisfied look on her face. This was exactly what she'd hoped for, or so it seemed.

Coleman and both deputies, who'd arrived in the nick of time, waded into the group and started sorting it out. Curtis was on the ground and the women had done a number on him. He held a tooth in his hand and looked like he was about to cry. Typical bully. I waved DeWayne over. He held two struggling and cursing women, one under each arm.

"Curtis started it," I told DeWayne.

"I'll get some cuffs on him when I can turn these two brawlers loose. Put a foot on his back until I get back."

I was happy to oblige.

Tinkie started into the fray, but I snatched her wrist and drew her out of danger. "You cannot mix it up with those people," I warned her. "Now stay here with Curtis. I have to find Roscoe. Someone is going to kill that dog because he has his snout in everyone's personal business."

"Can I sit on Curtis?" Tinkie asked. The red spots in her cheeks told me she was stoked and ready for combat.

"Whatever floats your boat," I told her, straining on my tiptoes to keep Roscoe in sight.

"I want to break his face," Tinkie said.

I sighed. "Wanting something never killed anyone, but if you get hurt, *I* will kill you. Oscar won't have to worry about you. Now stay put!"

DeWayne, who'd come up for the end of the conversation to claim his prisoner, laughed at me when I gave him the stink eye as I ran toward the dais, in the direction Roscoe had gone.

Dr. Diakos stepped down to say something to me, but I brushed past her. I was more than a little annoyed that she'd started a riot on such a lovely fall day. "Roscoe! Roscoe! Where are you?" I stepped into an area thickly planted with beautiful shrubs. Up ahead I heard Roscoe's evil growl. Whether he was angry or pleased, hungry or sated, happy or sad, he generally sounded like a possessed person. It was part of his charm.

"I'm going to bake you in the oven," I said sweetly to Roscoe. "With a meat thermometer stuck right up—"

I stopped in midsentence. Poking out of the bushes was the barrel of a rifle. The sniper's gun, like something from World War II, was propped up on a stand, but the shooter was nowhere in sight. I dropped to the ground to see where the gun had been sighted. No surprise, it was right at the dais where Dr. Diakos had been standing. Someone had planned to shoot her. I backed away from the rifle, feeling for my phone in my jeans pocket. I had to let Coleman know.

"Never touch a man's gun."

The voice came from behind me and I whipped around

to confront a young man—or upon closer inspection, a young woman. She carried a rifle and wore dungarees held up with braces, a long-sleeve white shirt, and a man's fedora. Her hair was cut short, and she stared down into my eyes with a steely gaze.

"Who are you?"

"Pearl Hart, at your service." She grinned. "I'm a lot more like you than you think." She cocked her hat to one side and waited.

"Should I know you?"

"If you had a better grasp of history, you might. I'm an adventurer, a highly educated person, and . . ." Her eyes were alive with merriment. "An outlaw. I'm the second woman to rob a stagecoach and the first one not to die while doing it. I did a stretch in prison. Eighteen months. I was famous in Arizona for my fearlessness and wit. When I was brought before the bench, I told the judge, 'I shall not consent to be tried under a law in which my sex had no voice in making.' He convicted me anyway."

"Jitty! What are you doing here in the middle of a riot!"

"Looking out for you and that baby incubator you hang around with."

Jitty seldom traveled to town to seek me out, but she always had something on her mind when she did put in an appearance. In her latest disguise as an outlaw, bank robber, and feminist, I didn't have to look far to see what her message might be.

"What's up?" I asked, even though I knew she'd never give me a direct answer.

"Equality has always been a dream for women. Too many have settled for second best. Not your mama, though. She demanded equality, and most often she got it. But your daddy had her back, every single hour of every single day."

"You don't normally stroll down memory lane without a reason. Why are you here?" I was eager to notify Coleman about the gun, but I also wanted to give Jitty every chance I could if she had wisdom to relay.

"I'm here to give you a caution. A lot of men don't like smart or uppity women."

"And?"

"Be careful. You think you can't get hurt but you can, and Tinkie's gonna need your skills with that new baby."

I had zero experience with babies. They scared me more than criminals, because babies were so fragile. "I'll always be there for Tinkie, but she can hire a nanny to do the hard stuff."

Jitty patted her rifle. "For friendship, you do whatever must be done." She pulled a bandana up over her nose and gave me a wicked wink before she took off. "Happy trails to you," she sang as she disappeared, accompanied by the sound of clip-clopping horse hooves.

I looked back at the area near the dais. Coleman had cuffed Curtis Miller and had him standing with Tansy, also cuffed, along with several prominent Zinnia women, not cuffed but certainly chastised for bad behavior. Roscoe was hard at work as well. He went right past the women and Tansy, stopping in front of Curtis Miller, where he hiked his leg and peed, the waterfall of urine splashing all over Miller's pants and shoes. Miller struck out with a kick, which Roscoe dodged easily, then doubled back and knocked Miller's support leg out from under him. The man went down hard, face-first.

"Get that dog," Coleman said to Tinkie, who waddled

forward, slow as molasses. She could move quicker; she just didn't want to. She was waiting to see what Roscoe would do next. I knew my partner backward and forward.

Miller was rolling around on the ground, grunting and threatening, moaning about his nose. Budgie, Coleman's second deputy, grabbed Miller by the handcuffs and pulled him to his feet. "I'll put him in the patrol car," he said, pushing Miller in front of him.

"You can't take my husband in!" Tansy hurled herself at Budgie. Tinkie's little foot stuck out and tripped Tansy, sending her stumbling into DeWayne's arms.

"I'll cut your throat. I'll poke your eyes out." Tansy caught her balance and turned on Tinkie.

"You keep defending that man and you won't live long enough to do anything," Tinkie warned her. "Wake up and smell the coffee. Don't you realize he could permanently harm you?"

"You don't know a damn thing about me and my husband," Tansy said.

"I know that love can't fix him or protect you," Tinkie responded.

Tansy made a run at Tinkie, but Coleman stepped between them.

"Break it up. Tansy Miller, you're in enough trouble. Calm down." He faced the crowd of spectators that had swelled to over a hundred. "There's nothing going on here!" Coleman dispersed the crowd while Budgie put Miller in one patrol car and Tansy in the backseat of another. "Budgie, could you and DeWayne take the Millers down to the jail? I think they need some time to think about things."

"Sure thing, Sheriff," Budgie said. "What about the women who attacked Miller?"

"I'll handle that," Coleman said. "Now ladies, line up. If you don't cooperate, I have another patrol car to fill or I can call the Baptist church and borrow their van." He rounded up the Zinnia women and took their names and gave each one a stern warning about the consequences of mob behavior before he cut them loose.

When almost everyone was gone, I led Coleman toward the dais. To my surprise, Dr. Diakos had also vanished. She'd packed it in while I was distracted. But the gun was still there—and Coleman gave me a look that telegraphed his suspicions were the same as mine. Someone had planned on shooting the professor.

He called out to DeWayne, "Let's bag this and anything else you find near here. Sarah Booth found it, so we can rule her out."

"What the hell?" DeWayne said. "Were they going to kill that professor?"

"Looks like that might have been the plan," Coleman said. "Until Sarah Booth thwarted them."

"No," I said. "Not me. Roscoe. I know he's frustrating, wicked, and possessed by the very devil, but he's smart. He brought me over here and showed me."

"That damn dog," Coleman said, shaking his head. "About the time I'm ready to send him to the electric chair, he does something wonderful." He nudged me on the arm. "Kind of like you, Sarah Booth."